Give Me One Good Reason

GIVE ME ONE GOOD REASON

by Norma Klein

G. P. PUTNAM'S SONS
NEW YORK

To Bobbi

PART ONE

"How come you're not going to England with Matthew?"

Jessie is wandering around my room, poking into things with seeming innocence, lifting things out of my still-unopened trunk. I sit in an armchair, one of the few possessions I brought from our old place, smoke my pipe and try to gather energy to unpack. The pipe is a not very effective replacement for cigarettes, only resorted to at moments of desperation. Up till about half a year ago, I smoked two packs a day, and for no special reason one day I woke up and decided I had to stop. Not that everyone—friends, family, etc.—hadn't tried for years to get me to stop, not that I hadn't, till then, embarked on hundreds of failed attempts. But for some reason this time it worked. It was agony of a grotesque, foolish but still awful kind. I remember one night, about three weeks after I stopped, just seeing a friend light up a cigarette and suddenly bursting into uncontrollable tears. She looked at me in amazement. But now all that's over, despite moments when I feel I'd sell my right leg for a few good puffs.

9

"Why *am* I not going to England with Matthew?" I consider. "Well, I don't like England, for one."

Getting this over with Jessie, my twelve-year-old sister, is a good trial run for learning to come up with answers for the rest of the family. Also, it's true—I don't like England or didn't the two years I spent there, studying at Oxford after college. I don't know if I should blame England. Maybe it was just that lonely in-between sort of feeling since I loved college and wasn't quite ready to face "real life." I always expected to like the English. I think of myself as someone who likes order, detachment, structure, reserve, all those un-American virtues, but somehow there, with everyone acting that way, not, seemingly, as a matter of choice, but just by reflex, it wore on my nerves. I think now I could handle it, or, at any rate, not handling it wouldn't bother me so much. But I came there fresh with the sense that I could handle anything and that cool, blank indifference to me—as a person, as a "scholar" as I thought of myself then was too much to bear.

Maybe, too, it was that I studied philosophy. It's not just that English philosophy is a hideous bore and that my tutor was surely not what has made the tutorial system revered for years. It was that I didn't belong in philosophy. I'm always attracted to the humanities, but they end up irritating me, and by the end of the first year I was already making out applications to colleges in the States to get my doctorate in biochemistry.

"Would you go with him if it weren't England?" Jessie is like this, which usually I love, blunt, wanting to know all, just "to know," not to pass it on in any gossipy way. So I'm not irritated by her as I would be if it were Calla, my other sister, or my mother who was asking.

This strikes me as an interesting question. Would I? I consider it. Say Algeria or Bengal. What then? No, of course, deep down I know I wouldn't, though maybe I'd have spent a few nights lying awake being tempted. The fact that it's

England—Matthew's going to be teaching there next year—makes the decision just that much easier.

"I guess you'll miss him," Jessie says. She's not a romantic. In fact, though I guess appearance doesn't really determine personality, she looks a bit like Tom Sawyer with her shaggy blond hair and jeans. So again her question, which I would ruffle at if it came weighted down with emotional overtones, I accept as just a desire to find out.

"I guess I will," I say. I'm really not sure. On the face of it you'd think how could you not miss someone you'd lived with quite contentedly for four years and seen more or less every day for the better part of six. I *will* miss him, but not, I suspect, in the tossing and turning in the dead of night did-I-do-the-right-thing kind of way. It's more: here's someone I really am fond of, love as much as I've seemed capable of it up till this point in my life, and that will leave a gap.

Jessie says, "It's really queer you never got married, in the end."

"Why?"

"I just thought you would."

"Do you wish I had?"

She thinks of this. "I don't know. . . . You don't seem like the type."

No, that's the trouble. I don't seem like the type to myself either. Otherwise I'm sure it would have happened, as a matter of course, as it did to almost everyone else of my generation. I've always had both the virtue and the vice of holding back. So I guess I avoided certain catastrophic mistakes, at the same time rather admiring those who make them.

In point of fact, Matthew and I came disastrously close to marrying a couple of times, and only the God or Goddess of Common Sense holding one or the other of us back prevented it. I'm not sure why I think: disastrous. In a way, I've often felt and still do we'd have made an exemplary couple. We were really good friends, and in our own odd way we lived together in what I gather from tales of my married and unmarried friends was unusual harmony. His being twelve years older—he's forty-four now—never really seemed to matter. We were both old-seeming and had been even as children. When I saw the photos in his family album of him at seven, staring out at the world with that "I am only a child in disguise, I am really sixty years old" look, I felt an instant pang of recognition.

As for our marrying or not marrying, twice it was a close call. The first time we actually sent out wedding invitations, largely because of his mother who adores the forms. It was all set and would, I think, have been a lovely wedding with music by Purcell and champagne on the wooded lawn of their Rhode Island house. But about four days before, I arose with a violent attack of stomach cramps, threw myself into my red Volks-wagen and drove in what I now see was a kind of subdued hysteria to a small town near Bryn Mawr, where I'd gone to college. From there I sent telegrams, first to Matthew, of course, who, at that time, was devastated and uncomprehending, though I think about a week later quite relieved, as anyone who has remained unmarried at the age of thirty-nine would be in such a situation.

Like me, Matthew is the opposite of a doer, and I think his first reaction of being devastated was due to my depriving him of having perhaps his one chance to perform an act which society, such as it is, would recognize as significant. By the time things simmered down, the main persons to comfort being his mother and my parents, we felt kind of exhausted but happy, as though we, in fact, had been the parents of a couple that had just eloped. We both, for some reason, comforted the other, for its not happening, for its almost happening.

The other time, about two years later, was a lower-keyed version with the sides reversed. I woke up, for reasons that are obscure now, feeling we must be married at once, and Matthew reluctantly agreed and then, on our way to driving to a justice of the peace, lost his nerve and said he just couldn't, at least not right then. So we went out and got drunk instead, and as he must have felt that earlier time, I arose the next morning thinking: whew, almost!

I'm always amazed how many people, everyone I know, it seems, is the opposite of us, constantly falling into insane situations, marrying hopelessly unsuitable people, having far too many children far too soon, pursuing hated professions, bungling through painful, far from amicable divorces. And here we both are, in professions we like—Matthew teaches French lit, and I do cancer research at a large hospital-connected laboratory in New York—pursuing our quiet but maybe quietly weird lives, apart from the mainstream. You'd think, in a way, two such oddballs finding each other is rare enough that we should have married at once. Maybe someday we will. I always envision us marrying when I'm seventy and Matthew is eighty-two, like those old people you occasionally read about in the paper who've been separated for decades and, sometimes each married with grandchildren, meet again while doddering down some cobbled street. I think we'd make a marvelous old couple since we've both, in a way, been in training for being old since birth, very tender and deferential, going on slow walks down the village green, arm in arm. Yes, the more I think of it, the clearer it seems. Which just leaves about forty more years of my life to fill in till then.

"Jess—listen, is there any coffee upstairs? Do you think you could bring me down some?"

"Just coffee?"

"Well, maybe some apples or raisins or cheese, just some snack-type thing."

"Okay."

I am beginning, just beginning, to get cold feet about moving back into my parents' house. It is, on the face of it, a supremely practical move. I'm not nostalgic really, but I didn't feel like staying in the apartment Matthew and I'd shared, so we sublet it. Well, I could have looked for something, but I feel kind of drained and demoralized—not just Matthew's leaving but that "this marks the end of an era" feeling. And it happens, which is convenient in ways, that my parents own a brownstone on the upper West Side of Manhattan. They bought it years ago when it was still possible to do such things for not much money. It's ironical because my parents are far from practical about money, and now they have this great thing—they live here free, still rent a good part of it, and the neighborhood, which looked as if it might decline, has, in the last decade, suddenly prospered, what with the East Side becoming so expensive. This spring, with Matthew's leaving imminent, it turned out they had a one-room studio apartment, which is all I need, really. I took it quickly, without thinking, or rather, thinking: well, by now, at thirty-two, I can manage the thing of living so close to my parents. I'll be paying rent, it will be detached, professional. It's not as if we'll be in the same apartment, after all.

Now I wonder. I still think I can do it. I just wonder how good an idea it was. And what my motives were, at bottom.

I've always liked the idea of family houses. It's the sort of thing I thought I'd like about England. I like the idea of one family living on for generations in the same place, which is hardly common in America, to say nothing of New York. So partly it appeals to me, which is leaving aside, as though one could, the human element—namely, my parents still living here, not just the house as structure to contend with.

They are, however, away during the day, even on Saturday. They own a gallery which sells art objects, and they both virtually live there so it won't be a matter of having them here hanging over me, every second. Also, I often work not only all day but at night and weekends, so I'm hoping I can swing it.

I don't know when I'll tell them about the baby. I guess as late as possible, which doesn't give me a hell of a lot of time, maybe a couple of months. I'm not foreseeing any real problems with them, and I wonder if that, too, is really smart. My parents aren't typical. They're European, they're sophisticated. I believe they will take this, if not in their stride, well, I guess I just hope they'll take it, somehow. I wonder, though, if taking this studio in their house isn't somehow a symbolic returning to the nest and all that kind of thing. I don't believe in symbols really, but I can't help wondering about it.

Jessie said about my getting married, "You're not the type." Which I think in most ways represents the current family opinion. My other sister, Calla, is twenty-seven and has been married eight years; my brother, Boris, who's three years older than me, is also married, though it's a bit shaky at the moment. So I think they've all been ready, for their various reasons, to think it okay that there be one oddball in the family. I wonder if their first reaction about my having the baby will be: "You? But you're just not the type."

I'm sure as hell not, that's the funny part of it. I hated dolls as a little girl. I used to always lose them on purpose or give them to friends. I only liked stuffed animals, especially bears, of which I had quite a collection. I also had a stuffed snake, Sebastian, a monkey with an orange button nose and a mouse that could wind up and play a tune. But the idea of motherhood, even in those early symbolic forms, horrified me. I remember, later, going around saying, "Even a worm can have a child," and when any of my married friends would announce she was pregnant, I'd try to cough up a congratulations, feeling, somehow, that I was congratulating someone on having lung cancer. Oddly, I'm not even sure that basically my feelings have changed. I just know I woke up one morning, deciding I wanted a child. I don't think, I really don't, it was the thought of Matthew leaving and wanting a "remembrance" of him. I'm just not that type.

The other funny part is that it took us about six months to actually get me pregnant, which seems, in all ways, fairly typical of us both. This must be one of the most planned born-out-of-wedlock babies in the history of man. In the beginning we left it to chance, thinking that, of course, it would work instantly, as it always seems to do with unmarried couples in books. No such luck. Then began the era of taking my temperature every morning, graphs of temperature rise and fall, screwing on command, remaining flat in bed for hours afterward so not even one tiny sperm might drip out. And even then it didn't work for months. It began to be comical. And Matthew, as I'd imagined he would, became very interested in the whole project.

Matthew can't stand babies. By babies I might well say any child up to the age of sixteen. I think he'd be a lousy father. He loves quiet and order and hates sloppiness and noise. So do I, in point of fact. I think if we'd married, we would never have had children. He would have gone into deep shock if we had, and odd as it sounds, I would have hated that. I mean, I feel I can raise a baby myself, but I would have hated having him there, but not there. It would have caused land mines of resentment, I just know it. On the other hand, like, I guess, many men, he rather liked the idea of siring a child. So the deal was I would have it while he was in England and would send him pictures and so forth, but he would be free of any responsibilities. He, in fact, wanted to contribute to its education etc. but I really didn't want him to. I guess, again, that would make me feel he ought to be doing more, whereas if he does nothing but plant the seed, I feel it's still all mine. And I can support it. I earn enough, and there's no reason to assume I won't in the future.

To get back, however, to my not being the type, I still wonder about that. What I wonder is if I'm doing it partly because I'm not, because I see my life stretching ahead so well planned and organized, so mistakeless, and I want to tangle it up. But, really, I don't think this will be a tangle. It may be a kind of vanity, but I see myself as being a terribly good parent, very solid and responsible and warm. I'm not sure what leads me to this view or even if it's justified, but I have it. So far, which may again be a kind of vanity, I've handled every important adult decision that has come my way. So this shouldn't faze me. And I feel, living in New York, though I may not live here forever, is good in that the anonymity is a protection. At the lab I'm friendly with a few people, but in my actual section I mainly have cordial—well, not even so cordial—but at any rate distant relationships. I almost relish what their reaction will be since most of them, especially my lab chief, with whom I do not get along at all, are men.

Jessie comes back with the snack supplies in a plastic bag and joins me in munching on apples and cheese. Sasha and Olaf, my two Great Danes, get the cores. The dogs are my first children. I love animals, and I hate feeling defensive about it, though I do when people say. "Well, *I* love *people!*" As though it were a matter of choosing. Jessie loves animals too—it's a bond between us because the rest of the family is of the won't-they-shed-too-much type of orientation. Matthew was a bit like that, too. He put up with the dogs, but somewhat reluctantly. I think, if he'd had to have a dog, he'd have preferred a Russian wolfhound, something elegant and small, whereas I've always loved big, floppy dogs.

"I'll walk them for you, if you want," Jessie says, sitting on top of Sasha, who never minds; Olaf is more aloof.

"That would be nice, Jess, thanks."

"We can wash them together and everything."

"They take showers, not baths."

She laughs. "Hey, neat! Can I help?"

"Of course."

She grins at me. "I'm really glad you'll be here, Gab. . . . I bet we'll have fun. . . . Can I sleep over sometime too?"

"Sure." I can see how life for Jessie must be very different from the way it was for three of us who were relatively close in age. Now, with all of us grown and with our own homes, it must be odd, being the only child of a couple in their sixties. Jessie seems to me the closest thing to a really American child my parents produced, not just her looks, but everything. Maybe by the time she came along all those strange conglomeration of European genes had simmered down or out.

"I guess I better do some work," she says, getting up. "Are you coming for dinner?"

I nod. I don't want this to become a frequent ritual, but on this first night it seems only right.

"See you at seven."

"Calla and Julian will try and make it after supper," my mother says, serving the chicken. "If they can get a sitter."

"Oh, good," I say. If they can get a sitter indeed! I'm afraid, meretricious as such feelings are, that something of my feeling in wanting to be a mother is to show my parents how much better I can handle it, married or not, than Calla. She could perfectly well get a sitter, for Lord's sake! Her children are eight and six by now. But she loves to make motherhood into a very big deal.

I've often wondered if the Calla syndrome is typical. Calla, as a girl, was the rebel of the family, and it was a role which seemed almost forced on her by nature. She got her period at eight and had pubic hair at eleven. I remember watching her take a bath and being amazed at the thick swarm of dark hair at a time when I had hardly any. Drugs weren't in at that era—it was the early sixties—but Calla did all the other typical bits, sleeping around with anyone and everyone. While I, of course, stood by disapproving and envious, being, at that time, the type who thought wearing lipstick or perfume was a mortal sin. She had three abortions by the time she entered college, all somewhat skillfully handled by my parents, whose ever-ready desire to understand was certainly put to the test. But the odd part is what followed. After going to college in California, "to get away" as she put it then, Calla dropped out in her freshman year, returned to New York, where she got some menial-type secretarial job, and then, a year or so later, met and married Julian; she was nineteen at the time.

I like Julian, I really do. He's a shy, sweet, stoop-shouldered fellow, freckled, with curly ginger hair who always looks like he's carrying the woes of the world on his shoulders. He's an electrical engineer. I gather he was married briefly and disastrously to an opera singer. He's eight years older than Calla, but when you see them together, you'd swear Calla was his mother. She's tall and heavyset, heavier than I am, with thick black hair swept up in some kind of twist, and she always looks, even in slacks, like something out of Picasso's hefty mama period. When Boris was in the clothing business, he gave both Calla and me leftover stock, and as I recall, it was the year that at-home outfits were in style, great flowing things which supposedly you changed into after work. Calla looked great in them, very queenly and, well, flowing. When I see her with Julian, I always imagine him curled up at her breast like a small, frightened child. They have two kids, Elizabeth, whom I love (she's the eight-year-old), and Timmy, who's six. Anyway, whatever it was—marriage, Julian, motherhood—Calla has turned in the last almost decade into the earth mother of earth mothers. It's not just that she has no help, even when she has a fever of a hundred and two, it's that she goes nowhere and does nothing and talks of nothing but things relating to the home, having children, private versus public schools, etc. I don't belittle these topics; they have a value, but it's so ironical somehow to me—Calla, the great rebel, come to this! *If* they can get a sitter! So I sit here at my parents' table, thinking private thoughts about how *I* will be different, free, independent,

19

unharnessed. Oh, petty family rivalry. Yes, I know it's petty. No doubt Calla turned to motherhood to find her niche since I had cornered scholarship or intellectualness in the family sphere. And I'm sure it's typical of me that I can't be content to leave her unchallenged even in that.

"How do you like the room?" Daddy says.

"Nice," I say. I suppose calling my father Daddy still after all these years is odd, but if you start off with Daddy, how can you suddenly switch and to what? Father sounds so formal, Dad sounds so all-American, and first names for one's parents seem funny to me, affected.

"Will you have room enough, what with the beasts and so on?"

"Sure, it's fine . . . I'm not at home a lot, anyway."

"When did you say Matthew was leaving?" Mother says. Yes, I don't know why she's Mother and he's Daddy, that's just the way it is.

"The twentieth of June."

"So soon? That's Friday!"

"Yes, so—"

"I just didn't know it was so soon," Mother says.

There is a weighty silence. What is it? That with the sailing of Matthew's boat will sail into the sunset my last chances at matrimony? No, I can't believe that; my parents are not like that, they've never over the years breathed a word about my single status, and I really respect them for that because I know they must have all the conventional parental feelings on the subject. My parents are unusual. All my friends always adored them and wished they had parents like that. I guess I'm a bit more aware of the unspoken undercurrents, but I do think that as parents go, they've been exemplary in many ways.

"I think it's such a fine opportunity for Matthew," Mother says. "He spoke so often about wanting to get to those papers on Baudelaire in the Bodleian Library."

Mother and Matthew have had many long, intimate talks in the kitchen over lemon sherbet and tea while I've lain prone with some biochemical journal. Mother is a flirt and a good one, a talent which I'm afraid neither Calla nor I have inherited. She's at her best with reserved intellectual men like Matthew, whom she usually has eating out of her hand in about half an hour. Mother is one of the few women in her sixties who is still really lovely-looking. I mean, you wouldn't say of her, "She must have been beautiful as a girl" (though in fact she was), because that implies that now she's on the way to being a wreck and she isn't in any way, shape or form. She doesn't dye her hair, it's gray, but she wears it in a sort of pageboy to her shoulders which is very soft-looking. Her skin is fantastic, and she has a very petite, dainty figure. Next to her Calla and I look like oafs. I guess in part we've both rejected that kind of slightly formal European charm which she's so good at, but frankly I doubt either of us could bring it off if we tried.

Mother was married once before she met Daddy. Her parents were Russian, but she was brought up in Paris, and it was there she met Bengt, a Swedish theatrical director whom she lived with in Sweden for nearly a decade. He's married a couple of times since. He sounds like a charming, unreliable type of man, not my type at all, but easy to see how she could have liked him. I think she was smart to opt for Daddy in the end. The funny thing is that when she lived in Sweden, Mother was quite a well-known artist. I remember almost falling over when we came to some public square and there was a statue she had done while she was in her twenties. It was representational, a girl leading a horse, but not the kind of thing just anyone could knock off. Yet somehow here in America she more or less gave it up, though she still has a studio and repairs there on occasion. I'm not sure why she gave it up. Partly, maybe, her style was too realistic for American art at that time. And I doubt she was able to face the commercial aspect of the New York art world.

Plus, helping Daddy in the gallery is certainly a full-time job and not unrelated to art. I just always feel it's a pity that she had this other life that went so totally underground.

"I think Matthew's looking forward to it," I offer, feeling I've been, up till now, too standoffish. Maybe I'm somehow steeling myself for the inevitable discussions when they know the baby is coming.

"I imagine he'll adore England," Mother says, smiling. Mother adores England. Well, she and Daddy go there every summer to look for art objects for the gallery and because, even now, I think they still think of themselves as being European. Whenever there's a financial crisis in the United States, they start talking about transferring money to a Swiss bank, and I wouldn't be altogether surprised if one day they retired there.

"Did you say he was flying?" Daddy says.

"Boat."

"Oh," Mother asks eagerly. "Is it the *France?*"

"Umm."

Then follows a reminiscence of one of their many boat trips. I hate boats myself. I took a student ship to Paris once and almost passed out with acute claustrophobia. But I guess you have to love the social part of it, which Mother and Daddy would, the long meals, the sitting in deck chairs having bouillon, etc. I always think of Mother as a bath person, meaning not only that she literally does take long, scented baths with bath mitts and bath pillows and soaps shaped like lemons and tomatoes, but that she's the type to lie back and relax. Whereas I'm somehow a shower person, too nervous and jumpy to be willing to soak for ages in hot water, even though I can imagine it's soothing.

After supper someone calls Mother on the phone; she disappears into the bedroom. Daddy, after circling around the living room for a while, says, "You ... have no regrets about Matthew, do you, darling? I mean, I don't want you to feel *I* feel that you—"

22

"No, no, that's okay." I love Daddy, and I don't ever mind his trying to be personal, maybe because he doesn't do it that often. "He'll be back in a year, anyway," I add, though that has nothing to do with it.

Almost at once Daddy picks up a statue on his desk and starts in. "Did I show you this, Gabby? We just got it last week. You know, it's impossible to get anything from this tribe anymore. Everything good is in museums, but Oscar, you remember Oscar Morovski, happened to. . . ."

I stand there, nodding, partly following. Daddy has a real passion for art. When he talks of other things—people, politics, whatever—I always feel part of him is held in reserve, but when he talks about some new piece they've acquired or something he's seen in another gallery, his big fisheyes bulge with excitement. I still think of Daddy as looking a little like a fish, though I think that's because I did as a child. He's a shortish man, shorter than I am, though taller than Mother, who is so small, and he's portly. Despite this, he's quite vain about his appearance but in a sporadic way. He'll have suits and shirts custom made, but on him they look a little funny, too big or just off somehow. His hair is white and shaggy, but his eyebrows are black, and he wears gold-rimmed glasses. He's also a nonstop talker, though never about anything personal. Boris, who hates him in a way, always says that Daddy has no real friends, that he cares only about objects, not people. I don't think that's true, though I know what he means. I guess it's just that loving him, I accept this. The only effect his garrulousness has on me is that I've become, more and more as I get older, a lover of silence.

I always wonder why people say, when two people sit together not talking, that this is a sign of incompatibility. I love sitting in silence with someone I'm fond of; it's a great luxury. As a girl I wanted nothing more than to be like Daddy, talking and joking with everyone, librarians, elevator men, waiters, pulling their leg in a jovial sort of way, but I was morbidly shy, terrified of people. Now I don't know if I'd even like to be like that, and I find myself drawn to men who aren't such great talkers.

When Daddy has stopped talking for a minute, I say, "I guess Calla isn't coming then."

Daddy says, "You know, Gabby, I wish you'd speak to her about this baby-sitting thing. . . . She should get out more, it's not right. We'd be glad to—"

Calla even now hardly trusts Mother and Daddy to baby-sit with her kids as though they were delicate vases that would break if you dropped them. They have to beg and plead to be allowed to take them even for an afternoon. I understand power plays, so it isn't incomprehensible. Now, smugly, I want to say: *my* baby you can play with whenever you like.

"I'm hardly the person who should tell her that, anyway," I say. "She'd resent it like hell."

"Would she?" He looks puzzled. It is amazing how parents, seeing all these murderous rivalries developing and brewing among their children for years, still seem amazed at their existence.

"Anyway, I'm worried about Timmy," Daddy says. "Mother says Calla told her he's been having these dreadful nightmares and—"

"All kids do," I say lightly.

He sighs. I think he would like a grandchild he could really call his own. No, I'm not having the baby for that reason. I admit as a child adoring Daddy I did have the usual fantasies of Mother being bumped off and Daddy and me living together in a great scholarly Jamesian relationship, but I believe that's faded with time. But I feel he would love a little girl, and since Calla won't give him Elizabeth, I'll present him with one. . . . God, that sounds awful. No, I swear, really, this is not my primary motive. If it were, I wouldn't even let myself do it. I just hate slimy, overly intense family relationships. No, it's merely a thought which to deny would be false, but to overdo would be wrong too. In fact, I'm not even sure I'll be living in New York after the baby is born. I've thought of looking for a job elsewhere, not at all because of the baby and wanting to make a fresh start, just that I'm kind of sick of the setup there which doesn't look as if it's going to change imminently.

"I read your paper," Daddy says, pouring me some sherry.

I smile. I'm so touched by Daddy's trying to follow my field. He once was interested in science, but that was years and years ago and genetics almost didn't exist at that time. None of the men I've ever been involved with has followed my work to any degree at all. I remember Matthew, who, I think, really would have liked to, staring in hopeless fascination at some models of DNA in a very simplified *Life* article. But he finally confessed he could see them only as shapes and colors; the meaning of it all, beyond the barest simplicities, escaped him. Not that I minded. In fact, I think choosing men like this was rather deliberate, men in fields which had no special appeal to me that I could appreciate, but at a great distance. I'm a very competitive person, and I don't really want to squelch that; I just never wanted my personal life to be a battleground on which those issues were fought.

I'm sure it's true, too, that I picked science because it's a field no one in my immediate family can fathom at all. As a girl, loving animals, I had fantasies of being a vet, an animal breeder, and that kind of thing. I also loved painting, and I remember going around to galleries with Daddy where he would say with a grandiloquent sweep to Saidenberg or whoever, "Someday my daughter's paintings will be hanging here." It was a bit too much. But science was safe and nicely beyond the reach of them all. I suppose, apart from Daddy's overinvolvement in my painting, I somehow—as I think Boris and Calla do too—associate "art" with my parents. And with art I associate their whole life-style, warm, passionate, horrendously disorganized. I

GIVE ME ONE GOOD REASON

wanted something cooler and more remote. It hasn't turned out
to be quite the dichotomy I imagined then, but I still think I was
right, at bottom.

Mother's feeling about my work is: "When are you going to
find a cure for cancer?" She likes thinking of research as having
a social usefulness; otherwise, it would be too remote. And it
isn't really unrelated. It's just that I think she sees me, single-
handed, as one day "discovering" some little thing that will be
"The Cure." I used to argue and try to explain about this, but
now I let it lie.

But when Daddy takes a paper I've written and really goes
over it word by word, trying as hard as he can to follow, to
remember concepts we've discussed, I'm touched beyond
words. I know partly it's his wanting to be in touch, modern,
but also I like to think it's wanting to understand me, my world.

"You still find things difficult with what's his name?" he says,
eyes still fixed on the newly acquired art object.

What's-his-name is my boss, Leonid Lobochowski, a
Polish-born biochemist, not yet forty. I won't go into
Lobochowski now—he's a thing unto himself—but he's certainly
turned me, in the three years I've been in his lab, into a
Polophobe, me who used to pride myself on loving all nationalities. The Poles oughtn't to be blamed for Lobochowski,
but I can't help blaming them anyhow.

"Oh, it's okay, really. . . . We just steer clear of each other."

"Is that possible?"

"To an extent."

To Mother and Calla I keep my feelings about Lobochowski
under my hat more. Maybe I want them to retain that image of
me, working silently and efficiently with no grimy human
elements intruding. Would that it were so.

I suddenly think of telling Daddy about the baby, wanting to
tell it now, unplanned, instead of the way I, in fact, planned it.
But after a second of not saying anything, I decide not to. I may

be deceiving myself when I think that my parents' reaction to this will be a test of them, not of me. I expect they will meet it admirably, but if they don't, that is *their* problem. That sounds hideously priggish, true. And I realize I can go around saying of anyone's reaction I don't like: that's *their* problem. But I just want to feel in this eighth decade of the twentieth century it's possible for such an event to take place calmly, rationally, without any hysteria or prejudice. To imagine its being like that in some small town in Iowa might, I know, be foolhardy. But this is New York, and my friends are enlightened, and so are my parents. So until proved otherwise, I'm going to expect everyone to rise wonderfully to the occasion.

So why do I have nervous flutters when I think of it? Well, everyone's entitled to a few nervous flutters.

"Daddy, I think I might. . . . Could you tell Mother I felt kind of tired. I have to be up early tomorrow."

"Done. . . . Sorry about Calla."

"That's okay. . . . I'm going to see her one of these days anyway."

"Give her our love," he says dryly.

"I shall."

I take the dogs for their evening walk and then the three of us settle down to sleep.

I sit in the cabin of Matthew's boat, sipping champagne, and munching on candied apricots. Someone, his secretary, I think, brought a big box of candy, and he automatically handed it to me since he has no sweet tooth and I love candy. I blame my parents, who always gave us such healthy food when we were babies—meats, fresh vegetables, fruits—for my craving as an adult for every kind of nonnutritious crap from Mars bars to Drake cakes to that awful slimy white spaghetti with red sauce that comes in cans to potato chips and the worst, all nonbeef hot dogs. I'll never get enough of those things, I love them.

"Matthew, did you leave me your address?" Sherman Berinbaum, one of Matthew's colleagues who also teaches in the Romance Languages Department, yanks at Matthew's sleeve.

"Just care of the college, that's all," Matthew says, distracted. He hates all these people being here. I don't blame him, I do too. It's not just being squashed in this tiny cabin with several people smoking and the noise level rising so that soon everyone is shouting unnecessarily. It's that it would be nice to have maybe two seconds alone with Matthew. I don't know why I say that. I hate sentimental good-byes, and we've said all that already. But then maybe I shouldn't have come at all.

"Don't get too fat," Matthew says as I slouch back, munching on chocolate nuts. He smiles, meaning my pregnancy, and I smile back, and for a second I feel better.

Champagne always ends up making me sad. Is it because you drink it on occasions which have something to do with endings? Anyway, I lie there, paralyzed with sadness, only comforted in a mild degree by the sweetness of the candy. I stare at Matthew. It's hard for me to describe Matthew. I should say that most women find him either great or very ugly, which is probably to say that he's both. He's about six feet four and gaunt. I think "gaunt" is the word for him, not just thin. He always reminds me a little of a scarecrow because he's always stooping and his clothes hang on him—he dresses abominably. His face is all cheekbones and lines; I think he'd make a perfect Christ in an Ingmar Bergman movie. He has that same light-reddish hair and light-blue eyes, almost anemic-looking, of some Scandinavian cousins of mine. He stutters at times and has an awful habit of cracking his knuckles when he's nervous which drives me clear up the wall.

Also, he's homosexual. Or was when he was younger. I never told many people about that—that is, those who wouldn't have known anyway—not because I dislike revealing personal things about myself or men I'm close to, but because I was sure, and I still think this is true, that everyone would have said: oh, well, *that* explains it. *That's* why you never got married, *that's* why this and *that's* why that. And it *isn't* why anything. I will stick to that to my dying day.

For one thing, it's something he was always ambivalent about. And doesn't really understand himself since, though he tried psychoanalysis a few times, he never could stick, always feeling, which I'm sure was true but not really relevant, that he was much brighter than the analyst. We talked about it at times, but there were never any great revelations. Unlike me, Matthew can scarcely remember a thing about his childhood before he was twenty. He says he's tried and just can't. So there were never any things of "then there was the time my cousin seduced me under a haystack when I was six" or "the time my mother did thus-and-so." Mothers are always the villains in these things, but I must say, having met Matthew's mother many times, that though she's not one of my favorite people, she's no more overbearing than many another mother I've met, no more hung up on sex or anything. So all I can say is that I understand it just to the extent Matthew seemed to, as something that was true, probably had an explanation if one had the time, money and patience to find out, but for the most part just had to be handled somehow.

The reason I say it wasn't the reason we did or didn't marry was that—which may be extraordinarily odd of me—I don't think I'd have gone off the deep end if Matthew had become involved with another man. It's curious, but maybe one reason is that all the relationships he'd had with men sounded so awful, so painful that I could see his wanting very much not to do it. I think our life together represented for him, as it did for me, a kind of stability, something quiet and peaceful. But for him, and for me—and to me this is the cause, if there is any, of our not getting married—maybe it was too peaceful. Maybe some of the pain that comes from something very deep wasn't there. I must say I fight that a lot. I don't see why pain should be necessary, why people should have to be entangled in that ugly way. I really and truly hope that's not necessary. So leave it that there was, on the edge, this awareness of something else which both of us didn't find appealing but couldn't reject out of hand either.

Matthew is not the type for whom the existence of Gay Lib has made the whole thing any easier; quite the contrary. It's a kind of snobbishness basically, I think, but just as there are those who take solace in finding there are myriad others with the same problems as themselves, there are some, like Matthew, who hate the idea of being part of some faceless swarming crowd of individuals with whom one would at bottom have nothing in common beyond that problem. I know what he means, I'm not a great joiner myself, but I think he makes it a little harder for himself by being so utterly, exclusively private.

I don't think I'm the savior type. There are women who are, I know. But I never wanted to convert Matthew one way or the other. I was, I remember, upset when he stopped his analysis because I really did feel that there was no other way for someone like him to come to terms with it. Like many brilliant men—and he is, I don't use that term lightly—he uses about ninety percent of his brainpower on ideas and has extraordinarily little left over for perceiving how people, including himself, tick. At times I found this almost naïveté lovely and at other times incredibly depressing.

"Gabby, would you . . . I wanted to. . . ." I've been sitting here in a daze and find Matthew guiding me out of the cabin. I follow him blindly, a million light-years away as usual.

We walk down to the end of the corridor.

"That's awful," he says, waving his hand directly at the cabin.

"Oh, it's always like that," I say.

"Will you call me next week?"

30

"Why call?" I feel, for some reason, scared. I want a definite end, not calls. Letters, okay.

"It's easy. . . . I called Henderson last week and it was like talking to New Jersey. I could hear him perfectly."

So much the worse! "Sure, well, but . . . I can write."

"Please call, I'd rather."

I can't believe this. I thought we'd made it so clear that until the baby was born, even after, this would be something I'd handle on my own. I can't bear to think of him holding my hand, even by long distance. "Look, let's not do the calling thing," I say. "I don't want to." I blurt it out too bluntly, but I feel as if he's pulling at my gut or something.

"What do you mean? It's easy."

"I know it's easy, it's not a matter of easy. . . . Matthew, come on, you promised, this is awful . . . I want to do this myself."

"You are such a stubborn son of a bitch."

"Bitch is the usual term."

"Why are you *like* this?"

I really, to my amazement, am about to cry and I am not a crier. "Stop it!" I yell.

Someone passing by with two suitcases in hand stares at me.

"If you make me cry, I'll kill you," I say grimly.

"Darling, Jesus!" He stares at me as if I'm someone he can't fathom. Matthew, what women want is so simple, really, compared to what men want. Men are the hard ones to figure. Please, give me a woman any day.

"I just feel funny." I'm sighing, gulping, trying to get back to my usual distance. "Too much champagne, I guess."

"Well, all I can say is, I don't want this complete cut-off thing."

"It's not that. . . . How can we be talking like this? You agreed, we had it all settled."

31

"What did we have settled?"

"This is my goddamn baby, and I don't want all this crap about call me next week. That'll do me in."

"Honey. . . ."

"We had this perfect agreement and you're screwing it up, already. . . . You hate babies, now remember that, please!"

"I know I hate babies, what's that got to do with it? All I'm saying is I'd like to hear how you're doing. . . . Why does that have to do only with the baby? Christ!"

"No, that's true." I feel suddenly calmer. I must be getting hypersensitive.

"I wonder if I should be doing this," he says vaguely.

"What?"

"Going."

"Going to England, you mean? . . . Why on earth not?"

"I don't know . . . I hate change and—"

"Matthew, come on, this is too much. You'll love it! You'll love every damn bit of it, you'll drink port in the evening and get gout and write a great tome on—"

"—on nothing."

"Stop it." Matthew, though he's probably the best known and liked teacher at the university, does have a horrendous block about writing. He's written a few articles which everyone claims are classics, and for years everyone has been waiting for him to finish the book on Baudelaire which he has, absolutely written out, in his head. This is something we discussed and discussed, and by now I feel I understand it and don't. But I am hoping that maybe this year away, in a strange place, will work some kind of miracle.

"You'll have a lovely year, no matter what happens."

"Will I?" He's looking mournful and distracted.

"You will, I promise."

We kiss and march back to the cabin, but I just grab my coat and leave.

On the dock I stand awhile, looking at the boat. Traveling is exciting, I guess, if you're not the one doing it. As a child I loved all those books about stowaways.

I feel, despite all my resolve not to, terribly torn. Not so much about going. But I feel Matthew is the last link with the baby as our idea, as something funny, to joke about. I feel what lies ahead is hideous long explanations, defenses, this is why I did it. And there'll be no one to laugh about it with. One thing Matthew and I shared to an almost eerie extent was a sense of humor. We always could just look at each other during a movie, when someone was talking, even at a name printed on a program, and know exactly why it seemed funny. That's not passion, it's not why Antony gave up everything for Cleopatra, but, Jesus, it was very very nice.

I hope I know what I'm doing.

"You're absolutely sure you can handle it?" Calla is saying.

"Absolutely, perfectly."

"No, I mean it, Gabby. . . . Because Timmy has been having these nightmares."

"I know. . . . You told me."

She is ruffled. Calla hates it when you tell her she's already told you something. "He may wake up several times at night."

"Cal, it's up to you."

"It's *not*. . . . It's up to *you*."

"Well, I've said I will do it, nightmares and all."

"And you'd really rather have them stay at your place than here? . . . I mean, here they have all their stuff, their toys."

"Have them bring a few crucial toys. . . . It'll be fine here. They like sleeping on sleeping bags."

"Oh, I don't know, I just wonder. . . ."

If this were anyone but Calla and we were speaking face to face instead of on the phone, I'd be tempted to sock her one. I mean, Lord! Here she's getting free baby-sitting for a whole weekend by a competent, genial, resourceful individual who is known to her kids, and still she's hemming and hawing as though she were about to embark on a six-week trip to North Vietnam and were leaving them to fend for themselves on the side streets of Saigon in the care of a blind beggar lady or something.

"What time shall I come by?" I say, cutting through or past her long, ambiguous silence.

"Eleven," she says slowly.

May I here take an oath? I have no witnesses but the dogs, but I want to say that never, *never* will I be like this. I will not believe that motherhood reduces formerly intelligent, rational beings into driveling, indecisive idiots. And if I start acting like a driveling, indecisive idiot, I'll—well, what *will* I do? "She's always the last to know." Don't be silly, me? Never, never, never, never. I'm going to leave this baby with strangers of all sorts right from the beginning, and she's going to love them and get to know not just me but the whole wide world.

Oh, dear, I'm starting to sound self-righteous, that's a bad sign too. Ye gods, what attitude can you take that's okay? Well, still, my point is valid, I think. Freedom for parents, freedom for children.

Saturday morning I rise early, get into my weekend blue jeans and shirt outfit, pack a picnic lunch in my knapsack and set off for Calla and Julian's house.

They live in a kind of crummy neighborhood. It's on the Lower East Side, just before Fourteenth Street, in a building which, I gather, is mainly swinging singles and that sort of thing. There's scarcely a playground in the neighborhood, and they've been looking forever for a bigger and nicer place, preferably uptown, but haven't found anything yet. Meanwhile, the kids share a room, which doesn't seem to me such a dreadful thing, but, naturally, it gives Calla untold worries about early sex play and the like. I got a big bang out of her story of how, when Elizabeth and Timmy were five and three, they used to take baths together and he would put his penis in her vagina. They both, evidently, thought it was a gas and did it whenever they had a bath together. "Should I tell him it's bad because she's his sister?" Calla used to say. "Or because he's only three?" Good question.

Elizabeth is also in blue jeans and a shirt. She runs to meet me and leaps into my arms. "Hi, Scrie!" She made up that name for me, I forget why.

"Hi, frog face. . . . How're things?"

Timmy is in his room playing. Calla is in a very pretty purple and yellow Marimekko dress and dangling wooden earrings. She's not pretty, she never was, really, her features are heavy like everyone on my father's side of the family, but there's something stately and nice about the way she looks. We don't look unalike. I'm taller and less heavy. Also, no matter what I weigh, I never, somehow, look voluptuous the way Calla does. She doesn't have that big a bust, really, but she's flowing and I'm rangy. Even when I'm fat, I'm rangy, which is something you have to accept on faith if you can't imagine it. Basically, I look like an Indian chief, which is not as much of a calamity as it might have been, say, fifty years ago when I might have been consigned to the upper wing of the family mansion as an un-marriageable freak. What I mean by Indian chief is that I have thick, coarse black hair, which I try to wear in a braid down my back. If loose, it stands straight out like something with four dimensions. I have black eyes and eyebrows that are as straight as pencils. My nose is hooked. It's not a beak, but neither is it your all-American pug either. Despite all this, I'm really not bad-looking, though no one has ever suggested I enter any beauty contests. I guess it's that in this age of everyone wanting to look individual, I look just that—individual. I don't have the kind of face that gets lost in a crowd. Calla's face is, I think, more conventional, though her coloring is dark like mine.

"Look at my bag!" Elizabeth said. She has a new bag with her things in it, a kind of duffel bag covered with big smile faces.

"Great."

"Can I bring my comics, my Barbie dolls *and* my Crissy?" Elizabeth wants to know.

Calla lifts her eyebrows at me. "Will you leave those fucking Barbie dolls home?" she says. "Oh, Lord, what made me get her those hideous, crummy things? I must have been off my rocker."

I have to admit to a hidden, indefensible fascination for Barbie dolls. It's probably akin to the Drake cake syndrome. Calla and I, as children, had such irreproachably good toys—carved lovely wooden horses, rag dolls, charmingly illustrated picture books, no TV, of course—that the perfect vulgarity of the Barbie dolls stirs a deep yearning in me, their platinum plastic hair, their expressions of utter, bright-eyed vacuity, the fact that their shapely rubber arms come off so easily and as easily can be screwed back in place, their giant wardrobes of grotesquely fashionable clothes with names like Bloom Zoom and Snappy Snoozers. It's all a world I never knew anything of in life, never felt influenced by or especially avoided. It's so American, I guess that's it, and we were, as a family, slightly odd in a way my parents never appreciated. When I see photos of us as girls, we were always dressed in charming but peculiar things, dark dresses with lace collars, heavy woolen tights. Mother even used to buy us things in the Salvation Army, which to her had no class connotations; she just thought of it as a wonderful place to pick up interesting bargains.

"Look, whatever she wants to take is okay," I say. "I don't mind."

Calla makes a face. She looks at me scrutinizingly. "You look fat," she says.

My heart takes an instant leap into the pit of my stomach. God, no, no, not so soon. I'm *not* fat. God, I have dieted unspeakably. For the last month, since I got the positive test from the lab I've been in a state of blind unspeakable hunger almost every second. And I normally *love* food. I eat when I'm happy, I eat when I'm sad. I'm the only person I know who actually gained five pounds while in the hospital with pneumonia. But despite this, I've been holding myself back so rigorously that I can't believe I really do look fat. I just shrug. Calla is, in fact, fatter than I am, so I think I'll try and put it down to envy.

"I guess you feel bad over Matthew leaving," she says.

I get it. He left; therefore, I've been overeating from sorrow. Why not? I nod. "Well, yes. . . ."

"Is he liking it?"

"I've just gotten one letter so far," I say. "I'm sure he'll like it."

Calla is staring at me. No, my dear, I do not regret not marrying him. Calla is one of the last people on earth, by the way, whom I would tell about Matthew's bisexuality. I go into a cold sweat when I even contemplate her attempts at analysis of the whys and wherefores—she was a psych major in college. She's always thought I should be analyzed, too, but I think we've reached a draw on that topic by now.

"You know, you're either crazy or very brave," she says.

"How so?"

"Moving in with Mother and Daddy?"

"I'm not moving *in* with them. . . . I have my own place."

"Still. . . . You wouldn't get me within ten miles of the place."

"I'm away all day. . . . I think it'll work; it won't be forever."

"Why not?"

I'm taken aback. Why not, indeed? "Well, I may not stay in New York after this year . . . I'm thinking of looking for a new job."

Calla's revenge on me, which I guess is transparent but bugs the hell out of me anyway, is that whenever I refer to my work at all, her face gets a blank expression as though I were speaking of either something unmentionable or something so dull that she can't be at pains to react in any way, however small. Why? Is it fair, is it just? I have listened to endless crap about her children, whom I admit I love, but in a way that's irrelevant. I haven't found all her blow-by-blow accounts of natural childbirth, her fights with her pediatrician, her struggles with nursing, etc. all that fascinating, but I've listened, oh, how I've listened! So, is cancer research such a dirty, weird little thing to be doing that every time I make the slightest reference to it, which it's hard not to do just because that's where I am eighty percent of my waking hours, she looks as though I'd turned into a roach before her very eyes?

"Jobs are impossible to get," Julian offers, walking in from the living room, harassed-looking as always.

"In general, yes . . . but Nixon has this big cancer thing. . . ." Oops, bite your tongue, if Nixon is for it, it must be bad, right? So, if he's against cancer, for whatever grimy, political reasons, he must be wrong. Let cancer flourish! A great campaign slogan for some aspiring Democrat. "There's a lot of money floating around."

"And you want to get it?" Julian says, not nastily, really more naïvely than anything.

"Not personally . . . I just think there'll be certain labs that are expanding, and if I can publish one or two things, I might stand a chance of—"

"I thought you did publish that one thing last year," he says.

"Sure, but one thing is one thing. . . . One thing will not get me a job."

Calla hates it when Julian takes even this peripheral interest in my work. She begins bustling around, getting the children ready.

"Have fun!" I call when we are all finally assembled.

They both stare at me gravely. As though that were possible! They're going to spend the whole time racked with anxiety that I am doing something unspeakable to their children. And I've done this before, mind you. I've taken the kids a couple of other times, and I'm a relative, I have a PhD, I take showers once a day! Oh, the hell with it!

The kids and I have a lovely picnic in the park. It's just beginning to be warm now, late May, and the benches are crowded with rows of old ladies and old men chatting or just sunning themselves. Oh, to be in England now that spring is here! As I recall, England's spring is a pretty shoddy affair, rain and more rain, not unlike New York. Ah, well.

"Take off my crusts," Elizabeth commands.

I have no knife, so I bite them off, which strikes both kids as terribly funny.

"You're so *silly,*" Timmy says. They're not quite used to grown-ups being silly. They like it, but they're not sure it's proper. Maybe in aunts it's okay.

Hertz Rent-a-Family. We're Number Two, so we try harder. Yes, I have, I admit, had the odd fantasy of Julian and Calla meeting a sudden and painless death on one of these infrequent trips of theirs. No doubt even if that happened, they have a will that gives the kids to some couple they know, some respectable married couple with children of their own. I mean, you don't give kids to an unmarried aunt, for Lord's sake. Still, in fantasies *you* set the rules, and in this fantasy there is no will and my parents are ruled too old and Boris and Eve are splitting—not that Eve would for a second tolerate two more kids in her house—and I am declared sole beneficiary.

It will be funny when I have my own child, I'm so used to being an aunt. What I hope and pray is that I don't just get a kick out of Elizabeth and Timmy because they're not mine, exclusively mine. It's Elizabeth I really love with a passion that is not fair, and I suspect it's purely and simply her being a girl.

Timmy is great, but when he lies there with his baseball cards, staring at the heroes of the day, I just have no sense of comprehension, no way of making that mental leap into what it must be like to be a small boy of six. Whereas it takes no leap at all to become Elizabeth. We're equals and companions, and that's all there is to it.

How did Calla do this fine thing, produce such a great daughter? It's not fair, is it? My other fantasy is that somehow Elizabeth really *is* my child in some science-fiction way. I mean, she does look just like me. I'm not the only one who has commented on that. Timmy is the spittin' image of Julian, ginger-haired with incredibly long eyelashes and freckles, a sweet, sweet boy, but Elizabeth already, at eight, has the Indian chief look, I swear. Her nose is getting more hooked day by day, and she has that shrewd, black-eyed, imperious, stubborn, dreamy expression which I recognize oh so well.

I fancy that as we lie here, people beam at us. Let them! Beam away, folks!

Elizabeth says, "I need to make a pee."

"So make one."

"Where?"

"Anywhere."

"But people will see."

"So? Most people around here have seen a vagina before in their lives; they won't faint."

"They're not *supposed* to see."

"Roo, it's your problem. . . . If you need to pee, pee."

She scrunches up her face and finally drags off to a semiprivate spot, where, spreading her legs apart about eight inches, she makes a fine pee. Then she walks back, her skirt up to her neck for me to wipe her with a napkin.

I love children's genitals. Why can't ours be like that, only bigger? I never saw the real purpose or beauty of pubic hair. In

40

fact, come to think of it, I always felt nature or whoever was responsible for the design of genitals could with a little more thought have come up with something both more practical and more esthetic. I can't believe this is the best that could have been done. Jesus, I read yesterday that the inside of a vagina is about as sensitive as the heel of a shoe. Now, if so, that wasn't smart. Not at all.

"So, what's on for the weekend?" I ask, drinking from the thermos cup.

"I want to go bicycle riding," Timmy says.

"*I* want the Junior Museum," Elizabeth says.

"I'll tell you, Roo, it's so nice today, let's do the bicycle riding and tomorrow the Junior, okay?"

She makes a face, hating the decision to go against her even if the reasons for it are good. Well, I understand that. I'm something of a mule myself.

Sunday morning I wake up at nine o'clock and lie there, feeling mysteriously happy and content. It's gone pretty well. Timmy did get up with a nightmare Saturday night—Friday he was fine—but after mumbling a bit about a "peach-colored skeleton," he dropped off to sleep. Now the two of them are in different corners of the room, Elizabeth scribbling intently in a large pad, Timmy with his baseball cards. I wonder how long they've been up. I sleep like a log, and anything short of a nuclear explosion usually fails to wake me.

I like watching them while they don't yet know I'm up. They look so wonderfully absorbed in their own worlds, so intent. Also, I just feel good myself. I guess I've been lucky in that I haven't had horrible nausea or morning sickness, not half so bad as some I've heard of. Instead what I've had is just some days that were awful from morning to night when I just felt as if I'd had an overdose of sleeping pills and could hardly drag myself around. It was worst when these came on days I had to go to the lab. Once it happened on a Sunday and I just slept all day, straight through till suppertime.

I think of a photo which keeps striking me in magazines. I believe it's an ad, but I can't remember what for. It shows a house in the country at dusk or nighttime. Everything is black and still except for a light or two in the window. Underneath it says something like: "When you feel that nothing can ever go wrong, that is called security." I'm sure the intense feeling this photo inspires in me now is more wishful thinking than anything else or maybe a vague memory of childhood, not specific since we never lived in the country or had such a house, but just that feeling of protection. I suppose what I mean is I had it as a child and lost it, as I guess one always does as an adult, and now wonder if I can possibly, especially on my own, create it for a child. Because I think it's important, and when I think of the baby really being here in six or seven months, I do have occasional pangs of fear.

I don't want her to have a slipshod bohemian sort of life. I'm not the world's most conventional person, but I guess about basics I do want to give, in whatever odd way, the sense that that photo inspires in me. I sigh. A minute ago I felt warm and serene, and now there's that slight-shadow-over-the-sun sort of feeling. But my sigh attracts Elizabeth's attention. She looks up.

"Boy, you certainly sleep a long time!" she says, continuing to write.

"It's only nine thirty," I say, smiling.

"*We've* been up since seven thirty," she says.

"*I've* been up since seven," Timmy says.

"You have *not*. . . . I was up before you," she says.

I yawn. "Hey, kids, how about breakfast?"

They are just cereal eaters, so that doesn't take long. While we're eating, squatting on the floor, Elizabeth says, "Do you want to see my list?"

42

GIVE ME ONE GOOD REASON

"What list?"

"It's a list of everybody in the whole wide world."

"What does it say about everybody in the whole wide world?"

She shows me the paper. "Everybody has a number," she says. "The best is a hundred. The only person who gets a hundred is Dorothy Landau."

"What has Dorothy Landau done to deserve this honor?"

"Dorothy Landau is my best, best, best, *best* friend. . . . She lives in 106 West Eighty-second Street."

"Aha, I see." I study the list. I cannot help being pleased that I get in the 80's. Calla gets two points higher, however, 88 to my 86. Poor Julian only gets 56. "Why only fifty-six for your daddy?" I say.

She shrugs. "Fifty-six is good," she says defensively. "What's wrong with fifty-six?"

Timmy is way down there with a 25, along with a few children I don't know. I sigh. There is something so horribly reminiscent in this idea of grading everyone so precisely, reminiscent of myself, though I can't remember actually having ever done such a thing. "What made you think of this, Roo?"

"I just wanted to," she says calmly. She picks up her bowl of Kaboom and drinks down the rest of the milk.

"Want to take a shower?" I ask.

"Yay!" they both yell, and instantly pajamas are flying in all directions. I do not know how Calla feels about my taking a shower with her children. I do not know if Spock or Gesell or any of the authorities have a footnote on the topic: showers with aunts, pro or con. Frankly, I don't even know if Calla knows about our showers. I'd feel like an idiot, saying, "Please do not tell your sacred mother about this because she may flip," so I never say anything.

Showering is fun. We all dance around, soaping each other back, front and everywhere. They are always curious about my pubic hair. "Why do you have so *much?*" Timmy says critically.

"That's just the way grown-ups are," I say. "It probably looks like more because it's dark."

They shampoo my pubic hair and my breasts, playing with the breasts as though they were rubber bath toys. Then I shampoo their hair. Timmy's penis is so small and white, almost more unlike an adult version than Elizabeth's vagina is.

When we get out and are toweling off, I say suddenly to Elizabeth, "Her name is Gwendolen," pointing to my vagina.

Like all lovers since time immemorial, Matthew and I had names for each other's genitals. Mine was Gwendolen and his Bunbury, both from *The Importance of Being Earnest*, a play we both loved. There must be something everyone feels about their genitals somehow having a life of their own which causes this naming, apart from the sheer whimsicality of it all.

"I want *mine* to have a name, too," says Elizabeth with sudden decisiveness.

"Okay."

She goes off and is intent and silent for a long while, evidently trying out various possibilities. Finally she says, "I think Lucille."

"That sounds like a good choice, Roo."

Timmy will have no part of this. He is back to his baseball cards.

But walking home later, Elizabeth looks up at me and smiles slyly. "How's Gwendolen?" she says.

"Fine," I say, smiling back. "How's Lucille?"

I love my gynecologist. I love her, but I hate her for having such a god-awful schedule in her office. I see her once a month and try to come during lunch hour, which is flexible in our lab. My disappearance may seem slightly odd since our section tends to lunch together, but so far it's been infrequent enough so that nobody has noticed, I don't think.

The trouble is her office is in Brooklyn, and the reason for that is that I wanted a woman to deliver my baby and women gynecologists are not all that easy to find. Why a woman? Maybe partly it's that my mother, though she's feminine in a certain way, if one can still use that word, isn't the least bit earthy. I can't conceive of discussing details of childbirth with her, and it's not only the peculiar circumstances of my particular pregnancy. She was of the generation where you were rendered unconscious as swiftly and totally as possible, and the whole idea of natural childbirth or of being interested in the process itself physically I think would be very alien to her. So maybe searching for a woman doctor is like searching for a certain kind of mother I've always partly imagined having, though no doubt it would have its own complications, someone hearty and basic and bread baking and jolly.

Dr. Hattie Armstrong is like that. She has five kids, though she says that if the population problem had been known about then, she wouldn't have. But I think she loves them and must be a great mother. She's heavyset and not really pretty, but she has a big, booming laugh and a round, freckled Irish face, though I don't think she is, in fact, Irish. She reminds me of a Renoir. I'm sure nude she has that heavy-breasted, hippy look which women nowadays shun like the plague. I wonder how she will take my decision not to breast-feed, which I haven't gone into yet. I think she will see it my way, I hope.

I wait till one thirty, and finally she ushers me into her examining room. Usually I'm back from lunch at one. This means I'll be back no sooner than two thirty. Well, what can you do?

I step on the scale, a little anxiously because of Calla's remark about my being fat. But Dr. Hattie just smiles approvingly.

"Terrific. . . . You just gained a pound." She whacks me on the shoulder. "You're in good shape, kid."

I smile ironically, but feel pleased as hell. "Thanks."

Afterward we go into her office, which is a morass of books, too much furniture, etc. But I prefer it to these very neat, formal Madison Avenue doctors' offices I've seen.

"Told anyone yet?" she says.

Dr. Hattie knows two things: that I wanted and planned for this baby and that the father is a "good friend," but someone I'm not planning to marry. I shake my head. "No, I'm putting it off as long as possible."

"Because of your job?"

I think about that a minute. "Not any more because of that than anything else. . . . No, just cowardice or common sense, maybe."

"You're planning to keep on working if they let you?"

If they let you! They sure better "let" me! But I just nod. "My job doesn't involve people," I say, carefully. "I mean, I do some teaching but just graduate students, mostly, it's just research. . . . So I don't see how there'd be any grounds, at my job, for . . . I mean, it's not like I was teaching high school."

She just looks at me. "These things are trickier than they should be."

"I know! Look, I know! But I do believe my job is safe. . . ." I put on a prissy expression, half-mockingly. "I will be shocked and offended if it's not . . . I'm the best researcher in the lab."

"Good," she says. "You'll need to be."

I like the camaraderie between us. I don't know if she approves or disapproves, but she accepts my decision, one which I've thought over and will go through. I guess she treats me with respect, is what it boils down to, and I need that now very badly.

On the subway back to the lab I wonder about what the reaction there will be. My technician, Frances, will be sympathetic. The rest is up for grabs. The institute is filled with middle-aged men who've hung on there, not because their research is any good but because the institute gets the money for research on its own and then doles it out to the fifty or so labs which constitute it. In short, instead of competing by way of grants for research money from the government the way most scientists have to, these fellows have an easy deal. Many of them really are jokers who would fall by the wayside instantly if they did have to compete.

I get along all right with most of them. We have to have dealings in meetings and so forth. Some of them are the sort who tell dirty jokes and then say elaborately, "Oops, I forgot there's a *lady* present." Let them tell as many dirty jokes as they like, though frankly their jokes are usually incredibly puerile, but the "there's a lady present" bit really bothers me. If they find out, I foresee nudging in the ribs, while I'm not present, of course, and dumbly coarse remarks about being "knocked up." Why should that bother me? I'm not a prude. I guess it's just that I'd like to feel some sense of human dignity about this. I can't bear, at thirty-two, a scientist who has done well and earned my keep, so to speak, to be the butt of locker-room-type jokes and that kind of thing.

Coming into my lab, I see Frances, who is just putting down the phone. "Lobochowski was in here before," she says. "You better go see him."

My heart sinks. Isn't this stupid and insane! Why guilt? First, it's clear no one on earth knows or could know now, but anyway, if I'm going to feel guilt before these people, then I'm in a bad way.

Of course, it turns out to be something completely different. We have a huge expensive scintillation counter in the lab which you have to sign up to use. There are always petty squabbles if there's any switch in the schedule, and now it seems Yoko

Nakimura, the little Japanese lady who also works in our section, wants me to give up my space because, so she claims, she desperately needs it by this afternoon.

"I'm down on the list," I say to Lobochowski.

"I know you are, Gabrielle," he says, "but could you possibly postpone...."

"No, I could not possibly postpone...."

He sighs. He and Yoko have a slightly comic relationship, almost like a married couple, though in real life neither of them is married. She is usually silent and self-effacing but occasionally has intense dramatic rages which terrify Lobochowski. He's always trying to get me or Paul D'Angelo, the other researcher in the lab, to try and calm her down.

"I'm sorry I was late coming back from lunch," I say. "I had to go to the dentist." Immediately I feel like giving myself a sharp kick in the shins. Why say anything? He's not asking. I must somehow figure out a way to exorcise this guilt thing or it will really screw me up.

Back at work, I think of Lobochowski. Why I smile as I contemplate his reaction is anyone's guess. Will I be smiling as I get booted out of this place? Basically, Lobochowski is my boss, and basically I feel that he cannot afford to let me go. His own work and Yoko's and even Paul's are a bit far afield from cancer research, which is supposedly what we're all engaged in. I feel he needs me to make his statement to the board of scientific advisers look official. When I smile, I am just wondering, slyly I guess, what he will feel personally.

What can you say about a thirty-nine-year-old Polish biochemist whose family owns a sporting goods store in Buffalo? Right there you have some, but not all by any means, of the Lobochowski problem. I know and sympathize with what it's like to have foreign-born parents in America. It's the great melting pot, sure, but it takes some longer to melt than others, and I bet in Buffalo fitting in may have been even harder than it was in New York. Lobochowski's family is huge. His father died years ago, but there are four sisters, all married with immense families, and I sense that Lobochowski was an enigma to all of them, being an intellectual, respected, probably, but also considered an oddball. He hasn't broken free of them in many ways. I gather they're rabidly right-wing, as probably small storeowners can be, and he is peculiarly so himself. I used to have great flaming political arguments with Lobochowski at lunch. I ceased, not out of fear for my job, but because it just wasn't worth it. I just felt that his right-wing thing was part of a whole. He's terrified of anything revolutionary at any level. Occasionally I still throw up the odd topic, almost out of a morbid curiosity to see how he'll handle it because partly he's a bit embarrassed at his views, without being ready to relinquish them.

He is a very, very strange fellow. It's not just being repressed to the utmost degree—I'm not the swinger of all time myself— it's that his sexual identity seems so utterly underground. If I had to make a guess, I'd say he was latently homosexual, but you'd have to underscore the "latent" rather than the "homosexual." It's not a bit like someone like Matthew, who may not go around picketing but is aware of his situation. With Lobochowski I'm sure that even if his best friend (and he has no friends) were to broach the matter in the dead of night, he would rise up and challenge him to a duel. There is no awareness, just an iceberg of antipsychological terror which runs deeper than I care to imagine.

Lobochowski lives with his mother, who is seventy-four and has a heart condition. Why the whole pack of multi-childrened sisters didn't take her in is more than I can guess. Only recently did he even get a kind of companion for her during part of the day. As it is, he still rushes home at lunch hour to fix her a hot lunch and rushes back here right afterward. She knows no English sinch I gather they always lived in a predominantly Polish neighborhood.

On top of all this, he still, believe it or not, runs the family sporting goods store in Buffalo. Again you'd think that after his father's death one of the brothers-in-law would have taken it over. Well, maybe they do in part, but Lobochowski, in addition to running the lab, which he does in his own peculiarly compulsive fashion, is often to be found brooding over stock lists of tennis shoes, squash rackets and the like. He has never, in the five years I've been here, taken a vacation. He is here seven days a week, often way past midnight. I often have moments of wishing I could steal up to Lobochowski and sink a tranquilizing shot into his leg the way they do to elephants that are sick but wouldn't, on their own, stay still long enough to receive medical attention. He is so wound up, talks so fast it's like a record player on 45. His smile flashes on like Charlie McCarthy, a sudden flip, then off again. Maybe someday he will shatter into a thousand tiny pieces, like Humpty Dumpty falling off the wall—or maybe not. I hope I won't be around long enough to find out.

He's a pathetic, driven person, and maybe, if I heard about him or read about him, I would feel more unadulterated compassion, but the fact is that he impinges very much on my daily life here, and that dilutes my feelings into what at times amounts to a murderous rage. Lobochowski did at one time do some good scientific work. But since I've been here he's become so compulsive even about that that he inevitably repeats experiments over and over until he is scooped by someone else. Which would be okay, if sad, but he also wants all the rest of us to repeat *our* experiments over and over and over. He himself shuns any general scientific meetings like the plague and is positively paranoid even about the people working down the hall. But if anyone in our section has to give a paper, say, he makes all of us stop and spend the entire day—and this can go on for a week—going over the paper, rehearsing it, criticizing it.

A few months ago Paul D'Angelo, Yoko and I were up for promotion. We each had to give a short talk on our work in front of the Scientific Review Board. Poor Yoko had a talk ready which, given her faltering English, wasn't so bad when she started. But by the end of a solid week of rehearsing it in front of us, Lobochowski criticizing her, rewriting it himself, having her rewrite it, he managed to reduce her to a quivering wreck and to render her paper more or less unintelligible. Naturally she wasn't promoted, whereas Paul and I, who underwent the same treatment but managed to keep our heads, were.

He doesn't do it to be sadistic. He's merely trying to be "nice," and I don't mean this ironically. He wants us to be as safe as he himself from making, God forbid, a "mistake."

On the whole my research is my own affair, and I discuss it with him as little as possible. But—and it's not such a small but—he has to go over any paper I write, any talk I give, and a truly immense amount of time can be wasted this way. To say nothing of the time involved in the almost-weekly birthday parties.

I think rebellion is brewing in the wings about the birthday parties; maybe, which would be delicious, a full-scale mutiny. Lobochowski decided that it would be a lovely custom if there were a birthday party for everyone in our section, not just the higher-ups like Paul, Yoko, himself and me, but for everyone, all the technicians, all the cleaning ladies. This is quite a crowd. So each time such an occasion occurs there is much secrecy, cakes and cookies bought, and virtually a mob scene of everyone jumping out yelling "Happy birthday!" at the supposedly dumbfounded celebrant. For Lobochowski's own birthday there is a real Polish feast—sausages, wine, etc. And of course there's the Christmas party too. Most labs or offices have

Christmas parties, but we have a real Santa—one of us, picked by drawing from a hat. We each write little ditties, buy tiny presents for someone else to be drawn from a big sack. I don't know who it was who finally said one day that, apart from the truly insane amount of time wasted on these functions, there were those of us who, being beyond the age of ten, didn't really care to have quite such a production made out of our birthdays and holidays. Lobochowski got very hurt and said he couldn't understand this, maybe it was just that he was a bachelor and therefore we were his "family," but he simply couldn't bear to give it up. Also, he felt that deep down we would all miss it terribly, no matter what we said. At this he often casts a meaningful glance in my direction, meaning, I guess, that I, being a "bachelor girl," must understand even if the others don't.

Like anything else, despite the weirdness of it, most of the time I give it not a thought and go about my business. Just occasionally the sheer madness of it all descends on me, and I wonder if I shouldn't look elsewhere for a job.

"There were two calls for you," Frances says as I return from talking to Lobochowski.

"Okay, but listen, did you run the sucrose gradients through yet?"

She nods.

I am lucky with Frances. She's not only good, but she's remarkably easygoing, which with Lobochowski breathing down her neck, as he does occasionally, is not so easy. Not that I feel exactly free to spit in his eye, but for a technician it's even harder, and I don't think her opinion of him is much higher than mine.

"Have a nice lunch?" she says and smiles.

Secrets, secrets.

I am still in my third month. I am still in the time when I

could have a miscarriage, but I don't think I will. Not that it matters, but I've been living in my parents' house for nearly a month and it seems to be working. Jessie comes down to visit me on her own quite often, but they don't unless I go up.

I miss Matthew, but it's been as I expected. I'm not anguished about living alone again, though it's the first time I've done so in five years. The trouble is—well, whether it's a trouble or not, I don't know—I don't mind being alone. I think it comes more easily to me than adapting my life-style to someone else's. I can keep the hours I want. I don't feel, yet anyway, lonely in the classic sense.

Sex may be a problem, we'll see. At the moment masturbation seems a sufficient diversion. I must admit, which I think is typical of me in a way I don't like all that much, that part of me never quite got past masturbation. It always seemed so easy and so quick, and it took me a long time to find intercourse a suitable substitute. I attribute this, apart from my shyness as a girl and the fact that I didn't sleep with anyone till I was twenty, to a certain conflict about physicality which I can't say even now I've really resolved. Even my way of masturbating is odd, though I never thought it odd until I thought about it at all—*e.g.*, when I was in my twenties and had been doing it for ten years or so. What's odd about it is that I never touch myself while masturbating. I just lie there and perhaps clench my legs together slightly and that alone always, if I'm in the mood, produces an instant orgasm. I've heard sex is largely in the head anyway and in my case that seems more true than it may be for many others. I can sit in a taxicab and have on my face the blankest expression and be having an orgasm, if I feel like it. It never even occurred to me that masturbation for most people involves not only touching but manipulating, squeezing the genitals, for me it was so cerebral. The good effect this has had on my sexual life is that if I'm in the right mood, I can have an orgasm with anyone. I never know or really care if the man I'm sleeping with is a "good" lover since it doesn't seem to have any effect on whether I get pleasure or not. If I'm in a mood to get pleasure, I seem to get it, and if I'm not, I think I could sleep with Casanova himself and nothing would happen. So I've probably made a lot of insecure men feel great and a few overconfident ones wonder what happened.

I accept this fact about myself without altogether liking it. It obviously serves to make me sufficient onto myself in some ways which for a single person is useful. But I admire passion, even self-destructive passion, and wish, at times, that it at least had the power to tempt me. For instance, I've always admired alcoholics, homosexuals and drug addicts solely because they all to me seem people who are driven, by a kind of passion, to pursue a goal which society disapproves of, which they'll pursue even to the point where it causes them acute pain. I drink wine at dinner and smoke pot from time to time, but I never detect in myself the ability to become "addicted" to anything. If I went mad, which I doubt I'll do, probably I'd become catatonic, just curl up into a withdrawn shell. Whereas I love and admire people who go off screaming and wild into the night.

With Matthew gone, I don't know what will happen about sex since I don't see masturbation as a really effective long-term proposition. The trouble is, I'm not used to casual sex; maybe I'll have to *get* used to it again. There was a time after college when I was in my early twenties when, even if I didn't sleep around on any grand scale, I did sleep with a variety of people for a variety of reasons, and whether it was pleasant or not, the mere idea didn't faze me. It was what you did, what girls of my generation did anyway. Behind it was the goal, which I certainly never attained, of being as free sexually as we imagined men to be. Certainly the men I've gotten to know at all well have been far from free sexually and I'm beginning to wonder how valid that is. But it was the goal, and there was a certain vroom or whatever from doing it. Am I getting old or what? Or is it just having lived with Matthew and having had a peaceful, pleasant sex life for six years? No doubt we were both repressed in complementary ways, but for whatever reasons, we always seemed to want to do it about as often, in the same ways. I don't think our encounters, if recorded on tape or screen, would have been exemplars of passion, but we were pleased, and for those six years nothing else seemed to matter.

Now I guess I'm in the open market again. Matthew and I always declared each other free to go off with anyone we fancied, but when it came down to it, neither of us did. So I am quite out of practice and also not in the least inspired to go to parties or singles bars or any of those kinds of things. "Let the world come to me," used to be my motto as far as men went, and I suppose it will be again. How far that will get me, at my age, with my peculiarities, I am not all that sure.

I think I'm more peculiar than I used to give myself credit for. On the one hand, being single suits me since I love being alone, love silence, love independence, love long walks with the dogs. But I would also like a regular sex life, and unfortunately these two are hard to combine. I'd been hoping that being pregnant might make me uninterested in sex, but no such luck. Maybe toward the very end, but frankly now with my breasts burgeoning I feel quite sensual and ready to be made use of. Ah, well.

"I don't want to bother you," Mother says. She's standing at the door. It's Sunday morning, and I'm in Matthew's Viyella robe, which he left with me.

"That's okay," I say. "Do you want to come in?"

Sunday mornings Mother and Daddy usually set off on long walks in the park. They look dapper and charming, Mother in her suede coat, Daddy in his silly Tyrolean hat and cane. They walk to Seventy-second and back and then have a long tea at home. "Would you come to tea later?" Mother says. "We're quite concerned about Boris, Gabby. . . . We want—well, I don't want to talk about it now. . . . Can you come?"

"Certainly. . . . Four or so?"

"We'll see you then, then."

After she leaves, I sigh and return to the Sunday *Times*. Then I sit at the window and wait to watch them emerging. On the one hand, our family track record on marriage is not all that great, which may explain my own skittishness on the subject. Mother was married before as I've said, and so was Daddy. Daddy's family is Dutch—hence our family name, Van de Poel—and he was married while in Holland, a marriage which dissolved by the time he came to the States. His first wife, Anika, is remarried to a physics professor in Berkeley, and we get Christmas cards from "Aunt Anika" every year, the kind with color photos of her children. Daddy speaks of her when he does with a friendly condescension, as though she were an overweight older sister. I gather their marriage was okay, but just dull and not very sexy, whereas Mother's first was not at all dull and quite sexy but just not good for other reasons. Then there's Boris, who married Eve six years ago and has separated from her twice. There's Calla's Julian, who was married before—even *his* brother, Teddy, is just getting divorced, and his parents split long ago. So there seems an ambience about everyone who even marries into our family which is not that conducive to matrimony. Which may be why Calla embraces her middle-class mama role with such a vengeance.

But despite all this, when I see Mother and Daddy—as I do now—trot off on their Sunday walk, I feel something akin to envy. They are such a "couple." I used to think Mother hung too much on Daddy. It's part of the European charm bit; she does all but wipe his behind for him when he shits. However, I like it, I like their calling each other "dear" and never quarreling in public and having separate bedrooms but still seeming very affectionate. I like the formality of it and the affection of it. I'm not sure, however, that it's a way of life that will be or can ever be mine.

Mother has a set of Arabia ware for her tea set. It's lovely, brown, grainy, solid. She pours now and remembers that I take milk and sugar.

Daddy is munching on a roll and some fresh scallions.

"Is it the thing of his business?" I ask, sipping tea.

"He's bankrupt," Daddy says dismissively.

"Dear, he's not really. . . . It's not quite *that* bad," Mother intervenes.

"Your mother knows so much about business," Daddy says ironically.

"He's not really 'cleaned out,' is he?" Mother says, the expression sounding foreign on her lips.

"He will be soon."

I nod. "That's too bad."

"What I wonder—I was thinking again," Mother said. "I feel Boris would be such a good architect. . . . He has such an eye for form. I don't say that lightly. He does."

"He does," I echo genuinely.

"So I just wondered . . . couldn't you perhaps mention to him again. . . ."

I sigh. "Mother, why me?"

She looks embarrassed. "Who, then? He never sees Calla. If it's one of us. . . ."

"Anyway, I've mentioned it before," I say, which is true.

"I know," she says, "but I feel now with the business failing . . . I mean, it must strike even him that he doesn't quite have the . . . touch for business endeavors."

"Umm." Ooh, do I hate errands of this kind. Like every child of parents born, I guess I take some pleasure in being the "good child," a role I played to the hilt while younger, and I liked hearing Boris and Calla abused or, if not abused, "the object of concern." So it's not a fluke that they are coming to me for this. I've encouraged it for years, and now it serves me right. "Well . . . maybe I'll see him soon," I mumble. "I told Eve I might drop over there some evening."

There is a small silence.

"How *is* Eve?" Mother says.

"She's well."

They look at each other. Finally I say, "I don't know what's happening with them, really."

Daddy shrugs. Boris' marriage is, to him, just another failure.

It's unfair. With Boris Daddy is so harsh and totally unforgiving, ready to take any failure as "typical," any success as a peculiar fluke which time will soon undo. Not that Boris' life hasn't been strewn with various kinds of failures so far, but I've always felt Daddy's attitude didn't help. In the last ten years Boris has started law school, business school, graduate school in economics, has worked in a publishing house, on Wall Street and in the Seventh Avenue garment district. He has talent, a fact no one seems to deny, but he can't seem to "get it all together." And the same has been true of his personal life.

I don't altogether blame Daddy. What I feel is just that the sons of self-made men—which Daddy is in a sense—seem to have a much harder time than the daughters of self-made men. Maybe because the competition is more direct and less softened by the kind of indirect sexuality which exists with fathers and daughters.

For me, and I know it's selfish to consider Boris' life mainly as it affects mine, but so be it, Boris is an albatross around my neck. I feel his success would free me and that his failure weighs me down. I'm not to blame for Boris' fate—I doubt either he or anyone else would suggest that. But I somehow never feel scot-free either. As children we were locked in a deadly murderous kind of competition. With Calla I never felt it.

We've had our ups and downs, but I never felt threatened by Calla, maybe because I was several years older than she. Whereas Boris, being several years older than I, was the one against whom I pitched myself and all my efforts to succeed.

In the beginning it was the good child versus the bad. He was wild and unruly; I was quiet and obedient. No doubt in a more "American" family his rowdiness might have been looked on with favor, but Daddy is about the least likely person in the world to go out pitching baseballs to his son, and all Boris' possibly natively masculine obstreperousness was held against him, whereas my sly, determined competitiveness was encouraged and seen as charming. In school I not only always did well, but did especially well in all those traditionally masculine subjects—mathematics, science—in which he might have been expected to succeed. In another family scholarly achievement at school mightn't have counted so much, but in a family like ours, newly arrived in America, seeing the children as the ones who would somehow scale the ladder either economically or socially, the ones to do well at school were the ones who were most to be valued. Boris was fair at sports, not remarkable, and even there, with sheer undaunted effort, *I* was the one who managed to become an excellent baseball player, hitting (I recall this afternoon vividly even today) three home runs and a triple in one game, shooting more baskets from the center line than anyone in the class, being the best guard on hockey, a veritable demon at whacking the ball away from the other team.

I think it started innocently—that is, I had certain abilities and applied them, and Boris had and didn't. But by the time we were in our teens it was more than innocent, though maybe not quite conscious, at least on my part. Chess was a perfect example. Boris, especially around the age of sixteen, loved chess and spent all his free Saturday afternoons at the Manhattan Chess Club, observing, playing, studying books on the game. And I, at the age of fourteen, sat down and for six straight months read every available book on chess I could lay my hands on, played and played until the day when I could beat Boris consistently. He, then, gave up the game completely and has never played it again. And I, having reached that goal, ceased to play anymore either. I still like chess and will, if the occasion arises, play the odd game, but the fact that, at fourteen, it was that important to me to go past him even in a hobby is a fairly grisly commentary on my personality.

Boris' one revenge, in these years, was in his social life. He was remarkably handsome at fifteen, not very tall, but with dark eyes, almost too perfectly chiseled features, but more than that, quite suave and nastily witty and quick and sarcastic in the manner of certain New York boys. He had all the girlfriends he wanted, whether he slept with them or not, and assuredly he tormented quite a few of them. Whereas I, at around this age, was abnormally tall, having reached my full height of five ten at the age of eleven, with a bumpy skin, huge feet, a morbidly shy, self-conscious personality, a wallflower par excellence. Boris played that to the hilt. If I was dressed to go out to some dance, he would say, studying me carefully, "You could look fairly good . . . *if* you had your nose done." Or he'd point out some pimple which I thought I had carefully concealed under tons of acne cream. Just what I needed to eradicate what small amount of self-confidence I had socially.

It was revenge, and maybe I "deserved" it. The only irony now is that at thirty-five Boris has lost almost all his hair and has to tease and fluff it around his head, he wears glasses—in short, whereas I may not have bloomed into the knockout of all time, our physical selves are no longer such poles apart. But—and herein lies the crux—he still hasn't found his thing intellectually.

Oh, I've suggested at times he be a dentist, a lawyer, anything, anything I felt to get him off my back, to free me. I've almost felt at times that his failure was almost deliberate, just to spite me, though I know that's not the case.

60

And maybe—which would be an amusing irony if so—I'd be very jealous if he did succeed. Maybe even now I get some subliminal satisfaction out of still being Number One. I don't think that's so either, but I'm not willing to clear myself one hundred percent.

After tea I go downstairs and call Boris and Eve's number. Eve answers.

"I thought I might come over some evening," I say as coolly as possible. "Is Thursday okay?"

"Sure, why not?" With Eve you never know, through her voice, what she's feeling.

"How's eight thirty?" I decide to eat at the lab and go from there.

"Perfect. . . . See you then."

I get Jessie to promise to walk the dogs since I'll be back late; she's delighted.

"Where's Boris?" I look around the living room. "Putting Miranda to bed?"

Eve waves her hand dismissively. "He'll be back later," she says, offering no further explanation.

I suppose I should have said on the phone that it was Boris I was supposed to see. But now that it's turned out this way, I'm more than a little relieved to have Eve to chat with for a bit before the sure-to-be-unsuccessful probing into Boris' career plans.

Miranda looks out from the door of her room but says nothing. She's a very beautiful, very sullen little girl of four, looks like Boris with those black, black eyes. Eve calls her a "bitch," and they've never gotten along, something Calla ascribes to Eve's being a terrible mother. According to Calla, a child is a "blank slate" upon which anything can be written, and if sullenness is there writ, the parent is solely responsible. Eve takes the opposite view, that children are born complete with personalities that are already formed and only become revealed in time, but were always there down to the last detail. I guess the truth, as they say, lies somewhere in between. I don't have any personal conviction one way or the other—yet.

On the table are some sketches—Eve designs jewelry and is very good at it, though I don't imagine she earns enough to support the family should Boris' business go under again. It's transfusions from Daddy that have kept them afloat until now.

"How's it going?" I say.

"Very well, actually," she says.

"I want a spoon," Miranda says finally, having been staring at us the entire time.

"So go get yourself a spoon," Eve says. "You know where they are."

Miranda emerges, walks slowly to the kitchen and returns with a spoon.

"You have ten minutes, Miranda," Eve says.

"I want to see Daddy!" Miranda says, aggrieved.

"Well, 'Daddy' is not here," Eve says, ironically and dryly.

Miranda with her spoon vanishes.

Eve raises her eyebrows. "Ah, children!"

Eve should make me nervous, I guess. She's someone who hesitated tremendously about having children and now regards it as a terrible mistake. How awful it must be to discover that so coldly and finally when your child is only four. Anyway, I guess it should prove to me that not everyone, simply by virtue of being healthy and female, is cut out for motherhood.

"Discovered a cure for cancer yet?" Eve says, pouring me coffee.

"Not yet . . . just trucking along," I say. I don't, for some reason, mind Eve's dry, sparing personality. I knew her at college, though she was four years younger than me and we weren't friends. What made me notice her, what made everyone notice her, was that, even as a freshman, at seventeen

62

or eighteen or whatever, she had it all together in a way most people I know never manage to at all. She was very smart, she was very pretty, she dressed charmingly, perfectly, not too fashionably, not stiffly, but always looking terrifically "right." I remember one male teacher I had saying of her, "If I'd met Eve Hammerling when I was eighteen, I'd have been scared out of my wits." My only other recollection of her from around that era was running into her one day on the library steps when I was getting my doctorate. I had, as a senior, won a prize for the most all-round something—otherwise I doubt she would have known or remembered me at all. At any rate, what she said was, "I do hope you're continuing with your work. . . . So many girls give it all up, and it's such a shame." I really felt like socking her one. There she was, twenty years old and speaking with such awful condescension and self-assurance. What did she know about what made girls give things up or not? I remember thinking as I walked away, "Someday you'll get yours, kid. . . . I wish I could be around to see it."

And then she married Boris. A total "coincidence." They didn't meet because of me or anything, but by now Eve has become, in her own way, another of Boris' failures. She's still terribly pretty with very, very short blond hair—only very pretty girls can wear their hair like that and get away with it. She has a tiny blob of a nose, "ice blue" eyes, which I've never seen except in Juicy Fruit ads, and the same air of absolutely uncrushable self-confidence. She claims she suffers, and I'm sure she does, but it's all done with such style that one doesn't, as it were, suffer along with her. She has affairs—in fact, she was married briefly before Boris, a marriage that was annulled—and it seems in the cards that one day she'll up and leave him. And in this, too, for some stupid reason I feel responsible. I didn't introduce them, they met, courted, married owing to reasons that had nothing to do with me. But I guess I feel maybe I somehow set Boris in that pattern of wanting to conquer unconquerable tough girls, of which I was, not at all in the same way, the early Platonic ideal. Oh, fooey! I should repeat over a hundred times a night: I'm not guilty, I'm not guilty.

"I hear you're living at home," she says, fixing me with her bright gaze.

"Well, only in the sense . . . I have my own apartment. It's working well."

"God, I'd hang by my toes before I'd move back within a hundred miles of my parents."

"Mine are different."

"In a way. . . . But they send out their own signals."

"I guess I've learned to duck when I see them coming." I wonder privately if that's so.

"You probably can," she says thoughtfully. "You've always had that ability to compartmentalize your life."

I know people see me this way as superorganized, supercool. It has a surface validity, so I don't rush to deny it.

"Actually, I'm here because they're worried about Boris," I say, deciding to get it over with in part with her.

"What *about* Boris?" she says coolly, implying, somehow, that there's more than one thing one could worry about if one were so inclined.

"I gather his business is . . . not doing so well," I say.

She snorts. "You might say that."

At times I feel exasperated with Eve. If you hate him—leave him. But in fact, she's done that a few times. And they do have a child. And of course, it's easy to rule other people's lives. I get along better with Eve than I do with Boris. She doesn't hate me, for one, and we have a feminine camaraderie which is missing in my relationship with him with nothing else to take its place. I've often heard it said that there's more competitiveness between two people of the same sex than two people of the opposite sex. I wonder. Maybe the former is more common, but it seems to me the latter, whether between brother and sister or husband and wife, is more deadly when it *is* there.

Without moving, Eve calls out, "Miranda, it's nine. . . . Will you please turn off your light?"

There is no sound. Then about a minute later there is a click.

"She'll stay up till he comes home anyway," Eve says.

"What does she do there in the dark?"

"Have fantasies. . . . Plan my funeral, God knows."

"If you get divorced, will you let Boris have Miranda?" I say, frowning.

Eve sighs. "Oh, Lord, Gabby, I don't know. . . . I'd hate myself forever. . . . Isn't it crazy, I've put more of myself into my relationship with her than I have into anything in my life, I can't believe it's worked out so badly. . . . I just don't know if it's vanity or what—how could I have screwed it up? I'm not crazy. I don't go off in a huff or walk out—but we just plain don't get along, as *people*. If we met at a party, we'd exchange two words and part. And I don't know why."

"And you think that's possible—with a child?" I say.

"I don't *think*. I mean, it's not something I have any thoughts about, just feelings. . . . I would that it were not so. . . . I hate myself for it, I think it's unfair to her to have a mother like me. . . . But I really do think that with another child, I'd have been different."

"You really do?"

She nods. "Maybe I'm deceiving myself or whatever, but I do."

"That's sad," I say after a moment.

"It is . . . for everyone."

As we sit there, I am aware in a physical sense of the baby sitting in my stomach, already, if Eve is right, a person with whom I will or will not get along, someone who will either be funny and great like Elizabeth or sullen and detached like

Miranda, someone utterly unknown. And with me there'll be no Boris to lighten the burden, to be a good father to my bad mother. It's win all or what—lose all? Help!

"Do you think you will get divorced?" I say, trying to shift the topic away from children.

Eve is silent a long time. "I don't know," she says finally. "I seem to go in circles and circles, it's absurd. . . . Maybe I don't really have the courage to be on my own—yet."

"On your own with Miranda?"

"Or without her. . . . Even with her, which would be easier in ways. . . . I like life to be comfortable, and I don't earn that much money, and the men I'd take up with would be bohemian screwballs with no dough, completely unreliable."

I smile. "Why would they be, necessarily?"

"Because that's the type I go for, unfortunately. . . . Only I don't really at bottom like that sort of screwed-up life. I like comfort and luxury and time to do what I want with my work."

I snort. "It's funny you picked Boris then."

"Maybe. . . . I still think Boris will make it, oddly enough. . . . I certainly thought so when we got married, and I still do think so."

"What if you stop thinking so?"

"Then I'll leave him."

"Does he know?"

"I imagine."

Eve is so damn cool. I can't imagine running my sex or love life this way. It's funny that she thinks I "compartmentalize" my life. She gets up to fix more coffee. From her kitchen she says, "I wish I could find a solution to sex somehow."

"In what sense. . . . Going off with people?"

"Umm . . . from time to time."

"Well, you do. . . . Or you did with what's-his-name."

She laughs. "What's-his-name is right. . . . Sure, only Boris hates it. . . . He doesn't want to do it himself. If he did, it might

66

make it at least fair. He took me back that one time, but I don't know.... Maybe he would again." She considers. "He might.... Only it was such a *thing,* so much guilt.... I hate being guilty, but I am somehow. And stupid as it sounds, I think I might hate it if Boris did it.... I guess I believe in the double standard in reverse.... I'd be jealous as hell if he even thought of it...."

I do like Eve. She's honest and funny, and it's only her "connection" with Boris that makes me uneasy. I wonder if I like talking to her because Boris comes out in such a—well, if not bad, not a very good light. Am I getting some sneaky pleasure out of hearing him belittled? I don't know if he knows how much Eve tells me. I doubt he'd be happy if he did.

He arrives at ten thirty, just as I'm yawning and wondering if I shouldn't take off. I'm a morning person, and by ten I start drooping. I certainly feel very, very unlike a big discussion of his future career.

"Oh, hi, Gabby." With me he's always carefully polite except when we're alone. Then he can be very cutting. So I like having Eve around for protection. "How's the great cure for cancer coming?"

"Okay." Needless to say, Boris is not that interested in my work either, though he knows more about science than Calla does. He likes hearing only the negative things, and I, in an awful masochistic way, usually dredge up everything bad I can think of in an attempt to placate him. It does no good. In fact, it may just incite him, and I know this and still do it; I can't seem to stop myself. I belittle my colleagues, make fun of my own experiments and, of course, ruthlessly conceal anything good that might be happening. Then, when I leave, I feel awful, as though the version I'd presented were the truth.

"Your boss gone off the deep end yet?"

"Not quite." Naturally I make Lobochowski even more insane than he is, which isn't so very hard.

I take a deep breath. "Listen, this is stupid, but I'm here on a mission. Daddy says your business is falling apart and Mother thinks you should think of becoming an architect and I have to go home to sleep."

"Amen," says Eve.

"Tell them I appreciate their concern." He disappears into the other room.

"Daddy!" calls Miranda.

He goes in to her.

I shrug and look at Eve. "I did my duty."

"They're incredible!" she says.

"Well, all parents are concerned about their children. . . ."

"He's thirty-five."

"So . . . they're even more concerned."

"And they send you as envoy? Incredible!"

"Well, if Miranda was somehow screwing up her life, wouldn't you care?"

"If she was thirty-five, I hope I'd have cut the cord and run years before. . . . However, my problem isn't exactly overconcern, so maybe I oughtn't to be the one to say."

I get up, looking for my coat. "I *do* think Boris would be a good architect."

"Sure he would. . . . So would I."

"No, I mean . . . really."

"*I* mean really. . . . Lots of people would be good at lots of things. . . . Which has zero to do with what they actually do or become."

"Okay." I feel put down as only Eve can make me feel put down. "Sorry, sorry. . . ."

She hands me my coat. "How's *your* sex life," she says, "speaking of irrelevancies?"

"Is my sex life that irrelevant?"

"I just meant in context. . . . No, I gather Matthew is now one of the dear departed."

"He's in England."

"That's what I meant."

"I'm a celibate at the moment."

"That doesn't sound like much fun."

"It isn't." I wave. "Thanks for the coffee."

"Anytime."

Waiting for the bus, I wonder if I need have handled that quite as badly as I did. The combination of Boris and Eve does something to me. I mean, I'm not a great one for fast repartee, but the tensions between them and then between me and Boris probably make me clumsier than usual. And maybe Eve is right. I have no business coming on such an errand. If his business is failing, it's their affair or his, certainly not mine, for Lord's sake. Parent pleaser.

A pregnant parent pleaser.

It is getting hot, and I hate the heat. My waist lines are getting tighter.

Going into the lab just before lunch to pee, I discover blood on my underpants. It is bright red, and there's quite a lot of it. Only the fact that I have on fairly heavy panty hose over the underpants prevented it from seeping through. Oh, no. . . . I thought I was past the miscarriage time or at least the time when it was most common, but no doubt it can happen anytime. . . . Oh, no, please, no! I sit here tensely. What now? One trouble is that, owing to my particular situation, I haven't discussed the pregnancy much with anyone. I guess if you're married, you hack over all the details with your friends, and no doubt if I had, I'd have discussed the topic of bleeding, the whys and wherefores. No doubt I might be comforted to learn it was common—please let that be possible—or to know how miscarriages occur when they do. Eve, for instance, had a miscarriage once, and now that I think of it at the time she described the whole thing in great detail, of which at this moment I can remember not one word. What's wrong with me? I've been told I'm such a great listener. The fact is, I listen and my mind wanders from here to Kalamazoo and back. When I want to concentrate, I can very well, but I can also get on a bus and arrive home two hours later having changed to two other buses, bought a pumpkin pie, mailed letters, and I'll have no idea how any of these things occurred. I'm a mind wanderer. My mind goes "walk about," as they said of that Australian girl tennis player. Blood, blood. I know I've read in my much-leafed-through volume *Pregnancy and Birth* about bleeding, but what? It must be tension, but it's all vanished from my mind. I know pregnant women do bleed, that bleeding often means miscarriage, and that is all I know on earth and not all I have to know.

Please, God, don't let me have a miscarriage! If I were God, I would say: blow off, lady! It's dames like you who say you're atheists or agnostics or what have you, but when the crunch is down, it's Oh, God, this and Oh, God, that. Okay, God, you're right. If I were you, I'd feel the same way. But just the same, please, I have to talk to somebody!

I planned this baby, doesn't that count for anything? I didn't have an abortion, not that the matter came up since I wanted it wholeheartedly. I'm going to bring it up myself, doesn't that impress you? I mean, I'm not just some screwed-up single lady who woke up to find herself pregnant and didn't have the courage for an abortion. I really want this baby!

I've been sitting on the toilet ten minutes. The blood is still dripping, slowly and quietly, but it's dripping. I can feel it. I go to the Kotex machine and buy some supplies, fasten a pad under my legs. Usually, when I have my period, I use Tampax, but now I want to see if the blood is going to continue to flow. It's lunchtime too, nearly twelve.

At lunch I sit like a zombie, smiling occasionally in what I hope doesn't seem like an insane way just to indicate my presence . . . not of mind, certainly. My only thoughts are for what is happening between my legs. I think it's stopping, no, no, it's not, yes, it is. Well, I'll check as soon as we get out of here. I'm almost desperate enough to turn to Frances, my technician, and say some spiel about: I have a friend and she's pregnant and she started to bleed and I wonder what it means, but no, that sounds too transparent, I just can't.

After lunch I race upstairs to the bathroom and lock myself in one of the little cubicles. There's more blood. It's hard to tell with blood how much is a lot. This is true. It's so red it shows so much it looks like a lot. I mean, if it were pale gray, it probably would look like less. . . . Will you cut it out?

I have to call Dr. Hattie and obviously not from my office. I go downstairs to a pay phone. I also happen to have a seminar in forty-five minutes, one of a series which Yoko, Paul and I share in alternating sessions. I have my notes, I'm all prepared. . . .

Dr. Hattie is at Mount Sinai, where she has her rounds or whatever at this time. I call that number, and they say they'll try and trace her. I stand in the phone booth, the pad feeling smelly and wet and heavy between my legs.

"Dr. Armstrong? It's me . . . Gabrielle Van de Poel . . . I'm just calling, I hate to bother you, I'm sure this is just a trifle, it's just I thought, well, it's that I've been bleeding and I thought, well—"

"Since when?" she says very quick.

"Oh, um, since, well, let's see, since about eleven thirty this morning."

"Steadily?"

"Yes, well, oh, wait a sec, I said eleven thirty, I guess probably it started a little earlier because I just noticed it at eleven thirty and there was already some there."

"It didn't begin when you woke up this morning?"

"Oh, no, no, not at all."

"What color is the blood?"

Color, color. Pale gray? "It's, um, red."

"Dark red or bright red?"

"Brightish, I'd say."

"Umm-hmm. . . . Well, Gabrielle, why don't you meet me over here as soon as you can?"

"Over where?"

"Over here. . . . At the hospital. . . . I'll meet you here and we'll see what we can do about getting you a room."

"What do you mean? Do you mean. . . . Does that mean you think it's a miscarriage?"

"Well, frankly, I can't tell anything for certain until I examine you, but I'd like to get you off your feet as soon as possible."

I go up in the elevator, my heart racing. I was so sure, somehow, that she'd say: tush tush, my girl, you're making mountains out of molehills, what's a little blood among friends, all that. . . . Oh, fuck it all, I'm having a miscarriage. God damn it, damn it, damn it.

Lobochowski isn't in his office, so I go to Paul. "Listen, Paul, something's come up with my family, an emergency, and I have to go to the hospital immediately. . . . So, could you—I have the first seminar today—could you go there and do whatever, tell them I'll reschedule tomorrow and post the new time on the board?"

"Sure."

I give Frances a few instructions about what to do in the next couple of hours and say I'll call her later.

I hail a cab and am at Mount Sinai by three.

Dr. Hattie seems different in this context. She seems more doctorly, more brisk and efficient. I'm still in my white lab coat, and she's in one too, and I guess neither of us has seen the other in working gear. She examines me silently and gravely, which doesn't help the butterflies which are leaping and dancing all around my stomach.

"Okay, well, I've arranged a room for you, Gabrielle. . . . Let me get you settled, and then we'll have a little talk."

I feel like weeping or yelling with rage. This isn't fair. Not fair! People all over this insane overpopulated globe are having unwanted *hated* babies, unplanned babies, women with four or five kids, teen-age girls who will dump on their mothers. Can't I have my one measly daughter?

I have been guilty of no moral sin. In fact, my motives for having this child are so good. I don't want a child so that she will be better than I am, so she will do what I left undone. I'm quite content with my life. I want a child for the purest, the simplest, the best motives. Oh, shit!

I am lying in bed staring angrily at a TV set which is hooked up in the corner. Dr. Hattie says quietly, "I don't know if you're having a miscarriage, Gabrielle. . . . You may not be. . . . There *are* some women who bleed all through their pregnancies, and it means nothing."

"Even as far as the baby's well-being is concerned?"

"Right. . . . It can mean nothing and can affect the baby not at all. . . . It may just be a fluke of a particular woman's metabolism. . . . Now, naturally it's easier to gauge this in a second pregnancy where you know the woman's patterns. . . . You've never been pregnant before?"

I shake my head.

"Never had an abortion?"

"Uh-uh."

"Well, we'll just have to see, then. . . . You have to rest, and tomorrow I'll check you out. . . . If the pains get worse and there's more blood, please call my office immediately."

Left alone, I try to take some comfort from the fact that there has been, now that she mentioned it, no pain. Look, what do I want? She's left some hope and I'll hang onto it as long as possible. But I feel exhausted and drained and as low as possible. Finally I fall asleep, and when I wake up, it's past five. I call

Jessie and tell her to walk the dogs. There's no need to tell anyone where I am, and I don't.

Oh, I do feel bad! I used to give blood sometimes while I was in college, and I remember right afterward that drained, zonked feeling, as though I were as hollow as a shell. In the room next to mine is an ancient old man—I saw him being wheeled down the hall, all crumpled up with his chin on his knees. Now, at night, he keeps getting up and going to the bathroom, and there's a great deal of bellowing for nurses and the nurses yelling out cheerfully (I guess he's close to deaf), "That's okay now. . . . You're doing fine!"

So it is three in the morning! What's it to them, or him or me for that matter? Have they put me in the geriatrics ward by mistake? Maybe that's where I belong. I can see myself in twenty or thirty years: sixty-year-old single lady finally gives birth after years of miscarriages, oldest living case on record.

I'm so healthy—that's what kills me. I eat tons of meat and fresh spinach and fruit. You'd think I'd be Popeye. . . . Well, I guess all that is irrelevant. I finally drop off to sleep around four and am awakened at what seems like a remarkably short time later for breakfast. Then, at seven thirty, Dr. Hattie appears, fresh and perky in her white coat.

"So, how goes it, my dear?"

"I don't know."

"How do you feel?"

"Psychologically rotten. . . . Physically okay, I guess, except for having about two hours' sleep."

She grins. "Oh, sorry about that. . . . At short notice we have to put down where we can find space."

"It doesn't matter."

"How's the bleeding, though? That's the main thing." She examines me again. "Hmm . . . Well, very good, very good. . . . It seems to have stopped."

I stiffen. "Does that mean it's all over?"

"It means we're out of the woods, I think. . . . Okay, well, great. . . . Want to check out at eleven? Or is that too late?"

I stare at her. "But—did I have a miscarriage?"

She shakes her head.

"The baby's still there?"

"Right."

"But . . . what now? I mean, what did the bleeding mean?"

"The bleeding may just mean you're a bleeder. . . . No, really, some people are and you may be one of them. . . . But I wouldn't let it bother you. . . . Check back to me if it happens again, of course."

"But why did I have to go to the hospital then?"

"You can't tell. . . . It might have been something. . . . Look, I'd rather be on the safe side, wouldn't you? Especially since you're not too far along." She leaves the room, obviously in a hurry.

I feel great but still slightly worried. I suppose in some way I feel a shadow over the whole thing. Not just the nagging feeling that the bleeding did have some effect and will mean something about the baby, but the feeling that this whole thing can't be as easy as pie physically once the moral decision or whatever is made. Well, everything's trickier than one bargains for, so it oughtn't to come as such a blow. Still.

Back at the lab, I go in to see Lobochowski. "I'm sorry about yesterday," I say. "My, um, sister-in-law is expecting a baby, and there was a false alarm. My brother's out of town on business, and I had to—"

People are rarely interested in the excuses you work over so carefully or, as in this case, throw together to suit the occasion. "Try to reschedule as soon as possible," he says. "Their exam period starts soon."

"I shall."

Wednesday night is writing to Matthew night. Matthew

75

writes me every two weeks, and his letters are splendid. They're a perfect representation of a certain part of his personality—witty, dry, perceptive. It's funny that Matthew who has such a writing block he can scarcely draw up a grocery list seems to lose it completely with letters. They're the kinds of letters that one ought to tie up with violet ribbon and put in the attic, if one had an attic, to reread in one's old age, if one has an old age. I'm afraid my replies hardly do them justice, but I enjoy the idea of a "correspondence." It's one of the few I've ever had. Most people I know hate to write letters, which means, sadly, if they leave town, like my college roommate, Phoebe, one has to resort to long-distance phone calls.

I describe the almost miscarriage. I guess it's nice to feel there is someone for whom the whole incident, even if it doesn't have the equivalent meaning it had for me, has some importance. I am sitting in my bathroom, my hair just washed, drinking a can of beer and feeling pretty good when the phone rings. It's Calla.

"Gabby, I have a bone to pick with you."

For some reason the literal image sticks in my mind, maybe because I am very fond of bones, especially steak bones. "Shoot."

"Since when do you take showers with the children?"

"Aha."

"Aha what? Answer me."

I take a gulp of beer. "You don't like the idea?"

"No, I do not like the idea. . . . And I also do not like the idea of your doing it behind our backs without even mentioning it. . . . Has this been going on for a long time?"

"Calla, come on!"

"Why come on? Timmy's been having these nightmares, as you perfectly well know, and I realize now what may be the cause of it all."

"You can't be serious."

"Look, if you look at any goddamn book on Freud or not

76

even Freud, *Spock,* for Christ's sake, they say it's just terrible, very destructive and bad for young children to see the naked bodies of adults. It's not this great blow for freedom it may appear to you!"

"I don't consider it a great blow for freedom," I say quietly. "I just don't see the harm in it."

"You don't see anything!" she says, furious now. "You live in this crazy off-key world and you just don't see!"

"I'm sorry, Calla. . . . I genuinely meant no harm."

"Christ, vou've been saying that your whole fucking life. . . . Well, maybe you did mean harm! Think of it! You like the idea of screwing up children just because you—"

"Calla, your children are lovely *un*screwed-up kids. . . . I don't see how you—"

There is a loud click. Calla is a great one for hanging up in the middle of conversations. It is, I have to admit, a rather effective weapon. However, I feel severely chastised, as though my knuckles had been rapped. Not that I hadn't contemplated the possibility that it would get back to Calla and she might be mad, but I hadn't foreseen anything on this scale.

Mea culpa. I will not call her back, however. I know she feels good now, both from screaming and from hanging up on me, and I'm not quite willing to give her the extra satisfaction of groveling for forgiveness. As I recall, I said I was sorry. I think I did, didn't I?

Families, families. . . . Does this mean I won't be allowed to see Elizabeth again? That I cannot bear. I feel at times as though Calla and I had been married and were now divorced and I was the pleading father who must submit to his wife's whims as to when he can be allowed to see his child. Well, soon I'll have a child of my own. So there, Camilla Nicole! . . . But I love Elizabeth, it's not fair. . . . Okay, I'll never do it again. I won't let one ounce of my great, frightening, hairy, sensual body be seen. I'll take an oath in menstrual blood. Fuck it!

77

I finish the beer, which luckily makes me feel pleasantly groggy, and finish the letter without referring to Calla. Matthew never took Calla seriously anyway. He said, and I quote, "She doesn't have a first-rate mind." Oh, would that I could put people down that easily! Maybe I do without knowing it. I think *I* have a first-rate mind; I guess feeling that just doesn't make me feel exempt from a lot of other things. Why not a first-rate body? Not that my body is so bad, but Matthew would have considered that beside the point.

Is it a pity Matthew didn't die a quick but painless death, isn't truly one of the "dear departed," as Eve said? Would it make everything easier or much harder? He's there and not here, as they say on that *Sesame* program that Elizabeth and Timmy watch. He is there, I am here.

I get dressed, and seeing me, Sasha and Olaf leap with excitement, knowing it's their turn to go out.

PART TWO

I'M afraid Sasha is pregnant. Which doesn't come as a great surprise to me. I knew she was in heat, and Olaf has been all over her while I'm here, as well, no doubt, while I'm at the lab. I can have her aborted. I'll have to since, though I'd love to raise a bunch of her puppies, right now doesn't seem the perfect moment. Also, she's very young, just over a year, a teen-age mother if there ever was one, and I hate to burden her carefree life with these responsibilities. I call the vet Saturday morning and explain the problem.

"How did this happen?" he wants to know. "Do you know the father?"

"The father is Olaf, my other dog."

"Well, didn't you know she was in heat?" He sounds testy and impatient.

"Yes, I did."

"Well, that doesn't show too much forethought, does it, Miss Van de Poel?"

I say nothing.

"You'll want her spayed after the operation, I presume?"

"No."

"Pardon me?"

"No, I don't want her spayed."

"Well, then, you want—what's his name—Olaf altered?"

"No, I don't."

"Well, what *do* you want?" I can just see his thin, irritable face, and I'm getting angrier by the minute.

"I'd like her aborted, and that's all."

"Then the situation is bound to recur, if you're planning to keep both dogs."

"It may."

"Not just may. . . . It will, Miss Van de Poel."

"Let's cross that bridge when we come to it."

"Miss Van de Poel, I don't think you realize. . . . I will abort your dog for you, but neither I nor any vet in this country is going to keep performing such an operation on a dog that should, under these circumstances, be spayed."

"Why don't you perform a vasectomy on Olaf?" Finally I say it, then wait for the predictable response.

"We don't perform vasectomies on dogs."

"Look, Dr. Marangella, it can be done. . . . I happen to know that because a good friend of mine is a vet and she has done the operation countless times."

"Then have your 'good friend' do it now."

"She lives in California. Otherwise, I would."

"Miss Van de Poel, I'm sorry, I cannot remain on the phone all morning. . . . My office is full. If you desire, bring your dogs down and we can pursue this discussion then." I'm hung up on again for the second time in twenty-four hours.

It's funny, I don't really think I'm a kook. I realize that one's view of oneself may not tally with the view shared by the outside world. But I give myself credit for at least a certain modicum of self-knowledge, and I believe that on the whole I'm quite a rational individual. In fact, too rational, if anything. . . .

But I just don't see why I have to either have Sasha spayed or Olaf altered. Of course it can be done, but the dogs aren't the same afterward, and I defy anyone to say they are. They gain weight, their whole metabolism is different. But, mainly, they have no sex life. One of them. Either he's altered and she'll go crazy every time she's in heat, or she's spayed and he'll go crazy, or you "fix" both of them and they sit around like eunuchs for the rest of their lives. Why shouldn't dogs be entitled to a sex life? If he were vasectomized, they could screw to their heart's content, enjoy it, and there'd be no problem. Every damn single person I know has two fixed dogs or cats, great, fat, ungainly creatures, and I hate that. What I love in animals is their freedom from all these screwy hangups, and here we go arrange their lives for them so they can't even enjoy sex if they want to. What if every teen-age boy or girl in this country were "fixed" as a solution to the population problem?

Oh, God, I *am* sounding like a kook, but I also do believe I'm right. Also, Phoebe, my former college roommate who lives in California, is a vet and does do vasectomies in dogs—it was from her I got the idea—and I could, I guess, at great expense, ship the dogs out there and then back. . . . But why? It seems so unnecessary.

I suppose I can also call the American Kennel Club and find out if there's anyone in the New York area who will perform this operation. It's just a lot of time and bother for something that could be very simple.

As it turns out, I can't even make it to Dr. Marangella's that Saturday anyway since I have an experiment running and have to get to the lab. I work straight through, stop for dinner and then come back. Yoko and Lobochowski are still there and probably will be, no matter when I leave. Paul D'Angelo, who lives in Hastings-on-Hudson with his wife and two sons, rarely comes in Saturdays anymore.

When I contemplate the idea of myself here with the two of

them, I feel a sad, rebellious desire to assert that I am *not* like them, we are not three peas in a pod, all unmarried, all asexual, all droning away on work that in a hundred years won't matter anyway. I don't want that kind of life, but more than that, I don't even want other people to think of me that way. Which is petty and so minor. What does that matter?

"How is your mother doing, Leonid?" I say when we meet and pause in the hall.

"She's much better, thank you. . . . She's visiting my sister now."

"The one in Buffalo?"

"No, that's Zina. . . . Stefania lives in Rhode Island."

I am on the verge of saying it must be easier without her when it occurs to me he might not like that remark, even if it actually is easier.

When I go back to work, it occurs to me that I am owed a three-week vacation this summer, and I wonder if I'll take it and, if so, where. New York is so awful in July; it would be nice to get away. Or in August for that matter. And since I'll be very pregnant by the fall, it might be a good break for that reason. I could plan to break the news to everyone after the summer, which would surely be as long as I could possibly wait.

I just have no idea where I would go. I could go to England and visit Matthew. He's suggested it. I'm just not sure.

On Monday, after work, I stop in briefly at Mother and Daddy's to "report" on the evening with Eve and Boris. "I think they'd rather be left alone," I say.

"Well, darling, of course," Mother says. She's embroidering some crewel work pillow in a great elaborate medieval design. "We don't want to interfere in their lives. . . . That's the last thing we want."

Then why in heck did you send me? is my first thought. All

I say or mumble is, "I guess I'm also not the perfect person to send on these missions."

"But Boris respects you so much, Gabby. . . . He really does," Mother says, deftly pulling the needle through. "You've always been a kind of ideal for him."

I can't believe, I just can't, that Mother doesn't sense the violent hostility that has raged between Boris and me over the years. Which doesn't contradict what she's just said but certainly puts it in another light.

I sit down in an armchair, but don't do anything. As an adolescent I used to bolt dinner and bury myself in magazines as a kind of protection while at home, and even now I can feel that sense of wishing I had something of that sort to hide behind.

"What do you hear from Matthew?" Mother says.

"Oh, he's . . . doing well," I say.

"It must be lonely for you without him," she adds.

I feel that, small as the point is in a way, it would be impossible to explain to Mother how I do and do not feel lonely without Matthew. Mother is such a man's woman in a certain way—just in the sense of drawing her life's blood as it were from flirtations, always having had some man, husband or lover as the main thing in her life. I don't know if she could fathom someone like me for whom the whole issue is both easier—*e.g.*, I can survive quite well alone, and harder, in that I'm not by nature a "celibate," if anyone is.

"Of course, your work is so demanding," she goes on, answering her own question. "It's not as though you have all that much time to sit around and brood!" She smiles brightly.

I nod vaguely, eager to be let off the hook.

The next day I decide that I had better get the dogs to the vet. His office hours on weekdays end at five, which means coming home by four at the latest, taking a cab to his office, which, unfortunately, is way downtown, and then, probably, having a long horrible wait since his office is always jammed full of people. But what else can I do?

Tuesday when I wake up, it's pouring rain. But I feel I can't put this off indefinitely, so at three fifteen, though it's still raining, I leave the lab, giving Frances instructions for what to do since she leaves at five, and head home. I leash the dogs up and walk them to the corner of Central Park West and Ninety-sixth Street—usually it's easier getting cabs there. Not a cab will stop for me. First, there aren't that many cabs because of the rain. But at least three pass by within half an hour with their lights on and just drive past despite frantic waving on my part. What am I supposed to do, throw myself under the wheels? Meanwhile, though I have a slicker with a hood and boots on, I'm getting sneezy and cold and angry and the dogs are soaked.

Usually I defend New York to all comers. I deny that its inhabitants are any more heartless or cold than inhabitants of any big city or, basically, of any place. I even, usually, defend cabdrivers, but now I am driven into a blind rage. Is there not one fucking cabdriver in the city who will stop? It must be the dogs. They're afraid the dogs will get the seat of the cab wet, even though I've trained them scrupulously to sit on the floor. It's incredible. I stand here, incredulous and furious at once as the fourth free cab slows down slightly, takes a look at us and then speeds deftly on.

What if the dogs get sick? And if I get there just as office hours are over, I'll have to go through the whole rigmarole tomorrow! This is just so unfair! Screw these people! Isn't there one kind person or one animal lover or just one decent human being in the whole taxi-driving population of New York?

A cab stops in front of us. For a minute I just stand looking at it, thinking there must be some mistake. He's stopping because he's about to change his sign to off duty or his aged mother lives on this corner or because he's so nearsighted that he thought the dogs were two big black bundles or something. No, the cab is still there, it's not pulling away. I wrench open the door, the dogs stumble in, and there we are.

I'm stunned. I get out a large bath towel that I always bring anyway and try to rub the dogs down a little.

"Where did you say you were going?" the cabdriver says.

"Oh, I'm sorry." I give the address. Then I go back to rubbing the dogs.

Somehow I am still furious. It's unfair—this driver was the one to pick us up, he's the one who certainly should be exempt from the wrath I feel at the moment toward mankind in general, but somehow I'm in such an angry mood that even he seems responsible in some indirect way for our forty-minute wait in the rain. I sit back sullenly, staring at his card. Rudolf Biedermyer.

"It's a hard day to get a cab," he remarks. I lean forward to hear through the grating.

"It sure as hell is . . . with two dogs," I say.

"Wouldn't anyone stop?"

"Are you kidding? They don't want to get their gorgeous cabs all slobbered up!"

This doesn't seem to surprise him. "Are those Great Danes?"

"Yes," I grunt monosyllabically.

"Where are you taking them?"

"To the vet."

"Are they sick?"

"No, one of them's pregnant. . . . She's going to have an abortion, and he's going to have a vasectomy."

He laughs. "Sounds like a logical progression."

"It may sound logical, but if you knew how hard it is to get a vet to perform a vasectomy on a dog. . . . It's like trying to get a cab in the rain."

He is silent. He has no opinion on the subject evidently. Well, why should he? Why should anyone named Rudolf have an opinion on anything? I feel angry again and sit back. We drive in silence the rest of the way.

As I'm paying the fare and trying to get the dogs together, he says, "When do you think you'll be done here?"

"Pardon me?"

"I mean, I thought, if it's still raining, you might have trouble getting a cab home, and if you like, I could come by."

It's funny. There are days or times when you don't want people to be nice because it doesn't fit into the general scheme of things. I stare at him rudely. "Look, I just have no idea when I'll be out," I say.

"When are the office hours over?" he says, seeming either not to notice or to be impervious to my rudeness.

"At five . . . but that doesn't mean a thing. That just means he doesn't let anyone in after that. It can take forever and usually does." I sneeze. "Thanks anyway." I walk away.

Dr. Marangella's office is jampacked. One thing that always strains my innate love of animals is going to a vet's office. I mean, the collection of weird types that are always there is a bit discouraging. Look, it's easy to explain. For many single people an animal is a child substitute. Why fight it? It's not illegal, there's nothing downright *harmful* in it. It's just that it seems that none of these people can take it lightly. There's such furtive adoration of whatever creature they have locked up in that box, such a welter of baby talk and intense whispers about what do you feed him and so forth that I wonder: do *I* appear this way to other people?

The Danes sprawl out and look inquisitively at the other varieties of animal life around them. Sasha is interested; Olaf looks sleepy and bored.

I keep trying to think whom Rudolf Biedermyer looks like. There was something very familiar about his face, which was freckled and long with a hooked nose and a reddish beard. . . . Finally it comes to me. My Uncle Willem, my father's younger brother, who still lives in Amsterdam and whom I've only met one or two times. There's something similar, not just the beard but something else.

I was mean to Rudolf Biedermyer, and now, sitting in the vet's waiting room, I regret it. I was just in one of my chip-on-the-shoulder moods, and maybe, who knows, I've become even worse since I've gotten pregnant. I think it's that I expect to get a lot of flak in the next year from strangers, and I'm almost steeling myself in advance. If people can be so beastly about something as simple as picking you up in the rain when you have two dogs with you, what will they be like about me and my child? I hate all those unknown people in advance, and maybe Rudolf Biedermyer just by putting himself forward stirred that reaction.

I'm odd, I have to admit it. I want help—like with the cab—but I hate feeling grateful. Why is that? It just kills me to feel grateful to people. Is it that I feel it's a kind of debt that must be repaid? No, that can't be so with someone you'll never meet again, but I feel it, still. I feel as if they're expecting some kind of response, and that freezes me up. I wish the whole world was an Automat and you could put in your nickel and pull out your food or sex or whatever and that was it. I don't always feel that, but there are times I do, and now, maybe owing to being tense about Dr. Marangella, I'm in such a mood.

It's not as bad as I expected. I feel exhausted. In fact, at one point I close my eyes and actually fall asleep in the office. When he finally takes me, I feel groggy but calmer also. He agrees to abort Sasha—I'm to pick her up in two days—and says he'll discuss the question of Olaf some other time. *He* looks exhausted, which awakens my pity, and I decide not to press it.

"Please do *not* spay her," I add as I'm leaving. "I will sue you if you do!"

"Miss Van de Poel . . . nothing but what we have specified." It's clear from his expression he thinks I'm crazy.

I don't think he'll spay her. He wouldn't, without consulting me, would he? No, this time I decide I should give humanity a chance. He's given his word, and why should I assume he will not keep it? I take Olaf, and we walk out into the street.

It's no longer raining, just dank and gray, but there's a nice leafy smell in the air.

"Hey there! You!" It's Rudolf Biedermyer peering out from the front window of his taxicab. He's parked on the other side of the street.

I stare at him, puzzled. "What time is it?" I ask.

"Six," he says. "His office must have been crowded."

"His office is always crowded." I get into the cab. I mean, what the heck, why not? But settling back, I think with a touch of my old resentment—what is Rudolf Biedermyer's *shtick*? Does he have a Great Dane fetish?

"This is very nice of you," I say finally, with some difficulty. "Thank you."

"That's okay. . . . I go off duty soon anyway."

"It must be a ghastly job, being a cabdriver in New York."

"It's not so bad. . . . I wouldn't want to do it all my life, though."

"I can imagine." What *is* he planning to do all his life? Oh, hell, do I really want to know? It's not a class thing, it's just—oh, what is it? I just don't know if I want to know.

"I'm a doctor, actually," he says. I guess luckily for him anyway he can't see my face, so whatever shades of resentment or tenseness are passing there don't register.

"An MD?"

"Right. . . . But I'm taking time off, as it were."

"That's interesting." But I feel so tired I could fall asleep right on the spot. Then suddenly it occurs to me that we're passing the lab and that I could get out here, if it weren't for Olaf, and then not have to make the trip back down tonight.

"Would you mind waiting for about twenty minutes in front

of this building?" I say. His meter isn't running—otherwise, it would be too expensive to even contemplate.

"Sure."

"I'll have to leave my dog in the back. . . . Is that okay?"

"If he doesn't mind."

"He may whimper a bit, but I imagine he'll be okay."

This is great! What a break! I race upstairs and manage to put the samples in the lyophilizer in fifteen minutes. When I get down, Olaf is pawing at the window. "Was he very bad?"

"No. . . . He quieted down once you were out of sight." The cab starts up again. "What were you doing?"

"I do research here."

We chat a bit about my work. He knows more than Matthew certainly, which isn't surprising if he's a doctor. I'm just not used, somehow, to talking about my work with anyone not from the lab.

When we arrive home, he gets out to open the door. "So, when will we meet again?" he says with mock formality.

I stare at him. Uh-oh. Is that it? "I don't know," I say. "Are we necessarily *going* to meet again?"

"I think so," he says.

God, I am bad at this kind of thing! And it isn't just not having done it for years. I was *never* good at it. I hate it. I hate all of it in advance, both this kind of thing and the worse kind of thing that comes later, all the maneuvering.

"Well, I live in this building," I finally mutter grudgingly.

"Would you like to tell me your name?" He's looking at me not with quite the expression of Dr. Marangella—"here is a crazy lady"—but with some irony as though he doesn't quite "get" me.

"My name is Gabrielle Van de Poel."

"Oh, are you Dutch?"

"My father's family is." I stare at him as though I were trying to identify him for a police lineup. No, it's not fearing he's really

91

an ax murderer, it's just that—well, human relations or things with men are not my forte. Oh, hell, it's not just being uneasy with the forms, not being able to flirt, it's a much more profound uneasiness about the whole thing.

"Would you give me your phone number?" Again he says it in this slightly ironical way as though not comprehending why I am so skittish and odd.

"555-0192."

"Thank you, Gabrielle." He smiles and gets back into the cab.

I like my full name, "Gabrielle," but no one has used it for years. "Gabby" or "Gab" isn't quite the same thing, but I've never felt strongly enough to make a point of it.

I lie down at home, make myself some tea and stare at the ceiling. . . . So—Rudolf Biedermyer, what are you going to make of it? Or me, to be more specific? Clearly, he must have some such thoughts—there's no other reason someone his age has even the mildest desire to get in contact with a woman. For years I fought the idea that men and women can't really be "friends" except as a side effect of a sexual relationship, but now I accept it. Sure, there are exceptions, and I've had a few in my life, but on the whole it seems just the way it is.

Damn it, I feel incredibly horny. It's funny. I can go along for months, masturbating away, sublimating, not really giving the whole topic much of a thought. Maybe because of that, when it does hit me—whammo! I think he was attractive—at least he was to me, my tastes not being utterly orthodox. But maybe it's in part just the fact that I've gone without for six weeks now—and he seemed, though God knows that could be a cover-up, a nice person.

I don't like being maligned by men. I really don't. I may have Boris with his slightly sarcastic, down-putting style to thank for the fact that when I meet a nasty, witty, charming type, I up and head for the hills in no time flat. Maybe deep down in my unconscious I want to be dumped on or clobbered or taken advantage of, but I'm quite content to let my unconscious handle all that as best it can. So if Rudolf Biedermyer hadn't, at least from the minor glimpse I got of his personality, seemed like a decent human being, I probably wouldn't be turned on at all, whatever I thought of his looks or lack of looks.

Well, we shall see. Relations with men may not be my forte, but I just don't see any reasonable alternative. . . . I could see being a lesbian in some ways, but what holds me back there is that I've always had good women friends whom I can see and feel close to. In short, you don't have to be a lesbian to feel close to other women, but you do—at least in my life it's been so—have to be heterosexual in order to become close to men. I see men at work, I have students who are men, my boss is a man, but those aren't relationships of "knowing." And somehow I don't feel able to rule out half the human race, quite apart from the fact that I think I need, for whatever reason, that sense of otherness that being close to a man gives.

What makes me uneasy is that although if I met a hundred women, I could probably feel at ease with and be friends with eighty of them on some level, out of a hundred men I'd be lucky to find one where that would be possible. When I was younger, I felt the main problem was I was too ugly, too odd, too smart. Now I see it quite differently. I think that I hold back much more than I'm usually willing to acknowledge. Somehow it's easier to see oneself as being rejected than rejecting, maybe because in the former the blame is on the outside world whereas in the latter you have no one to blame but yourself. I guess in essence with men I feel uncomfortably vulnerable and I don't really altogether like it. It's not just the simple or not so simple fear of being clobbered, humiliated, put down or whatever in a sexual way . . . though all that enters in and isn't irrelevant.

Maybe he won't call and my problems will be solved.

I hope he does, though.

*   *   *

He calls the next day, and we plan to meet on Saturday to go bike riding. It's getting a little hot for that, but I like bike riding, so I say fine.

The day is overcast, as though it might rain, very muggy. I'm in shorts, a sleeveless top and sneakers and feel edgy. He's in slacks and a plaid shirt of some sort, the sleeves rolled up. He's not good-looking—maybe it's his nose, which is too big. Also, oddly for someone that tall, he's rather heavy. But his eyes are very, very nice, a kind of greenish-brown color, but mainly, I think, kindly. Lord knows people put on fronts, but I don't think he's a Jack the Ripper type.

After an hour or two of riding we stop at the Sheep Meadow and sit under a tree.

"How come you're driving a cab if you're a doctor?" I say. It's noisy around us from all the families with children, baseball games, etc., but it's comfortable and nice. The grass smells fresh and newly cut, maybe because we've had a long, gray spring.

He shrugs. "I guess I didn't relish the whole setting-up-an-office bit . . . you know," he says.

"So, will you ever?"

"No . . . I hope not."

"But you won't drive a cab forever?"

He laughs. "God, no! . . . No, actually as of December first, I have a job in San Francisco at an abortion clinic. I'll be—" He looks at me with some concern, which may be justified. Since I can't see my own face, I have no way of knowing. "Are you against abortion? You look uncomfortable."

"Oh, no, no, not at all," I say quickly. "No, I think it's great. I mean, I never had one myself, but that's just—I guess I'm too horribly well organized to get pregnant by chance." I laugh a little hysterically.

He's still looking at me with a penetrating glance. Or is it penetrating, or do I just feel very transparent on this topic? "I think it's a very good thing," he says. "You know, there are so many of these girls who screw their lives up with some kid that they don't know beans how to look after or even want."

"Sure, sure!"

"They think being a woman will make it all work out. . . . That's crap. We've got to reeducate people about this."

I'm nodding frantically. "Why, um, San Francisco?" I say, just to radically shift the topic in any way possible.

"Well, I've always lived in the East and. . . ." He talks on and it isn't until a lot of time has passed that I realize that although I've been staring at him and probably murmuring "um-hmm" and "yes" and "naturally," I haven't heard a fucking word he's said for about fifteen minutes. Oh, mind wandering! What's wrong with me? Where was I? He's probably been into some crucial thing about his life, and now I'll never know. I'm feeling horny and edgy and sweaty, and it's not the world's greatest combination. I sigh involuntarily.

"Are you feeling okay?" he asks with some concern.

"Oh . . . sure. I just—I guess I'm not in shape," I mutter.

"Shall we go back?"

"Okay."

We ride back and check the bikes in at the places we rented them. Then we go to my place. It's four in the afternoon and getting darker by the minute.

"We're lucky," he says as we enter my apartment.

"Pardon me?"

"It looks like we just made it in out of the rain."

"Oh . . . right. . . . Would you like a drink or something?" I have nervous flutters and every other possible kind. Also a blister on my toe from not wearing socks.

"You wouldn't have any iced tea by any chance?"

"Well, as a matter of fact, now that you ask, I have a gallon of iced tea." It's true. From my Aunt Greta I learned the best way to make iced tea. You fill a huge mason jar with hot water and tea bags and then let the whole thing sit in the sun. Somehow the heat diffuses the taste, and after a few hours you have a beautiful amber-colored brew which you can then store and drink from all week long. His asking for iced tea cheers me up. While he's in the living room looking around, I get out glasses and hastily gulp down two aspirin.

I get headaches with some frequency, but I figure everyone has something. It's better than ulcers or high blood pressure, and usually aspirin helps. Not always. There are some really rotten days when I feel as if my head is in a vise and if someone said boo, I'd throw up all over them. I actually called a headache clinic once, and they said I could make an appointment in six months if I wanted, so I gather it's not an uncommon problem. (I didn't make the appointment.) Anyway, now I put it down in part to the heat and being pregnant, as well as the specific tensions of being with someone about whom I keep having uncontrollable fantasies of mounting and being mounted by.

He suddenly appears in the doorway and notices the open bottle of Empirin.

I wave my hand dismissively. "I really feel okay," I say. "I just get these headaches sometimes."

"Are they bad?"

"Well, they're. . . ." Oh, Lord, now he has a doctorly look of concern—tell me where it hurts. "No, really, here, have some iced tea." I shove it at him. "It's the heat. Sometimes the heat affects me this way."

The room is close. The dogs are lying in the corner eyeing him suspiciously. I have a sudden horror that if we do make love, they'll suddenly leap at his throat and rip him limb from limb. The trouble is, there's no other room I can put them in.

We talk about dogs and about living in New York, and my mind wanders back, forth, goes leaping around like a mad gazelle, undressing him, dressing him again, retreating, advancing. He drinks his iced tea and seems admirably composed.

96

Oh, God, I feel exhausted. I ought to have *myself* spayed. If, at thirty-two, a simple lay or just the prospect of it throws me to this extent, there's something wrong.

I go into the kitchen to get us more iced tea. He follows me, and just as I'm turning around to reach for something, the lemon or whatever, he has his hands out as though to reach for me, and then we both look embarrassed and jump back a little. And then we both smile awkwardly, acknowledging the hopelessness of the situation, and go into the next room, and then in a very short while it's all okay.

He's very good. In fact, he's just lovely. In general terms, I don't know what a "good lover" is. Somehow, for me, the term always evoked the image of a little man with a waxed mustache kissing a lady from the tips of her fingers to her toes. But what sometimes spoils things for me is a feeling of being pressured. I can't say specifically what that means. It's not a matter of a man doing this rather than that, it's just some men make me feel as though they're pressuring me and others don't, and he doesn't.

I think it's partly that for me—which I guess is odd—intercourse itself isn't the hard part. It always seems rather abstract and not that intimate. But all the rest, which supposedly should be easy, kissing, for instance, is very hard for me. I can sleep with someone I've met the day before, but kissing him is a whole other piece of pie. Well, either he senses this or he's just not that pressuring by nature. Whatever, it is very nice.

Nope, masturbation is just not the same thing. It's a pity, maybe life would be a lot easier if it were, and it's true, I haven't experimented with rubber dildoes or whatever, but I have a strong suspicion it would still quite emphatically not be the same thing.

"Why are you smiling?" he says.

"I was just thinking how nice this is . . . and how I forget that when I haven't done it for a while."

"How can you forget?"

"That's a good question. . . . I just do, though." I'm lying on my stomach. I do feel self-conscious about my body. I don't think I "show" yet, but I feel more physically aware and basically just very afraid he will notice and ask. I just don't feel up to dealing with that yet. For all he knows I just have a slight potbelly which lots of women do, and of course he doesn't know I'm normally much more flat-chested. Oddly, my body is probably better now than usual, but I feel much more sensitive that he'll make some remark about it.

"I'm glad the dogs didn't attack you."

He laughs. "I thought of that."

It's gotten very dark and rainy now. I'm glad of the dark, and I feel sleepy.

"Who was the last person you slept with?" he says after a moment.

Usually men don't ask that kind of question, so I'm a bit taken aback. Also—how to answer it? "A very good friend," I say slowly. "In fact, someone I lived with for five years. . . . He's in England now."

"I lived with someone for five years," he says. He talks a bit about this girl who sounds, from his description, a bit like Calla. That is, she was, when they lived together—which was when he was in med school—earthy and warm and open, and then suddenly she married and is now the earth mother of all time, and it bugs him.

"You should meet my sister."

"Why?"

"She's just like that."

"I don't think I want to meet your sister."

"Well . . . they say motherhood changes people."

"I wouldn't know," he says.

"Neither would I."

My remark hangs there with its—to me—double meanings. In some ways I'd like to tell him I'm pregnant, but on the whole not. I'm just not ready, and maybe I'll never be for even the possibly cavalier remark or joke. God knows, he doesn't seem that type, but I still feel too vulnerable even to chance it at all.

We have a very nice supper—spaghetti, wine—and Gwendolen is delighted. Poor thing, she has been neglected of late. She heartily approves of Rudolf Biedermyer—of course, her tastes and mine aren't always completely identical.

"Did they used to tease you about Rudolf the Red-nosed Reindeer?"

"Of course."

"Did you mind?"

"Yes."

There is one very good thing about Rudolf Biedermyer, apart from the more obvious good things. He is leaving in December. I'm glad to know that right from the start. It gives a structure to whatever happens in the next four months. It's like knowing the end of a story before you begin it. I'm the type that often picks up a book and reads the last chapter because I hate suspense. I like knowing how things will turn out, and this way I know.

"Do you get a vacation?" he asks a few days after "bike riding."

"A month."

"Where are you going?"

"Haven't decided yet."

"Do you like camping?"

"I love it."

He's from the South and is planning a camping trip to North Carolina. "If you felt like coming, you'd be more than welcome."

More than welcome, eh? I love camping. The idea is very appealing. I've never been South, but I know that country is supposed to be beautiful. When I see Dr. Hattie for my next checkup, I ask her if she thinks it would be safe. I'm just beginning my fifth month.

"Safe to go camping?"

I nod.

"I don't see why not. . . . You won't be miles from civilization, will you?"

"Nooo. . . . But what if the bleeding starts again?"

"You'll call me. . . . Frankly, I think you'll be okay. Just don't overdo."

"In what?" I say a little nervously. I don't quite have the courage to ask directly about sex. Later ̇that bothers me. If I were married, I'd ask perfectly easily, I'm sure. Well, according to The Book, anything up to the last weeks is fine, and I'm far from that.

"Oh, no hours of tennis in the hot sun—you can figure it out."

"I don't play tennis."

"So, you'll be fine. . . . Just relax, Gabby, and have a fine time."

She smiles at me so warmly, so sweetly that I melt. She's become my mother again, that ideal earthy mother who wants only the best for me. "I'll try," I mumble.

My technician, Frances, is going on vacation, too. She has a hobby—weaving—and she's going to spend the summer in some commune in upstate New York making great gorgeous woolly rugs. I wish her luck. I'm delighted I'll be out of reach of Lobochowski. Last summer I rented a house in Long Island with some friends, and he spent the whole time bugging me by phone. He has to make out an annual report around this time in which he describes the research of everyone in the lab. In fact, we all write up our own work, and he really could just organize it slightly, put it together and hand it in. But being Lobochowski, he makes it into a very big deal, rewrites it a dozen times and wants everyone else to rewrite his contribution. There's literally no end to it until the deadline arrives and the secretary more or less snatches it out of his grasp. Anyway, this summer he can writhe on his own. I'm leaving no phone number because I'll have no phone.

I need to get away. I feel tired and run down, and I want out. Blessed be Rudolf Biedermyer. I love camping. Matthew hated it. His idea of a picnic is a cold roast chicken, chilled white wine, watercress sandwiches and a red-and-white checked tablecloth. I don't mind that kind of thing, but I also like just the grubby parts of camping, sleeping on bumpy branches, hiking in the rain, getting bee stings on my nose, as I once did, and Matthew would never have any part of that.

To my parents I just say I'm going camping with a friend. Being the kind of parents they are, they don't ask. I say I'll send them postcards. They'll be in Europe anyway and immersed in their own travels, so I feel perfectly free.

We're going in his car, a very ancient station wagon. The dogs have plenty of room to stretch out in the back, and we tie the tent and other stuff on top. I insisted on bringing the dogs, and he said fine. I hate putting them in kennels, even though last summer on Long Island Olaf was almost shot by an irate summer house owner, who claimed he ate three porterhouse steaks out of a box of grocery deliveries left on this fellow's back porch. I'm sure it was true—Olaf was only eight months then and quite rambunctious. But on a camping trip, we'll have no one but ourselves to be responsible for.

I'm glad he accepted the dogs. As we set out and I glance back to see how they're doing. I feel a bit like a divorced mama who is bringing her two kids along. Take me, take them. Anyway, they're a lot quieter and less bother than kids, I'm sure.

We take turns driving. It's going to take a day and a half of driving pretty steadily to get there. I don't mind. I like driving. Lobochowski's lab section used to be part of a research division in Great Neck, and I had to commute out there every day. It was a forty-five-minute drive, but I quite liked it. I find driving relaxing, even when I'm tired.

It's late at night, past one, and I've been driving since suppertime, which was a perfunctory affair at a Howard Johnson's. The dogs are sleeping peacefully, and even Rudolf Biedermyer seems asleep, sitting next to me, slightly slumped over, his long legs crossed in front of him. It's always nice to sit next to someone who's sleeping. It makes me feel protective and good, as though they trusted me enough to fall asleep. Also, people's faces always look different in sleep, sometimes sterner, sometimes more peaceful. I reach over to turn on some radio music quietly, and he stirs and stretches.

"Hi," I say.

He puts out one hand and rubs my shoulder. "Getting tired?"

"Not really."

"You're good, Gabby."

"I like to drive."

"I didn't mean that."

I feel myself grow hot—personal comments of any kind affect me that way.

"Let's stop just for a few hours," he says. "We can start again early. . . . I brought an alarm clock."

"Thinking ahead, eh?"

"Don't you, usually?"

"Yes, actually I do," I confess. "I'm horribly well organized."

"Why horribly?"

"I don't know . . . I guess I admire sloppy scatterbrained genial people who don't know what day it is tomorrow."

He scratches his head. "What day *is* it tomorrow?"

We sleep right near the car, just in our sleeping bags. It's a clear night and not worth bothering with the tent. I lie awake a little after we make love. The baby is moving. I've felt it before, just lightly, as though my belly were a goldfish bowl and the baby were a very small fish just flicking its tail from side to side. Now it's a more pronounced feeling. "Oh!" I say involuntarily.

"Hmm?"

He's just about asleep, so I just mutter, "It's nothing." I feel I probably should mention it to him, but not having done so so far makes it that much harder. I guess I want to put the whole thing off—facing people's reactions—as long as I possibly can. I want this trip to be a final interlude, a last time before all that. But still, I'd like to share the feeling with someone since it's a lovely feeling.

We find a beautiful campground. It's really deserted, way off the main road, and for two weeks we hike around, driving just a little or not at all. It's secluded enough to swim naked. Even though we see a bear once, they don't bother us at night since we hang our food in a sack above the ground. The air is incredible and clear and smells of pines. It's an idyll, and in a way I'm not one for idylls. Partly I don't believe in them, but partly I always felt that even if I woke up in the middle of one, I'd be uncomfortable, not knowing how to react. I have a hard enough time on an average vacation which isn't even going well. But for some reason this time I just let it happen. Physically I feel better than I've ever felt in my life. I don't feel self-conscious being naked in front of him anymore. I rationalize this by saying that only a man who has seen many pregnant women would be able to tell that I'm pregnant. I'm sure he can't, yet I feel that its being pregnant that makes me feel so bursting with energy and relaxed and strong.

"You look like a completely different person," he says one night when we are fixing the fire before supper.

"Was I so wretched before?"

"Not wretched. . . . Just exhausted and harried-looking."

"I guess I get too wrapped up in my work."

"If you care about it, that's okay."

"I do, but I still sometimes wonder."

"New York does that anyway," he says. "Everyone looks that way. . . . That's one reason I want to leave."

"But then you go somewhere else, and it's the same thing."

"I don't think so. . . . I think if you're in beautiful physical surroundings, things fall into a different perspective."

"Wouldn't you care about your work, though, anyway?"

He smiles. "I don't in any case . . . the way you do. . . . I mean, I want to do something, but I don't care that much about getting ahead or making it to the top and that kind of thing."

"Don't you? How odd."

"Why is it odd? . . . Your attitude is odder, especially for a woman."

"Well, maybe that's it then. . . . Men don't feel they have to make it anymore, but women do. . . . I mean, I feel as a woman one would get nowhere if one didn't put everything into it, given the odds."

"That results in such a driven, lousy life, though."

"Maybe . . . I don't mind it so much."

He looks thoughtful, bemused. "I can imagine you leading a completely different sort of life."

"You mean like now, just . . . taking it easy and so forth?"

"More in that direction."

"Well, I never will," I blurt out defensively.

"That's too bad."

We stare at each other, puzzled, me puzzled at his lack of ambition, he puzzled at my caring so much. Somehow Matthew, though he was tormented and blocked in his work, was more like me in considering it the center of his life. And of course I've constructed my life so carefully around my work that the very idea of removing that center makes me unspeakably nervous.

"I'm not really like this, anyway," I say finally, unable to leave it.

"How—relaxed?"

"Yes . . . I mean, you're getting a false image of me."

He smiles. He has a wonderful smile and eyes. And he seems completely unaware of that which appeals to me. "Funny girl."

"It's *true*."

After dinner we go for a swim and then sit naked near the river while the dogs wander off into the woods.

"The dogs are like your children, I guess," he says.

I tighten a little. "No! They're dogs, that's all."

"I just meant—you seem very fond of them."

"I am. . . . But I hate it when people make dogs into people, which they're not."

"I didn't mean that."

We're sitting so close, and I feel we have a kind of physical intimacy by now which bothers me just a little. There's no justification for this, but I feel deep down I disapprove of people having a good physical relationship when they don't really know each other. That sounds priggish, but I guess with most men I've known at all well the friendship part has come first and the sex has followed, which just may mean that, deliberately or not, I've wanted friendship more from men or felt too uneasy to think of sex by itself as being that crucial. Gwendolen seems in such a good mood of late and of course Rudolf Biedermyer, not knowing her as I do, I think *is* getting a false impression. Half the time I don't know what Gwendolen will be up to. At times she can be surprisingly good. I can be feeling detached and off in various obsessions and she is suddenly warm and moist and eager-seeming, or I can feel quite responsive and she'll be as tight and dry as a drum, which is more than a little disconcerting. They say women can just lie there and not have to worry about "performing" about sex, but I feel that Gwendolen can ruin everything by being as tight as a clam or can save the day by being very open-seeming. I just wish I could predict her moods! But my being pregnant seems to have really changed her personality. I suspect Rudolf thinks of me—which in some ways is

105

a persona I admire—as much more earthy and warm and re-sponsive than I really am. I'm not consciously putting on a false front—right now I feel earthy, warm and responsive. I just feel the "real me" is more the harried, exhausted drone he picked up in his cab that rainy afternoon.

He's quiet. Sometimes we'll talk and sometimes not. He doesn't like to talk about ideas the way Matthew did, which rules out certain things I can be obsessed about—politics, literature. On the other hand, he can understand a lot about my work, and he loves nature and animals and seems at ease doing things like chopping wood for the fire, and I like that.

We are getting mosquito-bitten and slowly put on our clothes. We've worn the same jeans and shirts the whole time, just rinsing them out occasionally at night and hanging them to dry on a tree.

Walking back to our campsite, he says, "I was thinking we could visit my sister."

"Does she live around here?"

"Well, she lives in the town I grew up in—on the outskirts."

"With your parents?"

"No, she lives alone."

He talks a little about his parents, who, it seems, were professors of history at a small college but are now retired. His father had a hobby of studying maps and now, in his retirement, travels a lot with his mother, gathering material for books.

"They sound happy together."

"*I* think they are. . . . Ellen, my sister, thinks—well, she thinks my mother dominates my father."

"Does she?"

"Well, I don't think so. . . . It's just—she's a more rigid—she's religious and strong-willed in a sense and he's easygoing, but I think they've had a good life, despite their differences."

"Is your sister married?"

"She was, briefly."

"Now what does she do?"

"She lives alone and breeds hamsters for scientific laboratories." He looks at me for a long moment, frowns, and finally says, "She's mad."

"At your parents, you mean?"

"No, I mean mentally ill."

"Oh."

"I mean, she did have a breakdown and she has tried to kill herself. . . . Now I think she's okay. . . . But she's just strange. . . . I just wanted to tell you before we meet her."

"Sure."

"She writes poetry, she's a . . . well, you'll have to see."

"You sound fond of her, though."

"I am . . . but she can be very angry and. . . ."

"There are just the two of you?"

"Yes."

After quite a long while of lying looking at the stars, I say, "So, your parents have no grandchildren?"

"No, they miss that, but . . . well, Ellen wouldn't have made a very exemplary mother, I don't think."

"And you?"

"I'd like a family. . . . I wouldn't mind quite a large family, actually—five or six children."

I sit upright in my sleeping bag. "Six! What do you mean? What about the population thing?"

"Oh, there's adoption. . . . Look, anyway, it's not a practical thing, just a daydream really. . . . It's likely I'll never marry."

"Your wife would be exhausted. . . . How can you *think* of six?"

"Gabby, calm down! . . . Don't you ever daydream about things?"

"No!" What a lie. I'm the greatest daydreamer on two feet. I have a fantasy life in three D, Technicolor, smellovision, you name it. "But that's terrible," I rush on. "*Six* children!"

"How about four then?"

"It's the whole *idea*. . . . Who's going to look after those four children? You'll dump them on some poor girl and go off to your abortion clinic and—"

"Of course I wouldn't. I'd certainly want to help in bringing them up."

"Oh, come on!"

"Why, oh, come on? . . . Are you so reactionary? You don't think a father can take any part with children?"

Why am I so angry? My whole body is trembling I feel so upset. "Of course he can take a part. . . . But it just seems so many times the wife is overworked and konked out and the father drifts off."

He is sitting propped up in his sleeping bag now, looking intently at me. "It happens my best friend, someone named Karl Harper, has three kids, boys, and they're the center of his life. He's a writer, so he's at home a lot, but he says if he could, he'd love to do nothing but be with them all day long."

"Bull!" I say violently.

"Don't say bull! It's true."

"It is *not!* I just hate that. . . . I hate men like that. They are such hypocrites. . . . Does his wife work?"

"No."

"That's what I mean."

"His wife doesn't *want* to work. . . . He's not preventing her at all, in any way whatever."

"So let *him* stop work if he wants. . . . She probably spends the whole day running herself ragged while he's in his damn book-lined study with his pipe and all that and then when the mood strikes him, he saunters out and plays with the kids."

"You'd have to meet him, you—"

"I don't *want* to meet him!"

"You're painting an image of someone who doesn't exist."

"You just don't know!" I say. My face is burning, not just

108

from sunburn. "Those men, those are the worst, that go dump on their wives and then say—oh, no, I'd really love to be doing all that crap myself, I just can't because I was made for higher things." I know I'm sounding incoherent. I have that feeling that my sentence structure is breaking down, as it often does when I lose control.

Rudolf is silent for a few moments. "Is that why you never got married—for fear of being dumped on?" he asks quietly.

"No!" I shout. Then I mutter, "Well, it's part of it. . . . Why didn't *you* ever get married?"

"It just didn't work out."

"So it just didn't 'work out' with me either! . . . Why is it that when a man doesn't get married, it's fine, he's just exercising his perfectly okay right of free choice, and if a woman doesn't, she has to be some kind of crazy freak?"

"Did I say that?"

"What?"

"Did I say a word about crazy freaks?"

"Well, that's behind this whole thing. . . . You know, I really lose patience with this. . . . If men could be honest, the world would be in much better shape." And for some incredible reason I burst into tears.

I never cry. I'm not a crier. I've prided myself on this for years, so that all I can put it down to now is being pregnant and somehow in a sensitive state. I try to swallow all the tears down before they come. Rudolf keeps stroking me and saying, "Gabrielle, darling, please."

Finally I blurt out, "I never . . . cry!"

"You should."

"I should not! I *hate* criers."

Finally I lie back, exhausted, on my back and stare up at him and the tree which I can see behind his head. His face is shaded, but my eyes are used to the dark, and he has that concerned, tender expression. God, he's going to do me in! I should have realized. I liked the fact that he didn't pressure me at first, but the trouble is that made me at ease with him and now what? Whenever he looks at me that way, especially if I feel he's about to make love to me, I feel scared out of my wits. It reminds me of a fantasy I used to have as a child. I would be—in the fantasy—on a beach and a tidal wave would rise up. I don't know what tidal waves are really like, but in my fantasy it was a huge dark wave rising suddenly in the distance way way up in the air, and when it would crash down, it would destroy everything instantly. I would see it rising up and start to run away from the ocean, but then a small dog that I'd be holding in my arms would get loose and start running toward the ocean again. And to save it I'd have to run back too while the wave kept rising higher and more ominous in front of me.

I don't know if it's sex that's the tidal wave or just emotion or what—I've never been good at analyzing my own fantasies. All I know is that I now see the physical relationship I had with Matthew as being so much safer, so much easier. We simply didn't ask any more of each other than each of us could easily give, and I never thought till now of what a blessing that is.

While he's in me, moving back and forth, he suddenly says, "Sweetheart, relax."

"I can't. . . . And please don't ask me to."

"Of course you can."

"I can't. . . . I'm like this. . . . You have this false image of me. I'm not this earthy, warm person. I'm not."

"Gabby."

Afterward I have the feeling of panic I had the morning I woke up and drove to Bryn Mawr, the morning Matthew and I were going to be married. I've got to get out! Let me out of here!

In the morning we drive to his sister's. It's a long drive, and we don't arrive until nearly dinnertime, around five. It's still light since it's summer and warm. She lives in a small white frame house outside the town. He had stopped and called her from a store we passed earlier in the day, saying we might arrive on time for dinner or might not, but not to go to any trouble.

For a long time we stand on the doorstep, and no one answers the ring. I look at Rudolf. "Maybe she's not there."

"No, she's always like this. . . . She'll come."

Finally the door opens.

A girl stands there, girl, woman, probably in her thirties somewhere, but she's so strange-looking it's hard to judge her age. She looks childlike and quite old the way certain people do, with a pinched, unattractive face, very short hair. There's a raccoon slung over one shoulder and at her feet a large Labrador retriever with only three legs that ambles out after my dogs. "Ramma!" she yells after him. "Come back here." She laughs, a very dry, almost barking laugh. "He always feels he has to prove his masculinity in front of me when he meets a new dog. . . . Really he's as meek as a lamb."

I point to the raccoon. "What's his name?"

"Oh, that's Margaret."

"Are raccoons tameable?"

"Not really, but I found her and we get along, don't we, Margaret?" She looks at Rudolf. "Did you folks eat or what?"

Rudolf shakes his head. "But don't—"

She laughs. "I'm not a gourmet cook, so you'll have to eat what I'd be eating myself."

"That's fine," I answer, and we walk into the house.

It's quite dark and, on the whole, a shambles, furnished piecemeal with a couch here, a chair there, clearly a house no one enters but her.

"Ellen keeps her hamsters downstairs," Rudolf says, "in the cellar." To Ellen he says, "Gabby is a research biochemist. . . . She might have used some of your animals sometimes."

"Where do you work?" She's going into the kitchen, and we follow her.

111

I name the institute, and she says, "Oh, yes . . . I ship to them."

Dinner is hash out of a can and frozen string beans. Ellen dumps a lot of catsup on her hash and mops it all up with a roll. I'm hungry enough not to care, but I wish there was some wine, even Gallo. She's not exactly a conversationalist. Everything she says is barked out in a way that seems a cover-up for shyness but a cover-up that probably runs quite deep.

After dinner we take a long walk with the dogs, something she evidently does every evening.

When we get back, she shoves some blankets at us and shows us a small room upstairs with one narrow single bed in it. "Hope that'll do," she says and disappears.

"I wish she had served wine," I say, yanking off my shirt, which smells sweaty and ancient.

"She never drinks. . . . Hey, what about that grass you said you had?"

"Oh, Lord, it's in the car." Frances gave them to me before leaving on her weaving trip.

"I'll go get them. . . . Tell me where."

We sit in the small room smoking, and I'm glad Rudolf thought of it. I feel more relaxed. The room has a peculiar smell, dust maybe, or animals.

"She *is* strange," I say. We both talk softly so our voices won't carry.

"She was an excellent student, an excellent athlete."

"Who was the guy she married?"

"Someone awful. . . . She was nineteen."

"Has she ever had any psychiatric help?"

"I think she did for a while. . . . She won't talk about it. My parents hate the idea of psychiatry. They couldn't fathom her breakdown. It was like a car crash—something that 'just happened' and you try to put the pieces together as fast as you can. . . . But I think for several years she used to drive to Chapel

Hill to see an analyst. She'll never talk about it, but I think she liked the person—I believe it was a man."

"Well, she seems to have a sort of life."

"That's just it, that's just what she has . . . a sort of life."

"She sees nobody?"

"Nobody."

"She seems fond of you . . . I felt there were warm vibra-tions."

"Probably. . . . The fact that she let us stay here. . . ."

"What are we going to do about this bed?"

He laughs. "Sleep on top of each other, I guess."

"Try again."

"I'll sleep on the floor . . . I'll get my bag."

"Are you sure? . . . I'm just kind of konked."

But despite that, despite the pot, I lie awake long after Rudolf is asleep. He sleeps like Elizabeth, mouth slightly open, not quite snoring but heavily, heavily asleep. I think I can hear the hamsters in her cellar rustling around. She bothers me.

Living in New York, you get immune to craziness. There's just so much of it everywhere, so many little old ladies ranting drunkenly on Broadway or just vacant, insane faces across from you on the bus that it becomes part of the landscape which you notice no more than a tree that's been hit by lightning and therefore cracked or bent. But Ellen Biedermyer gets to me. It's not her connection to Rudolf. I don't think it really has much to do with that. . . . I guess it's that I have more than just a passing sense of—there but for the grace of God. Her love of animals—like mine, only more so. Using them as a shield, relating to them but not to people. Her quasimasculine but still oddly vulnerable, shy manner, as though she has never found, will never find, a way of dealing with life or people. And the scars on her arms and throat. I'm not going to kill myself, but I feel as though I know exactly how it would be to have tried it, to have almost succeeded, and I bet anything she came very close to succeeding, didn't just swallow a few too many pills and then wait for someone to rescue her. She came close and then came back and now has, as Rudolf says, "a sort of life." So everyone has a "sort of life." What's wrong with that?

It's curious his family has, in a completely different way, the failure-with-marriage thing. Maybe it's more common than one realizes.

The next morning, although I fell asleep very late, I wake up very early. It's not the bed. I just wake up with a headache, stiff.

Ellen is downstairs, dressed. For all I know, she gets up at four or six. She has that kind of face where it's hard to tell if she looks tired or peppy. She serves us eggs and bacon and good coffee. It's a good breakfast, and food always manages to bring me back to the living. We sit almost comfortably over second and third cups of coffee, Rudolf describing our travels, the animals we've seen. Then suddenly, for no possible reason I will ever understand, she turns to me and says, "Are you having a baby?"

It's like a game of statues. I freeze and turn to salt. If I had expected the question, expected it even remotely in any way shape or form, I could have said anything, denied it, explained it, but as it is, I just say, "Yes."

She looks at Rudolf and smiles just slightly slyly, thinking evidently that he's the father. And I look at Rudolf, and his expression is something it's going to take me the rest of my life to forget.

"When is it coming?" she says.

"January."

"Are you having natural childbirth?"

"Pardon me?" My mind is not just wandering, I'm blanking out completely and then coming back.

"Are you having natural childbirth?"

I think my brain is paralyzed. I'm having a very hard time

recognizing words. Natural childbirth. Childbirth means the act of giving birth to a child. Natural means without the use of drugs. She wants to know if I am going to, without the use of drugs. I still can't even get a grasp enough to say either yes or no.

"I guess it's no worse than having an abortion, the act of it," she says.

"I never had an abortion."

"Didn't you? How funny."

"Pardon me?"

"I would've thought you had."

"No, I just. . . ."

"Babies scare me half to death," she says. "Always have."

"Me too," I say, and we smile at each other, and despite myself, I like her, although she's done the most awful thing anyone has ever done to me.

"Are you going into town for supplies?" she says. "I can drive you."

"We'll take our car," Rudolf says, his first memorable words since her initial question.

We had planned to stay one more night and get an early start Friday morning. I'm due back at the lab Monday. Silently we get into the cab. Ellen has disappeared into the cellar.

Rudolf says not a word during the drive into town. We do our shopping and drive back. I am damned if I am going to say a word either. We can not speak for three days if he wants it that way. But I feel furious and also extremely hurt. There are things I hate worse than others, and one is people turning off. Just turning off completely. Matthew, for all his being repressed in some ways, was the type that, when he got mad, would rant and rave, and then it was over. I liked that. I hate people who run hot and cold. Get your fucking reaction over with, I don't care what it is, I think, glancing at his severe, remote face.

I'm going to become a lesbian. I just can't take men. I really can't. It's too much. They are so inconsistent. In theory it's one thing, in reality it's something else.

"I'm just curious why you never mentioned it," he says finally, not looking at me.

"You are not 'just curious' why I never mentioned it."

"Well, I am, among other things, curious why you never mentioned it."

"Why should I have?"

"You mean, it's such an irrelevant, minor fact in your life it wasn't worth bringing up?" He is looking so cold and so hostile I feel frozen from head to toe.

"Look, it's a fact of *my* life . . . not of yours. . . . If I don't feel like mentioning it, why should I?"

"Well, I thought you put this great premium on being honest and open."

"So, I'm inconsistent. . . . Sue me."

Another silence.

"So, you're in your—what—your fifth month?"

"Right."

"I thought you said you approved of abortion."

"I do. . . . Only I *wanted* this child." I stare at him, furious. "Look, I planned this goddamn child. I did not wake up one morning pregnant by some guy I never knew or heard of or whose name I could barely remember. This is something I thought about for *months,* for *years.* . . . So don't look at me like I'm some screwball who's—"

"Who's the father?"

"That man I told you about, that I lived with for five years."

"Does he have a name?"

"No, he calls himself Mr. X. . . . Of course he has a name!"

"What is it?"

"What difference does it make what his *name* is? Christ! It's Matthew! Shit!"

"Was he in on this famous plan?"

I smirk. "In on it? Yes, he was 'in' on it, if you mean it that way."

"I didn't mean it that way."

"Yes, he knew about it, we talked about it."

"So why did he go to England?"

"Because it's my child and he hates babies and I'm going to bring it up alone."

"All by yourself?"

"Yes, all by myself. . . . 'Cause I'm a big girl and big girls have babies. Lord, I'm ten years older than the average American girl or woman is when she has a child, I'm of the age of reason, I can fasten a diaper."

"Will you stop work?"

I stare at him, dumbfounded.

"Well, will you?"

"Yes, I'm going to sit at home and live on welfare."

"Some women stop work after their children are born."

"Well, I am not one of those women, and if you know that goddamn little about me, then you must be as dense as a door-nail. . . . Of course I'm not giving up my work!"

"Who'll look after the baby then?"

"I'll put her in a day care center near the institute. . . . They have them in case you weren't aware, just for women like me who peculiarly don't want to throw away ten years of what they peculiarly consider something important in their lives!"

"Well, you seem to have it all planned out."

"I do. . . . I have it beautifully planned out. I've planned out every goddamn detail."

"Good."

I sat there one second. "Though why the hell I should have to feel defensive with someone like you. . . . It's my baby! If I want to bring it up in a shoe, that's my business."

"Of course it is."

"Just because you feel every woman should be aborted the second she gets pregnant if she happens not to be married—"

"Did I say that?"

"You feel it."

"I do not."

"You do. . . . If you could see your face! . . . You know what I wish? I wish men could be pregnant. I think that's the only answer to this whole thing. To make them feel physically for one second—" I stop, thinking of this. I've thought of it before. It's true, test-tube babies are not the answer. The answer is for men to know, know in their gut what it's like to have a child.

"I don't think I'd mind being pregnant," Rudolf says. His voice is slightly back to normal, more quiet and musing.

I look at him to see if he's joking. "You really wouldn't?"

"No. . . . I don't think so. . . . Gabby, look, you're going off the deep end, as usual. Have your baby. . . . I just don't understand this secrecy. . . . What if Ellen hadn't mentioned it? Would you ever have brought it up?"

I shrug.

"I'm sure you'll be a great mother."

I look at him suspiciously. I am ready, I have thought of rebuttals to remarks about how can you do this to a poor child, it will have no father, you're a career woman, women like you should be sterilized or—you, you're a kook, how can you manage, etc. But the last words I ever expected ever to hear from anyone were those. "Don't be sarcastic, please," I say softly.

"I'm not! You're so defensive, it's incredible."

I look out the window. "Look, I don't know if I'll be a great mother or even a good mother. Maybe I'll be lousy. It's something I want very much to do. . . . And I have had great friendships with some children, so—"

We sit a long time in silence. There's the feeling of a truce, but also a feeling of exhaustion. I am defensive. I shouldn't be. How bad that I am. Why can't I be simply proud and straight-

118

forward? Why the hell *didn't* I tell him right from the beginning?

"Matthew must be an odd bird," Rudolf says, a little coldly
again.

"How so?"

"I don't know. . . . Just, what, siring the child and going off
like that?"

"It's been done since time immemorial."

"But, you still write him and. . . . It just sounds odd to me."

"Well, he is odd and I'm odd and it just happened to work . . .
for a certain era in our lives."

We leave it at that for the moment, but Rudolf still looks
extremely detached. Talk about holding back! I am not forgiven, on some level, that much is clear and partly I feel like
saying, "Go fuck off with your forgiven and not forgiven." Am
I supposed to go groveling for something which he has no right
on earth to have any opinion about whatever? I don't think men
know *what* they feel. Maybe it's not their fault. Maybe they're
brought up to think so much about "ideas" and to repress feeling
to such an extent that they wouldn't know an emotion if it hit
them in the face. . . . I know I'm not a great one to talk. I block
off and go underground, but I think I at least try to keep the
lines of communication with myself open.

After lunch Rudolf goes upstairs to nap. Somehow I don't
feel like going up to that tiny room with the one narrow bed
again. Things are claustrophobic enough in the open air. I go
down to the cellar with Ellen to see her hamsters.

It's very neat. Clearly this part of her life is altogether
different from the messy upstairs. I'm sure she does a very good
job at this. The cages are all lined up, one after the other.

"Your dogs are lovely," she says.

"Thanks. . . . I kind of like them."

"I never had a Dane, but I admire them. They're beautiful."

We talk a long time about animals. For once not only do I not

119

have to be defensive about loving them, I'm with someone who's more extreme than myself. We get some apples and go for a walk with the dogs. She takes Margaret, the raccoon, on her shoulder again.

"Ellen, you know . . . this isn't Rudolf's baby I'm having," I say, looking off into the woods. "I just met him a few weeks ago. It's, well, not his."

"Oh, that's too bad," she says in her flat funny voice.

"Why?"

"I think he'd like a child. . . . Only I doubt he'll ever get married."

"Why shouldn't he?"

"He's just not the type. . . . No one in our family is."

I admire her life in a way. Maybe it really would be easier just to rope off certain disturbing essentials. If it could work without them. I'm not sure for me it would.

"Oh, Rudolf's crazy!" Ellen says suddenly with her barking laugh.

"In what way?"

"Why did he go to med school? It was stupid! He didn't want to. Just because Mom and Dad forced him, said he'd never make it in art."

"Was that what he wanted to be—an artist?"

"Well, he loved to paint. . . . He's very good. . . . Half the stuff in my living room is his. . . . I think he's wonderful. He draws animals wonderfully. . . . And they got into such a state that, oh, my God, he'd never earn a living, the whole spiel, and he just knuckled under. . . . He'd dropped out of college and they made him go back. At least study art professionally, they said. . . . So he went to this awful stuffy college where all the art was abstract and he hated it and now he's given it all up. He never draws. . . . I'll never forgive them for that!"

She speaks with a passion that is unusual in her. Also, I never imagined she would speak so much all at once.

120

"He never mentioned it," I say, half to myself.

"Oh, he never does. . . . They made him feel ashamed of it. . . . You need a profession, they said. . . . Now his whole life is ruined."

"That sounds so final."

"Well, it is! He'll be a lousy doctor, he hates blood. . . . Once Ramma hurt his leg in an accident—that's why he has only three legs now, and Rudolf almost fainted."

"I think I would too."

We walk back in silence. I'm not sure how I feel about all this. Touched partly, though I'm not in a mood to be touched, touched that she seems to care so much. I think how much more wariness there is among Boris, Calla and myself.

When we get back, Rudolf is up and reading in the living room. I gaze around at the paintings which she has said are his. They're rather powerful, dark, somewhat expressionistic, though there are a few watercolors of animals that are more delicate. I can never judge about art, but he certainly is or was good. As soon as I come into the room, he gets up and goes out. Finally I see him outside getting our stuff ready. I walk out.

"Listen, I can take the bus back. . . . Just drive me to Chapel Hill."

"Don't be silly," he says curtly.

Ellen comes out and says good-bye. "Come down again, Gabby," she says. I feel I could be good friends with her, and if it weren't for the unpleasantness of this few days, I'd be glad we came.

We drive for four hours, till eight o'clock, then stop for dinner, which we eat in absolute silence. It's become, for me, a game. I will not say a word. I will not in any way defend myself, explain, grovel. I did it, I gave my views. I can be accused of nothing, and if he has some *shtick* of his own, fine. I won't be a party to it.

"Shall I drive?" I say as we come into the cool evening.

"No, I can do it."

"I know you can. . . . I thought you might be tired."

He just gets behind the wheel and we're off on our silent marathon. At midnight we're somewhere on Highway 102. "Should I take over now?"

"No."

So, the hell with him. Let him drive. He had a nap anyway. I feel very tired. I close my eyes, and in about two seconds flat I fall sound asleep. I have low blood pressure, and sometimes I feel that when I sleep, I sink deeper than most people. Waking up is like rising from the bottom of the sea. I have some vague dream about my mother and Calla. Someone is angry at me . . . then it shifts and I'm at school, about to take an exam. . . . I wake up suddenly. The car stops short, and I fall forward, knocking my head on the front window.

"Sorry . . . I didn't see that sign," Rudolf says.

I groggily come to and glance at my watch. It's three thirty.

"Why don't we stop?" he says. "I'll set the alarm."

I think of our trip coming down and how nice it was and how ugly and awful this is. Idyll turned to nightmare. It sounds like something off a Forty-second Street movie marquee. We each get into our sleeping bags and lie there, wide awake. Suddenly Rudolf puts out a hand and lays it on my shoulder.

"Stop that at once!" I yell, surprising even myself.

"What?"

"If you think I feel like screwing right now, you must be out of your mind!"

"Oh, fuck it, Gabby. . . . You're impossible." He turns away and goes to sleep.

The sad and very unfortunate fact is that I feel horny. Why is Gwendolen so insensitive? I just think she lies there absolutely unconnected to any brain waves or anything. I masturbate, which takes about two seconds and doesn't do much good. Suddenly the baby wakes up and starts kicking. She's moving

122

much more now, and I lie there quietly, enjoying the sensation of her vigor and good spirits even if I can't match them.

"You didn't even tell me you wanted to be an artist," I say suddenly into the absolutely quiet night.

"What—did Ellen mention that?" He sounds wide awake.

"Yes. . . . So you see, you have this thing, I'm so closed off, I never mention things. . . . Well, neither do you."

"It's different." He sits up.

"Why? Is it such an irrelevant small part of your life it wasn't worth mentioning?"

He is silent. Got you there, I think spitefully.

"Gabby, it's different. . . . I mean, say, I had gotten some girl pregnant, a girl I was still in contact with, whom I intended to continue seeing, whom I had 'planned' a baby with and I just had happened not to mention it and then you found out. . . . You wouldn't feel the least bit angry or resentful of me for not telling you?"

This time I was silent. "Well, maybe I would."

"Just maybe?"

"Okay, I would. . . . But I've told you, it's over, so why go on and on forever?"

"It's not 'over.'. . . You're still pregnant."

"No, I mean my not telling you is over."

"That's just due to pure chance."

"I wonder how Ellen could tell," I say.

"I don't know, she's like that. . . . She can be weirdly perceptive at times."

"You had no suspicion yourself?"

"I just thought what a nice round belly you had."

I snort. "She's jumping."

"Can I feel?" He puts out his hand and places it over my belly. Suddenly the baby stops. "Maybe she's gone back to sleep," I say.

He moves his hand over my belly and up to my breasts.

"They're usually half this size," I say.

"Then I'm lucky, aren't I?"

"Huh?"

"To have you now."

Those words hang briefly on the air, and I decide to let them drift by, "to have you now." I'm feeling turned on, and I've had enough semantic arguments for one day.

He keeps stroking my breasts. "Will you nurse?"

"No, I will not nurse."

"Why not?"

"Because—I don't know, first of all, Calla, my sister, made it into such a big deal. Her husband took these great shadowy photos of her with her boobs sticking out. . . . I mean, I can see doing it if you live in a primitive civilization and can just yank out a breast whenever you need to, but in New York? If you're the type that can yank out a breast on a Fifth Avenue bus, okay. I'm not. . . . Also, I don't know, I just hate that idea of men gazing at me fondly, being the object of 'fond admiration or adoration' or whatever just because I have these . . . things."

"They're so lovely, though."

"Okay. . . . But your penis is lovely, do you feel like exposing it to everyone who comes to dinner, which is what Calla used to do . . . whether they felt like looking or not?"

"Do you think it's lovely?"

"Don't beg for compliments!" He does, though, have a lovely body. While we're making love, I feel how nice his back is. Men's backs are so nice. And their behinds and legs. I can see how looking at a woman's body might be nice, but I think the feel of a man's body is much nicer, harder. So here I am again with my legs wound around his back. . . .

What am I going to do about it? I think of that motto: "Mother made me a homosexual." If I give her some wool, will she make me one too? There's really no choice, I guess, about being heterosexual. You're stuck with it for good or ill.

It's odd that I really care if a man has a good body. I would hate to sleep with one who didn't, who was too fat, for instance. Yet if a man ever made a comparable remark—that he liked sleeping only with women who had good bodies, I'd want to shoot him dead. Male chauvinist pig etc. Ah, inconsistency!

"You do have a very nice body," I say, regretfully, later.

"Thank you." He looks pleased, which always surprises me.

"It's funny men care about their bodies."

"Why in the world should it be funny?"

"I don't know. . . . I guess I just don't think of men standing in front of the mirror wondering—are my hips too wide or my waist too thick or my thighs too flabby?"

"They do."

"I guess I always think of them as just being content with the way they are."

He is silent a long time and then finally says, "Gabby . . . have we reached the end of this thing about your being pregnant?"

I tighten again. "I don't know. . . . Have we?"

"Look, I'll say one final thing, since you accuse me of not being open which has some justification. . . . I'd rather the child were mine. If that's an evil, male chauvinist thought, I have to plead guilty. That's all."

I ponder this.

"Somehow, I just can't find it in my heart to think that well of this guy who just disappears. . . ."

"I *wanted* him to disappear. . . . That was part of it, don't you see? If he hadn't been about to, I wouldn't have gotten pregnant. . . . If I'd gotten pregnant by chance, I'd have had an abortion—at *once.* . . . Can you understand that? For me the whole thing was in *my* planning it, *my* wanting it. . . . I'm not in any way shape or form seduced and abandoned. It's the opposite."

"I still don't like him."

"Okay.... That's your privilege." I understand jealousy
I'm very jealous myself, though I don't approve of jealousy. S
I can't quite put him down for that kind of feeling.

I know it would be very easy to quiet that feeling by jus
mentioning Matthew's bisexuality. He'd feel or think at once
well, then he's someone one doesn't have to bother about o
worry about, not a real "rival.". . . But I just can't. I guess I hav
a thing about not betraying people, and I do feel that to say tha
would be a betrayal of a kind. Matthew may not be "Th
Rival," but I don't want him put down for the wrong reasons b
someone who doesn't know him.

"Maybe I even envy you slightly the fact that you can, as
woman, just create your own family that way.... It does mak
women more self-sufficient.... What I don't like is the ide
that men are just to plant the seed and then 'disappear,' as yo
put it."

"I didn't say that."

"You said if he hadn't been about to 'disappear,' you wouldn'
have gotten pregnant."

It's also true as I now recall that I didn't embark on sleeping
with Rudolf until I knew he was leaving in December. There is
as they say, a grain of truth in his indictment, maybe more thar
a grain. "I don't think I regard men as just planters of seeds,"
say carefully. I recall, though, meeting a girl at a party this year
She wasn't much older than I, in her late thirties maybe, but she
had five kids, all from different fathers. I forget if she'd ever
been married, but she went on about how men were, just as
Rudolf said, mainly for getting you pregnant, which she
regarded as good since she loves babies. She regarded them as
fun for some things like taking you dancing, but basically not tc
be relied on, frivolous. "I guess it's my Italian heritage that
makes me feel that way," she said. No, I'm afraid that isn't me.
Put on your dancing shoes, Rudolf.... No, it's different. I envy
women like that. I wish I could say or feel: men are to gc

dancing with. Men are to make you pregnant, any generalization, really, that would sew the whole thing up. . . . In an odd way I think I've made it harder for myself due to the very thing I pride myself on—that I don't pick nasty, sarcastic, male chauvinist types. Maybe if I had or did, I could say more easily: men are no damn good. . . . But Matthew and Rudolf just aren't. God knows, they both have problems, but not in a way that makes it easy to file them under: Men, problems of. . . .

"Did you used to say, 'I love you,' to him or were you completely silent?"

Oh, God, this is like an endless series of Chinese water tortures. I turn over on my stomach and don't look at him. "I know I have a thing about that . . . which maybe I justify by saying it's not what you say but how you feel or act that counts." I know I am horribly silent during lovemaking. I cannot, will not moan, grunt, murmur anything—either sweet things or obscenities. I know, I *know*. It's all of a piece. I do hold back, I am guilty. "You've got to take me as I am or not at all," I say with mock defiance. "That's just the sum and total of it."

"I'd like to understand you."

"I'd like to understand myself. . . . Look, maybe I'm a puzzle with a missing piece. . . . You're not five easy pieces yourself."

"No," he admitted.

"So let's just try to take it as it comes, as it were."

"Okay."

We lie quietly, looking at the stars. The moon is half full.

"I liked your paintings," I say.

New York is grimy and still hot. It's a real shock to return. Mother and Daddy are still away. They never come back until the end of September, which is smart—by then it's usually cool and crisp. I go to see Dr. Hattie, who says, "I see you've finally expanded."

"Well, it had to happen eventually."

127

"Start wearing maternity clothes," she says. "It's about time. . . . You'll be more comfortable."

Wearing maternity clothes, of whatever sort, is the next big problem in that it means heralding the whole thing to the world. Nothing, I hope, can be worse than the thing with Rudolf. Still, I don't relish the next few weeks. I once read of a woman who got pregnant while unmarried, decided to keep the child, but hid off in some place, I think actually rented a new apartment and saw no one for nine months, even, I think, arranged to make it seem as though she'd adopted the child so "no one would know." That wasn't a hundred years ago either. Well, it's a test of my mettle, and I know I'll survive. I just don't exactly look forward to it.

It would be nice if one could send out carbon copies of a letter to everyone one had to tell the way some people do with letters to family. "Hello, you all. . . . This is from Gabby who wants to say. . . ." I guess one thing that bothers me is that when you're married and pregnant, all you have to "tell" is: I'm pregnant. But in my situation you have to explain why you're doing it, who the father is, where he is, in short go into a big spiel. It's not just the revealing of a physical fact: I am pregnant.

I get a bunch of maternity clothes, mostly slacks and smocky tops. There are some unspeakable tent dresses that look as though they're designed for women about to give birth to baby elephants. I hope the things I've picked look reasonably like the clothes I normally wear. I don't want to conceal anything, nor do I want to flaunt it.

The first person to "tell" is easy. I'm on a bus going to work the first day back, and who should get on the bus but Eve. I'm sitting toward the back and I watch her come down the aisle. Eve always makes a kind of entrance—I can see people staring at her. She's wearing a long gray coat and a floating feathery scarf in shocking pink. It's all theatrical and great.

128

"Hey, you!" I say, and she looks down, sees me, slides into the seat next to me, does a double take and then says, "I don't believe it."

"Okay."

She pokes my belly. "What is it—a pillow? You didn't buy one of those—"

I burst out laughing. "Eve!"

"Lord a mercy. . . . Can I say you're the last possible person—"

"You can."

"No, I *really* can't believe it. . . . What is it—Matthew's?"

"Right."

"You? How come? You're crazy! You're stark raving out of your mind!"

"How so?"

"God, for years I've thought of you as being the one sane member of your crazy family, the one sane person I *know!*"

"Are sanity and pregnancy incompatible?"

"Yes."

I can't help laughing again. "You're the first person to know, Eve . . . feel honored."

"Your parents are still away, aren't they?"

"They don't come back till September twenty-seventh," I say. "I don't think they'll be a big problem, do you?"

She ponders this. "Hmm. . . . That's a good one. Can I watch when you tell them?"

"Stop it!"

"No, I'll be curious. . . ."

"They've always been so good," I say lamely.

"It'll be very interesting."

"Will you get that little smile off your face?"

She smiles. She looks so pretty, and it's so early in the morning. "Look, I'm a sadist, Gabby . . . I'm really curious how this whole thing comes off. I've always hated you for managing it all so well while the rest of us were stumbling and groping and all the rest of it. . . ."

"*You* don't stumble and grope."

"Of course I do. . . . So I can't help feeling some small pleasure at how you will handle this rather, shall we say, 'human' situation."

I've always liked Eve's honesty. But at the moment it gives me pause. "Oh, dear."

"Why oh dear?"

"I hate to think of everyone gloating from the sidelines."

"You didn't think of that?"

I shook my head. "It's funny . . . I *think* I thought of everything. . . . But it's different now that it's happening."

"When are you due?"

"January."

"Ha, just when Miranda was born. . . . I hope that doesn't put a jinx on you."

"I *want* a little girl."

She's silent, no doubt absorbed in her own family thing. I get up—I change buses at Lexington.

"Let me know how it goes," she says. "Really. . . . If you need any, you know—"

"Sure."

At the lab I tell Frances, who is amazingly blasé. I guess being ten years younger than I, she moves in circles where this is more common. What a relief! I'm delighted to have someone *not* react for a change.

Lobochowski doesn't seem to notice. I know I could tell in one second if he did by his eyes, which reveal everything he tries to repress. Huh. Hadn't thought of that possibility. It now strikes me that unless I actually tell him in a formal way, he may just not catch on. Now that I think of it, Calla mentioned something like this, that when she was pregnant and working, most of the men in the office just plain didn't notice even though she was huge and coughing from their cigarette smoke and the like.

A formal presentation to Lobochowski. I'll have to think of it that way. Go home, draw up the salient points, decide how best to phrase them and then select what seems like the best occasion.

"How was your vacation, Gabrielle?" He always manages to make it sound as though having taken a vacation at all were slightly a misdeed.

"Very fine. . . . I went camping."

"I've left your part of the annual report on your desk. . . . You know it's due Friday? . . . Could you please redo the parts I've put a red line next to?"

"I shall. . . . Is the rest okay?"

He nods vaguely. If something is okay, he never thinks that worth mentioning.

I glance at the report. I can probably do it by working evenings all this week. Back to "real life." But in some ways I don't mind it. I like the structure of working, especially now. I like the fact that I'll be distracted by a whole mess of trivia, committee meetings, preparing seminars, all the things I usually balk at at least mentally.

Rudolf is back driving his cab. He stays here evenings most days. After we got back, we went once to his apartment. "I'll let you see it if you can restrain yourself from cleaning it up," he said in advance.

"Okay. . . . What makes you think I'd want to?"

"Well, anyone who's so neat that they always have precisely three sharpened pencils placed at a right angle on their desk has *some* hangup about order."

It's true. I am obsessed with order. As with other things, I blame it on my parents. It seems most other girls of my generation had immaculately neat housekeeper mothers, and they all rebelled by becoming arch slobs. Whereas since my mother couldn't have cared less about neatness or housekeeping, I have this thing about liking things in their place, the fewer things, the better. My idea of a perfect desk is a huge plank of wood with, as Rudolf noticed, three pencils and maybe a pad.

In the evenings we read and play chess. He noticed the chess board one night shortly after we returned and asked if I played.

"I happen to play a very bloodthirsty game of chess," I say, "and I refuse to lose on purpose, but if you want to play, fine."

Rudolf looks at me ironically. "Okay. . . . You've thrown down the gauntlet, now shall I take it up?"

Our first game is decidedly grim, scarcely a word spoken. It's a draw. He's very good, which is a relief. Though I enjoy winning, it's still more fun to play with someone with whom there's a possibility you can lose.

After that we play quite often. All my favorite games are ones which pit one person against another like chess. Matthew always loved bridge, but I couldn't for the life of me understand the appeal of sitting around a little square table with three other people, bidding and making jokes and all that; it's a whole other thing.

One evening when I'm lying on the bed wrapped in a towel after showering, I notice Rudolf looking at me and drawing something on a pad.

"What're you doing?" I say, startled.

"Just sketching you."

"Well, don't!"

"Why not?"

"I don't know." I try to explain. "That always seems such a classic thing. The nude lady in some stiff, awkward erotic pose, a blank smile on her face while the man, the 'artist,' quote unquote, draws her likeness."

"Even with the drawings of Degas and Rubens?"

"Anyone! It's the idea, not the finished product, I object to."

132

After a second I add, "And if you want to know, I feel you probably have some thing about thinking the female form, while pregnant, is so lovely, so round and. . . ."

Rudolf smiles. "As a matter of fact, I do. . . . Do I get a three-year jail sentence for that?"

"Yes!"

"Is this part of the not-wanting-to-be-gazed-at-with-fond-adoration business?"

"Something of the sort."

I hate to see myself being so rigid, so I give in. Also, I feel, if what Ellen said is true, that it's a pity Rudolf gave up art so completely if that's what he really enjoys doing most. Seeing him draw me makes me remember how I used to love to draw as a girl, and one evening I try drawing him as he's lying reading. Only the results aren't so great—I was never good at drawing the human figure, only animals.

"You've made me look about seven feet tall," he says later, inspecting it.

"I can't do people."

But he folds it up and puts it in his pocket.

I have set Monday as the day to tell Lobochowski about my pregnancy. I guess I want to be the one to tell him, not to have him pick it up through some rumor or lewd joke. I lie awake till three rehearsing my speech, and the next day, right after lunch, I ask if I can see him alone. We go into his office, and he closes the door.

"Leonid . . . there's something I felt I wanted to tell you. I don't think it will affect anything about my . . . position at the lab, but I wanted you to know that I'm expecting a child in January. I intend to come back to work after a week, and of course, Blue Cross will cover most of the expense so that. . . ."

He looks terrified. I can't think of any other word to describe his expression. Maybe it's that Lobochowski, being a bachelor, being so repressed, being Catholic, whatever, somehow thinks of all women as virgins unless given active, undeniable proof to the contrary. For a woman to be married, I suppose, would in his eyes be that kind of proof. His expression now is like that of a father whose fourteen-year-old daughter has just confessed that she slept wth someone the night before. He looks hurt and confused.

"Who is the father of your child?" he finally stammers.

"He's a very good friend, a professor, who happens to be spending this year abroad." His nervousness makes me sound by contrast very composed, the last thing I feel.

"And do you—is it your intention that, upon his return you will . . . the child's existence will be legalized?"

"You mean—will we get married?"

He nods.

"No, we aren't planning that." I say this almost gently, sorry not to be able to give him this comfort, which he seems to need.

"I see." I'm not sure he knows himself what he sees or doesn't see. Lobochowski isn't the world's most composed person, but in the years I've worked at his lab, I've never seen him look as distraught as at this moment. His face is really drained of color, and he's holding onto the chair as though he'd sink to his knees without its support.

"Naturally, if you feel this will in any—dislocate—the laboratory as a whole, I can look elsewhere for a job," I say, staring at him challengingly, to which he says, "Oh, *no,* of course not. . . . No, *no.* . . . I'm terribly sorry, Gabrielle, if anything I said led you to believe. . . ."

I just stand there, giving him rope enough to hang himself, if that's his intention.

"You said—January was the. . . ."

"Yes."

"Which hospital will you be . . . attending?"

"Mount Sinai."

This shift to the practical aspect seems to soothe him. He's looking calmer by the minute. "Oh, yes, they have excellent facilities," he says, "excellent."

"I just felt you should know," I mutter. We seem to have exchanged roles. He's calm now and I'm ruffled.

"I appreciate your confidence, Gabrielle," he says. "Believe me, it won't be misplaced."

Huh? Misplaced in what sense? What on earth does he mean? That, if anyone asks him, he'll deny it? Or say I'm really married? But I decide to let it go. In a sense he's risen to the occasion, and I really don't want or expect anything more.

The next day, however, after lunch, he asks if I would come into his office for a moment. Once again the door is closed behind us with great care.

When he begins speaking, he doesn't look at me. "Gabrielle . . . you know, I've been thinking of what you, of the situation in which you find yourself and I wanted to say that, if—for the sake of your child, you feel his having a name, that is, I would be quite willing to undergo a ceremony which would insure your child of a name. . . . Which would tie neither of us down in any way, of course. . . . It could be undone at any time. . . ."

He's speaking in such a crabbed, indirect way that it takes me a few seconds to realize that, in effect, this is a marriage proposal, the first formal one I've had in my life. "You mean, we should get married to give my child a name?" I repeat, trying to make sure I've got it right.

"Well, I realize how difficult. . . . People aren't always so. . . . I feel you would then have the confidence of starting off . . . on the right foot. . . . Unless, of course, this man you have referred to intends to give *his* name to the child?"

This thing about "names" really gets me. "No, he doesn't," I say quietly.

"I feel his behavior is certainly open to question," Lobochowski says, looking at me feelingly.

If I were in the mood to have any sense of humor about this,

I would laugh at the idea that poor Matthew, the very soul of honor, morally upright and conventional to a fault, is somehow seen, both by Rudolf and now by Lobochowski, as the "seducer." I just can't believe, first that that's possible, but it's true they neither of them know him. But how about me? Do I look like the "seduced and abandoned" type? I would have thought that would be the last interpretation anyone who had ever known me longer than five minutes would put on this situation. I'd not have been surprised at being accused of being too cold-blooded in planning this myself and all that. But that both men see me as the wilting flower, "I must give your child a name." It floors me. Also, in an insane way, I do feel touched. It must cost Lobochowski something to have made such a proposal.

"Leonid . . . that's terribly sweet of you," I finally manage to say. "I really appreciate it. . . . I think I can manage myself, though, I really do. . . . But I appreciate your having the thought."

"Please regard it as an offer which will always be open. . . . If you should decide later. . . ."

"I will, definitely." I can see me, while giving birth, suddenly calling for Lobochowski and having his whole pack of Polish relatives dance in, ancient mother and all, and a big swirling wedding feast taking place as I go into labor, with a great black-gowned priest holding our hands.

I'm touched, but by the time I get home I'm in a tearing rage. Rudolf usually gets off work at nine, and we have a late dinner or, if I've eaten, I have a can of beer while he eats.

"What the fuck does he mean—give my child a name?" I explode. "She'll *have* a name! *My* name!"

"I'm amazed he made the offer," Rudolf says calmly, tearing off a hunk of bread. "For a man like that. . . ."

"Rudolf, for God's sake, don't you see my point? I *have* a

name. Why do men think that only *their* family names are names?"

"It's not the name. . . . He's thinking, which may, I admit, be old-fashioned, about your 'reputation.'"

"But don't you see how demeaning that is? My name isn't even good enough for my child. If I don't borrow a name from some man, even one I hardly know, my child will be nameless. . . . I just can't tell you how that infuriates me!"

Rudolf reaches across the table and takes my hand. "Darling—"

"Don't darling me! Please!"

He looks cold. "Well, don't go off on one of your bits about 'men.'. . . You know, if I made half the generalizations about women that you do about men, you'd behead me."

"I just feel very put down."

"Because someone offered to marry you?"

"Yes!"

"Well, you have to admit that's a slightly unusual reaction."

"Well, I'm a 'slightly unusual' person."

He smiles dryly. "Okay."

"And why must every man I meet regard me as this poor wilting flower, seduced and abandoned? God, I've spent my life trying to be strong and reasonably self-assured, and yet every man I meet assumes I must be only having this baby because some madman raped me and tossed me in the gutter. . . . I mean, what view of women does that assume?"

"Perhaps a chivalrous one."

"Chivalrous!"

"Men like to feel women need their help. . . . I can't, somehow, regard that as a deadly sin."

"Maybe if you were a woman, you would."

"Maybe. . . . But since that's not likely to happen, I say that acknowledging that you need help is something a man or a woman ought to be able to do without going off the deep end."

Sometimes Rudolf gets this very stern, almost moralistic expression, and I hate it. He reminds me of a teacher, a woman, whom I loved in second grade who was always getting angry at me and only later revealed it was because I was her favorite, that I reminded her, as she wrote in my autograph book, of herself as a child.

"People aren't self-sufficient," he says. He gets up and stands looking at me.

"I didn't say they were."

"You try to live your life as though you wanted to be."

I turn away, I feel hurt and depressed. "Okay . . . but isn't that my problem? I'm the one who'll suffer from it, right?"

He's stroking me, hugging me, "comforting" me and for the millionth time turning me on despite myself. Sometimes I wish Rudolf had left for San Francisco right after we got back. As he kisses me and we move to the bed, that feeling of being closed in on comes back, the tidal wave, walking down a long corridor whose walls are made of burning hot metal, walls that are slowly closing toward me, another horror fantasy I used to have.

Van de Poel is such a *nice* name. I love the fact that my daughter will be a Van de Poel, and I look forward to taking her to Amsterdam, a city I happen to love, and having her meet all the Dutch uncles. Marie Curie Lobochowski. Matthew used to refer jokingly to our unborn daughter as "Marie Curie," and I became rather fond of the name, though I'm not positive I'll use it. . . . But with Lobochowski added on, it becomes a joke. . . . Maybe I am being off-key about the name thing. It's a detail, why get hung up on it? . . . Men want to protect women. Okay. . . . Why fight every single inch of the way? I'll be exhausted by the time I'm thirty-five.

Tomorrow my parents get back. That, too, is something I dread. I guess I've said to myself so many hundred times that I know they'll "rise to the occasion" that I literally go into a cold sweat when I think they may not. I know that for all my seeming independence I am still close to my parents, which has in part to do with our geographical closeness, my never having left New York, as well as my living here in their house at the moment. But it also has to do with the sort of people they are. In high school, in college, how I envied those friends whose parents were openly bigoted, narrow-minded, gross in some classic way, never read Freud, hadn't heard of Nietzsche, only watched TV, were right-wing politically. All those traits seemed so enviable in parents because they would, I felt sure, be freeing. Then you could go your own way, create your own way, and have no regrets. Whereas, as someone once said, "You really have a problem. . . . Your parents are human beings." My parents do have their problems, but they're all personal, not cultural. There wasn't a cause they weren't on the right side of, they don't, to this day, even own a TV. All those superficial, ugly sides of American culture which the kids I grew up with rejected and despised, my parents weren't even aware of. If you'd show my mother or father Malibu Barbie, they would just look blank, not even understanding this was something to reject—to them its appeal would be too incomprehensible for that. I feel that, in some subtle way, I was robbed of a context in which to grow, to test my ability to hate and feel angry. I became, even more than I need have owing to my personality, a parent pleaser, a conformist.

Which is why this whole thing now, my having this child, is ironical in a way. I'm not really in any sense a rebel. In some things I've gone my own way, and Lord knows I can be as stubborn as a mule, but deep down I want people's approval. I want to be liked. Rudolf calls me "porcupine" as a nickname because of the way I shoot out quills when angry, but, really, my quills are not half so deadly and barbarous as I'd like. I wish I *were* a porcupine.

Mother and Daddy are due back Tuesday evening, and sure

enough, at around nine, there is the phone call I've been tensing myself for. It's Mother.

"Hi! How was the trip?" I say. Rudolf, across from me, is gazing at the chessboard, contemplating a move.

"Oh, marvelous. . . . We had such a good time. . . . We met Hilda Garda on the plane, isn't that an amazing coincidence? And she said—"

"Mother, listen, I'd love to hear about the whole thing, but I was about to wash my hair. . . . Could I come up tomorrow after work?"

"Come for dinner!"

"Um. . . . I don't think I can tomorrow . . . I have an experiment that's running late. . . . Could I make it around nine?"

"Certainly, darling. . . . How are you? Have you been well? Did the camping work out?"

"It was wonderful," I say hastily. "I'll see you tomorrow then."

Rudolf offers to come along for moral support, but I can't do that. It would be too much of a dodge. Anyway, why I should be more nervous about this than about telling Lobochowski is hard to fathom. Or is it? I don't really care much about Lobochowski as a person, and I guess I still care enough about my parents to want their Good Housekeeping Seal of Approval.

It was a lie about the experiment that was going to run late. But I stay at the lab till eight anyway and catch a quick dinner at a luncheonette at the corner. Rudolf has a key and can let himself in, so I decide to go straight to my parents' apartment, not home first.

My stomach is in knots. I'm wearing one of my new maternity outfits, a pretty one, I think, a red blouse with pink butterflies on it and dark slacks underneath. Looking anxiously in the mirror in their hall, I feel I do look well, prettier than usual, if anything, not that that has any bearing on this occasion. I wait perhaps two minutes, then ring the bell.

Unlike Lobochowski, they notice at once, so there's a pause before I even step across the threshold.

I smile ironically, awkwardly. "I was planning to tell you tonight."

"Looks like it's beyond the telling stage," says Daddy.

They both look tan and fit, very well. My mother is in a long at-home outfit of some purple and yellow paisley silk. I walk in and sit down on the nearest couch. "Look, the details of it are that it's Matthew's and I wanted it and it's coming in January," I say, talking very fast before they even come around to the other side of the couch—in short, my speech is delivered while they're over my shoulder.

"I assume you're *not* planning to get married?" Mother says coolly.

"You assume right."

I look at their slightly grim, concerned faces and feel more of a sinking feeling than I did while standing on the threshold of their apartment. "I think it's something I can manage," I say. "I earn enough and, well, I just felt I wanted a child."

"Why?" Mother says.

I do a small double take. She had four kids after all! "I just . . . wanted one. . . . I mean, I feel I get on well with Elizabeth and I think I could—"

"You'll do a *fine* job, Gabby," Daddy says heartily. "I think it's just marvelous."

Mother looks at him as if he were off his rocker.

"Why did Matthew go away then?" she says, puzzled. "I would have thought—"

"Nooo. . . . Mother, you know Matthew," I say, smiling.

"What do you mean?" She looks indignant. "I think Matthew would be a very fine father."

141

"Maybe for a ten- or fifteen-year-old. . . . He hates babies."

But of course, for my parents that's no argument. My father didn't do much with us when we were babies either. That's the European way—certainly of their generation. It's not necessarily the mother who does it, but the nurse or the governess or the aunt or the grandmother.

"Did you give him a chance?" she asks.

"What?"

"I mean . . . if he had wanted to help you raise the baby, would you have let him?"

"It just didn't come up that way. . . . Mother, look, you know . . . Matthew had certain problems. I really don't know, at bottom, if he would have been a good father, and I don't say that to belittle him in any way."

Mother does know about Matthew's sexual "problems" or whatever; they discussed it. It's funny that this discussion should be centering on him, in any case. "I feel it's somehow cruel to leave him out like this," Mother says, looking at Daddy. "Don't you, Hans? I mean, Matthew might have wanted—"

"He didn't! He didn't!"

"Did you ask him?"

"Ask him *what?*"

"Ask him—if he wanted to help you . . . raise the child and so forth?"

I scratch my head. It's odd how you get so hung up in irrelevancies in these things. "Mother, having the baby at all, the whole *idea* of it was mine. . . . Matthew would no more have thought of it than he would have thought of flying to the moon."

"I didn't mean that. . . . I meant once you thought of it, did you really give him a chance, really see if he—"

"I did. . . . I did give him every chance."

"I wonder," she mutters, almost to herself.

I glance up, astonished, at Daddy, and he just smiles his

let's-not-get-into-a-quarrel smile and says, "I think this calls for a glass of champagne myself." He disappears and returns a second later, "Only we'll have to make do with white wine . . . the champagne isn't chilled. . . . You're looking gorgeous, darling."

"Thanks."

"Isn't she, Olga? I've never seen you look so well!"

My mother sits there silently, sipping her white wine and just gazing at me appraisingly.

"Don't overwork yourself," he says, "will you? Take it easy."

"Well. . . ."

"You haven't run into any . . . problems at the lab?" he adds.

"Not really. . . . They've been very understanding. . . . My boss even offered to marry me."

"Lobochowski? I don't believe it."

"I didn't either. . . . He wanted to donate his family name to the unborn child."

"What a thoughtful thing to do!" Mother exclaims. "Is this that same boss you always said was so awful?"

"Umm-hmm."

"Well, I think he sounds remarkable. . . . Don't you think, Hans? I mean, goodness. . . . What did you say?"

"That I already had a family name and I was quite happy to use that."

"He sounds like a very considerate, unusual person."

Maybe it's that Mother always almost automatically sides with the man in these things—first Matthew, now Leonid. Whatever it is, it's beginning to get to me. "He's nuts, but he has his moments," I say curtly.

"He doesn't sound 'nuts' to me."

I finish the glass of white wine, and Daddy quickly pours another. "Have you told Calla and Boris?" he asks.

"Well, I ran into Eve on the bus and told her. . . . So I imagine she told Boris. . . . But I just got back a week ago and. . . ."

"Your trip was fun, you say?" Daddy says. "Where did you go, exactly?"

I run on about the trip. The wine is beginning to get to me in a way that makes me not relaxed, but more tense. I feel the beginning of a headache coming on. At around ten I get up and say I have to go. Suddenly my mother darts off and returns with a very pretty dress that she bought me in Finland, a Marimekko. "Of course you won't be able to wear it now," she says after a second.

Back home, I don't even feel like talking about it to Rudolf. I lie on my side, and he massages my back and that feels very good. Suddenly there's a knock on the door. I jump up, buttoning my blouse, and go to answer it. It's Mother. "Dear, you forgot to take the dress," she says. "You know, I was thinking—" She sees Rudolf.

"Mother, this is Rudolf Biedermyer," I say. "Rudolf, my mother."

Rudolf ambles over, and my mother looks at him rather coldly. "Hello, Rudolf . . . I'm glad to know you." And a look to me to say: who the hell is he? And I look back as though to say: what's it to you?

"What a beautiful dress," Rudolf says. I knew he would like those colors, purple and green, and that somehow warms my mother up a little.

"Yes, I adore their fabrics," she says. "They have such an eye for color! It's amazing."

"I've never been to Scandinavia," he says.

"Oh, you should! You'd love it. Especially Finland."

"I hope to go someday."

When she leaves, I collapse on the bed. "My head's going to fall off."

"Take more aspirin."

"I've taken six.... They say you shouldn't take more than that."

He starts rubbing me again.

"No, I'm glad in some ways.... Now they know both."

"Both what?"

"Well, the baby thing and you."

"Would I be such an object of controversy? I thought you said they were sophisticated."

"Ya, only Mother adored Matthew.... They had quite a 'thing' together.... As far as I can tell, her main reaction tonight was how mean I was being to poor Matthew by excluding him from fatherhood."

Rudolf's face hardens a little. God, everyone in the world has his *shtick*. I'm sick of it. "Don't *you* go off on something!" I say warningly. "Right now I can't take it."

"She's beautiful."

"Who?"

"Your mother."

"Oh sure! ... She's had a million lovers and husbands and...."

"Really?"

"Oh, lovers somewhat.... Not since she was married, I don't think, but before, between marriages.... And she has lots of men friends who kind of lap around her."

"Why do you sound so critical?"

"Maybe because it's a talent I didn't inherit."

"Would you have liked to?"

"No ... I don't think men and women can be friends." I glare at him.

"Just sex, huh?"

"Rudolf, stop it!"

"I'm just repeating back what you said."

"You know damn well what I mean. . . . Now stop!" I crumple over.

"Stop worrying so much."

"I'm not worrying."

"Porcupine."

"Shit . . . I thought they'd be happy."

"I thought you said your father was."

"Oh, I don't know. . . . He pretended to be. . . . I can't tell."

Rudolf snaps off the light and starts undressing for bed. "Pretending is okay."

"No, it's *not* okay!"

"I didn't mean that."

"*You* seem so detached about your parents. . . . I wish I could be."

"I only see them twice a year . . . at best."

"You're smart."

"It doesn't mean I'm unaffected by them."

"Still, it's something." In the dark my headache is a little better. Rudolf lies, his arm around my belly, feeling the baby jump. I feel too disheartened to care about that tonight.

"Maybe you'll have twins."

"Don't!"

"He's certainly active."

"She, please."

"She."

"Actually, I can imagine you very well," Rudolf says, "with a little girl just like you with those very black eyes."

"You should meet my niece Elizabeth. . . . I want a little girl just like her, as much like her as possible."

"I'm sure you'll get one then."

Matthew and I never slept in the same bed. We both said—I don't remember who said it first—that we slept better separately, the whole issue of who needs or wants more blankets etc.

But Rudolf likes sleeping in the same bed, and now, perhaps owing to being pregnant, I've gotten to like it. It is crowded, and at times that's just plain annoying, not sexy, but at times it's nice, the warmth and solidity of another person right there. I feel as though the baby is doubly closed in, protected, and that must make her feel good.

The next evening, returning home at eight thirty, I find the apartment empty and a note from Rudolf on the table: "I'm at your parents." I feel dumbfounded. Why? If it were he who had gotten me pregnant, I could conceive, though just barely, that Daddy wanted to have a "serious talk" with him. Under the circumstances that exist, I can't imagine any possible motive.

I go upstairs and ring their bell. Mother is sitting in a chair with a glass of sherry, Rudolf is standing next to her. Seeing Rudolf there, that is suddenly, without forethought, drawing these two areas of my life together, I have the illusion I'm seeing my parents' apartment for the first time, through his eyes. I think it was in fourth grade that I first had this embarrassment about my parents' apartment. I had been out of school several weeks, recovering from tonsilitis, and my teacher came to visit, bearing various letters from the other children in my class. Taking one look around the room, she managed, after a long pause, to say brightly, "Well, this house certainly looks lived in!" Even at that age, I guess I could tell that that wasn't all she was thinking or feeling and I shrank back, hating my parents for being so unusual, so odd. If they hadn't earned enough money to send all of us to private schools where the average child had a lawyer or a businessman father and a Park Avenue duplex apartment and a poodle and a mother who either didn't work or who was in show business or interior decorating, maybe my parents wouldn't have stood out. If *I* hadn't seen a dozen apartments with everything just in place where the living room was redone each three or four years in purple instead of red, where the coffee table changes mysteriously from glass to chrome to wood again, depending on the current style, I might never have "seen" my parents' apartment at all.

It's such a strange conglomeration. There's some fantastic artwork, much of it the kind any museum would be glad to inherit, but the walls are covered with paintings hung one on top of the other, right up to the ceiling, many tilted slightly or jutting out. There are eleven African masks, clumped all together on a closet door. It's a welter of beauty, confusion, furniture from various European relatives, tables literally from the Salvation Army, discarded night tables from Calla or me or Boris plopped in the middle of the living room. The couch is the same couch that has been there for twenty years, always carefully recovered by some little European lady who comes to the house specifically for that purpose. There are Persian carpets so worn their pattern is almost indistinguishable, there are Persian carpets that are radiantly beautiful and in perfect shape. But it's all jumbled together. There's no room which has the best, no "oasis" of order or calm. There are times when I get physically dizzy in my parents' apartment. I want to just rush in and set it all to rights. But, even if you had the time and the energy, you couldn't. If it exists at all, it exists as it is.

Mother, seeing me, looks up almost guiltily. "We thought Rudolf might like some sherry."

Rudolf looks at me a little guiltily too. What's been going on here, folks? Some "deal" behind my back? I feel very paranoid and must show it a little because Daddy comes over and says, "Rudolf took a course once with Gerhard Mandelbaum at Cornell. . . . Imagine! It was his last year teaching, I gather."

Rudolf! Have you been betraying me? I scowl at him menacingly, and he just smiles his gentle daydreamer's smile. The three of them look so cozy with their sherry and their confidences, I feel totally left out.

148

"Darling, can I show you the poncho I got for Elizabeth?" Mother says, getting up. "I think she's going to love it."

I follow Mother into her bedroom. It's a jumble, too, like the rest of the house, with books piled nearly to the level of the bed, novels she's been planning to read for a hundred years, old *New Yorkers,* all her strange European medicines and creams on an ancient brass tray, her *mundwasser* and camomiles. Mother is a great believer, as many Europeans are, in "cures" and "mud baths"—she and Daddy sometimes go to some arcane place in Switzerland where they immerse you in peculiar ointments for weeks and supposedly rejuvenate you. She knows what I think of all this and never mentions it any more, no more than her various transient religious enthusiasms, which have ranged over the years from Catholicism to the various Eastern religions back, inevitably, to her own Russian Orthodox church.

I admire the poncho, but laconically, still detached.

"Gabby," Mother says, "I feel you misunderstood me last night."

"In what way?"

"Well, I felt you went away feeling I disapprove somehow of this baby. . . . It's not that, really. . . . It's just . . . I guess I just take such great pride in your career—you've done so wonderfully, and I suddenly felt afraid you might throw it all over, not be able to go on."

"Why? Do I seem like the type that would 'throw it all over'?" I ask a little coldly.

"No, darling, but no one thinks of themselves as the type. . . . I didn't think of myself as the type either."

I look at her, puzzled. I've never heard my mother express the slightest regrets about not pursuing her career. I can't even believe the innuendo in her last remark.

"But you've never really faced that, did you?" I say tentatively. "I mean, you've always done both."

"Both what?"

"Well, I mean, you and Daddy have had the gallery and yet you've had children and—"

"Well, I was once an artist, you know, Gabby," she says dryly, a little ironically. "Not the world's greatest perhaps, but one nonetheless. . . . And I'm not anymore."

"But if you felt children would stand in your way, why did you have so many?"

She smiles a little sadly. "Darling, you won't believe this, but as a girl, even after my marriage to Bengt, I was such a bohemian girl of a certain kind, you've never been like that, Calla was more so, everyone thought I was a scatterbrain, artistic maybe, but wild, silly. . . . My mother was forever telling me I should never have children, that I'd toss them out in the bath water, I suppose. . . . And I wanted to show her I could. . . . Silly, in fact she was dead when Calla and Jessie were born, but I think I still wanted to show her."

Now that she's mentioned it, I can easily imagine my mother as she might have been then, as I've seen her in old photos, incredibly pretty with dark hair flying, a loose cape, funny stockings and shoes. I sit silently, digesting all this.

"You're not like that," Mother adds suddenly.

"No, not exactly," I say.

"You're so organized. . . . I've always admired that. . . . I never could be . . . in anything. It's not my way. . . . So maybe you'll do both. . . . If anyone can, you can."

"So, it's not my not being married you're worried about," I say, incredibly relieved for some reason.

"No, it is . . . just in that you'll have to do it all yourself. . . . You'll want to, I can see that. . . . But it'll be that much harder."

I wish I could say with utter vehemence that I know I'll do it. I do feel I will, but her uneasiness has affected me.

We sit in silence for a while.

"Rudolf is such a darling!" she says suddenly, leaping up. "I love him."

How can she love so many men? Even casually, even enough to make such a remark off the top of her head. "He's kind of nice," I say, embarrassed. Oddly, I think for her the shift from Matthew to Rudolf is now accomplished with a lot less sweat than it took me.

"He knows so much about art," she goes on, her old bright, eager self again. "Daddy was amazed."

"He once studied it, I guess." I sigh and get up. I don't want Rudolf drawn into the honeyed web, I guess, I wish we were off camping in our own ugly, personal world.

Later, when we're back at my apartment, he says, "You know, your parents are hippies, in a way."

I laugh. "Sort of."

"I've never seen anything like that. . . . I thought they were great."

"I used to wish they'd be more materialistic," I say, undressing. "Maybe you can't understand that."

"No, my parents have that too," he says, "in a different way. . . . We never had a TV."

"Neither did we. . . . So you know."

"Umm. . . . They're so proud of you."

"That's what makes it sticky."

"Leave New York."

"I will someday . . . maybe."

He's looking at me. We've never discussed what will happen after December, and I don't, at all, want to. Rudolf seems to have almost a sixth sense about my not wanting to be pressured. Now he just keeps looking at me, but keeps whatever he's thinking to himself.

"Thanks," I say after a moment.

He just smiles.

151

*   *   *

From Calla I get a breathless phone call—at the lab, no less. She's heard the news and thinks it's the greatest thing ever.

"Gee, thanks, Cal. . . . That's sweet of you."

I want to believe it *is* sweet of her. She's the first person who's unequivocally said as much. But I can't help feeling it's the same sinister wanting me to "get mine" that I've sometimes felt for her. Motherhood, the great leveler. I endow Calla with fantasies of me buried under grimy diapers, screaming for help.

"Elizabeth is thrilled out of her mind. . . . She wants to call you about it."

"Fine. . . . I'd love to hear from her." I didn't mean to sound testy about the showering episode, but Calla says right away, "We'll be going away for a weekend later this month. . . . She'd be so happy if you could take her, them, if you're feeling up to it."

"That would be great."

"What do you want?"

"Pardon me?"

"I mean, a boy or a girl?"

"Oh, girl, of course. . . . As much like Elizabeth as possible." Calla laughs. "You would!"

"What?"

"Want a girl."

"Why shouldn't I?"

"No, it's great, you'll probably have one, first babies always seem to be girls. . . . It's just everyone else I know always wanted a boy first."

Well, bully for them! I think, annoyed. "Cal, I really have to . . . attend to something. . . . Thanks for calling, though."

Fie on it. I feel much more pleased when, that evening, I hear Elizabeth's voice on the phone. "Well, Miss Scrie, I hear you're pregnant," she says slyly.

"You hear correctly, Miss Roo."

"Can I be your baby-sitter?"

"Sure."

"Really. . . . All by myself, do *everything?*"

"Sure."

"I'm almost nine," she says importantly. "That's pretty old."

"That's ancient. . . . I think you'll be too old, Roo. I need a bright young thing."

"Blah!" she says.

"Blah to you!"

"You *have* to have a girl," she warns.

"I'm planning to."

"I've thought of the name . . . Flora."

"Why Flora?"

"I like it."

"I'll consider it."

"You can add some other names for the middle, if you want."

"Thanks, Roo."

"You know, we're staying with you in a month. . . . Did you hear?"

"I did."

"Are you so fat you can hardly move?"

"Nooo. . . ."

"I bet you're huge!" She laughs uproariously. "I bet you look like an elephant!"

"More like a rhino."

"Oh, boy! This is going to be something." She's still chuckling quietly. "Wow!"

I hang up, smiling. Crazy kid.

The next day I get another unexpected phone call.

"Is this Miss Gabrielle Van de Poel?"

"Yes."

"Miss Van de Poel, we've been requisitioned to get in touch with you by one of your relatives, a Mr. Rudolf Biedermyer."

"Yes?"

"Mr. Biedermyer has been injured in a car accident, and he wished that you be notified."

I sit down. "What kind of a—a car accident?"

"Yes."

"Could you tell me—how serious was the accident?"

"I'm sorry, Miss Van de Poel, we're not allowed to release information on patients over the phone."

"What hospital *is* this?"

"Mount Sinai."

"Well, could you at least tell me—is he conscious? I mean, just give me a very general idea of what—"

"We cannot release information over the phone."

"Can he be visited?"

"No, he. . . . Oh, wait a minute. . . . Yes, it says here, Dr. Glutton says he *can* be visited."

"What hours?"

"Visiting hours are five to six."

"Thank you very much."

I hang up and sit there in a daze. . . . A car accident? His cab? It must be that. Yet somehow I never think of cabs having accidents. New York cabdrivers drive so wildly, I've often sat back, wanting just to close my eyes and wake up when we get there, but *they* seem supremely self-confident, having mastered this special art, weaving in and out of city traffic. But Rudolf? God, his head was probably in the clouds! You idiot! You daydreamer!

There's one saving grace. If he has visiting hours, doesn't that mean it can't be fatal or near fatal? I try and think if I have any precedents for thinking this, but I've rarely been to a hospital. "He asks us to notify you," implying he was, at least when he said that, conscious.

For the next few hours, while with part of my head I do my work, the other part is racing wildly around trying to construct elaborate reasons the accident can't have been as bad as I am scared sick it may be.

First, I'm not the kind of person to whom such things happen, even indirectly. I mean, I'm not someone out of *Love Story*. All that is too melodramatic for me, doesn't fit my life-style. I'm not the kind whose lovers die sudden dramatic deaths. I'm the kind whose lovers drift off with a lot of chat and talk and letters exchanged for a hundred years afterward. So this just wouldn't fit the grand scheme of things. . . . Is there, however, a grand scheme of things?

By late afternoon I'm on to another tack. It's incredible how someone like me who despises horoscopes and any kind of mysticism, who elevates common sense almost to the level of a deity, sinks, with alarming speed, to the most gross kind of superstitiousness when I'm scared. Now it's back to offering up sacrifices. If I agree that I will die ten years earlier than I would have otherwise, will that make Rudolf be okay? Or will I agree not to have any paper I write published for this whole year? Or for my whole life? My whole *life?* Come on! What is this? Then, it's the baby. Will I accept a baby with some deformity in "exchange" for Rudolf's safety? Blindness? Six toes? Six toes are easy. I know one can be snipped off, but blindness? Why am I *doing* this? Is it just a way to keep my mind busy, or am I really at bottom a believer in "exchanges" of this kind? I did it compulsively as a child. Which parent would you save? Would you save them before yourself? Etc.

And finally at six I find myself at the hospital, having been juggling "sacrifices" for several hours, having somehow evidently rounded up my work, bid Frances good-bye, none of which I can remember at all.

Dr. Glutton? If I were in the mood, that would be amusing in a morbid kind of way. Maybe they made a mistake.

Ellen said Rudolf was squeamish about blood. *I* am squeamish about blood. I, too, thought of med school and felt I just couldn't take it. Maybe it would have been good for me if I had, but as I walk into Rudolf's room, I pray: don't let it be messy or awful. Let him be well bandaged, no matter how serious it is. Oh, what a coward I am. A moral coward, a physical coward.

He looks fine. That is, from the waist up, he looks fine. His legs are all bandaged and hanging from ropes so he can't move to see me until I come around by the side of his bed.

Despite everything, I feel so relieved I laugh, nervously. "Well, at least I was right in *part*."

"About what?"

"You didn't just up and die!"

"I'd never do that to you, honey." He smiles ironically.

"How the heck did it *happen?*"

He explains. It wasn't even really a car accident. He was unloading someone's luggage from the trunk of the cab when another car came up from behind and rammed into him. If they'd just rammed into his cab, it probably would only have been a minor smashup.

"So what do you have?"

"A mass of broken bones. . . . Compound fracture, as they call it."

I make a face. "Will you have to stay here long?"

"A week or so. . . . Then I'll be on crutches awhile longer."

"Jesus!"

I sit down facing him and then begin having an odd sensation. I have the feeling Rudolf, lying in bed, is becoming smaller, receding, like something out of *Alice in Wonderland*. It's a little frightening, and I sit very still, hoping it will pass in a minute. Gradually it does, but the uneasy fear that accompanied it lingers on. I think it's that I am bad about people being sick, not just the gory aspect, but the idea that as a woman this should be an occasion when I rise supremely to the test, become warm and compassionate and nurselike, Florence Nightingale, hang over

he bed with hot noodle soup, tend, wrap bandages. And instead
feel a horrible coldness at the prospect of this, not the physical
doing of it, but the idea of being in that role, the "tender."... I
don't know if it's that my parents overdid "caring" so much,
hat to care at all this way puts me off. I want to up and leave the
oom and not come back until he's all well.... You did this on
ourpose, Rudolf. You got hit by that car on purpose just to do
his to me.

"I'll be well soon," he says, mistaking my look of acute
anxiety.

"Umm," I murmur.

"Come over and kiss me."

"Is that allowed?"

He nods.

Very slowly I go over and kneel beside the bed and kiss him
softly on the lips. He puts out one arm and tightens it on my
shoulder. About one second later a nurse bustles into the room,
and I leap up as though electrocuted.

She smiles warmly. "Oh, don't stop for the sake of me! Just
coming in to change the water.... How's the leg, dearie?"

"The same," Rudolf says.

"Want another of those pain-killers? They help, you know."

"I think I better hold off.... I'm getting a little too groggy."

I hadn't thought, for some reason, of his being in pain. I
shrink back into my chair. The nurse beams at me and at my
stomach and says, "Now, what a time for him to go and do this
to himself, eh? Aren't men *like* that, though?"

I just nod, frozen.

She trots out.

Of course, she thinks I'm his wife and this is our child. I could
say, "No, I am not his wife," but then she'd just think I was his
girlfriend who was having his baby. And to say, "No, I am his
girlfriend, in a sense, but this is not his baby," is more than I feel

157

it's the privilege of any stranger to know. So between the truth and her assumption lie too many knots to unravel. Let me be, for her, his wife.

"Are you in pain?" I say after a moment.

"Some." After a second he says, "It was worse before."

I stare at him. It strikes me that Rudolf resembles a man angel in a play I once saw in Germany. Maybe it's those large greenish daydreamer eyes and the somber expression and his long face. I can imagine him with large stiff wings coming to announce the Annunciation.

"What are you thinking?" he says.

I swim back to the present. "That you look like an angel."

He smiles.

"Is your doctor really Dr. Glutton?"

"Isn't that great?"

I stay until the loudspeaker begins shouting that everyone must leave.

Rudolf gives me a list of things he might need, and I promise to bring them the next day.

"How about the abortion clinic?" I say. "Aren't they expecting you December first?"

"I think I can still make it," he says.

"On crutches?"

"Sure. . . . I don't need my feet, just my hands. . . . Anyway, I can report in. . . . There may be some other work I can do there."

He seems not unhappy in the hospital, which puzzles me. It reminds me of how, as a child, I used to love being sick, those enormously long afternoons immersed in various fantasy paper doll, coloring book worlds. I bring him some *Life Nature* books from the lab, and each time I come he's reading with great interest about the desert or mammals. I guess it puzzles me because when I was sick as an adult, in the hospital ten days with viral pneumonia, I almost went out of my head, I felt so claustrophobic and eager to be doing things again. Rudolf is funny. Watching him, I can imagine him as a boy, spending long afternoons as he's described, looking at his father's maps and planning imaginary journeys.

That evening, when I get home, it's Wednesday night, which is writing to Matthew night. It's easier without Rudolf there. I don't feel really guilty about Rudolf since even when we were together, Matthew and I agreed to feel free to have other relationships. But I don't feel utterly unguilty either. Maybe it's not guilt. It's that before this Matthew was my "best friend," and now he's not anymore. Maybe that would have happened in any case with our being apart, but I'm more aware now when I write him that the things I'm confiding, even about the baby, are things I've already confided; they're secondhand.

I sometimes wonder how he and Rudolf would get along if they met without either of them knowing me, just as people. Probably they wouldn't. I think Rudolf would find Matthew stiff and much too intellectual in a kind of self-conscious way. It's partly the Harvard thing, the sense of being part of an elite Matthew always had, which Rudolf doesn't have at all. In some ways they're both daydreamers, but in different ways. Matthew could be intense and brisk and sharp, give dazzling lectures, then disintegrate into self-disparagement and self-mockery. Whereas Rudolf seems more content with his own dreaminess. He doesn't even seem to want the fame or whatever Matthew would have possibly gotten if he had been able to finish that tome on Baudelaire.

"Is this your first?" the nurse, Miss Buffington, asks me when I arrive a few days later.

I nod.

"Oh, you'll have a beautiful bouncing boy, I'm sure," she says. She's a lady in her fifties, perhaps, with dyed blond hair piled in an elaborate beehive and quite fancy makeup. I suspect her sex life is still very much a thing of the present, though she confided she's a widow and has been for twenty years. Evidently back in England she has a daughter and grand-daughter. Her son died from drowning when he was twenty, just two months after he'd gotten married. She's a warm cheerful person, a bit of a compulsive talker. Her life has certainly had a tragic side, and maybe the talking is a cover-up. Anyway, I don't think it would bother me so much if it weren't that she has these false assumptions about my being Rudolf's wife which I can't quite bring myself to disabuse her of.

"I'd like a girl, actually," I say finally.

"Oh, no, you'll have a boy, I can tell," she says.

"How?"

She gestures vaguely. "Oh, your face. . . . You don't have that puffy funny look some women get. . . . That always means a girl."

It's begun to irritate me that whomever I meet, a cabdriver or shoe salesman, always predict a boy for me and always on the basis that I look well. It seems that, being strangers, they want to literally wish me the best and wishing someone they'll have a girl is evidently equivalent to wishing she has a Mongoloid.

"I think girls are . . . easier," I venture, lacking the courage to announce my real reasons for wanting one. "More verbal and. . . ."

"Oh, no! Not a bit of it!" And she goes on about her son and how he adored her and always came to her and told about his girlfriends and how much easier he was than her daughter. "Your husband'll want a son," she said. "Men *always* do."

When I go into Rudolf's room, she even says to him, "What name are you thinking of for the nice little boy your wife is going to give you?"

Rudolf's face gets that deceptively angelic, bemused expression. "Sebastian," he says finally.

"Sebastian! Well! Yes, that is a nice name, an unusual name. . . . He'll be a blondy, I bet, like you, babies always are,

160

oh, I bet he'll be a beauty. . . . Too bad you're having it over at Mount Sinai, I'd love to drop in and see him when he's born."

"I'll send you a card," I say.

"Will you? Oh, do, darling. . . . I just miss my granddaughter so much, I can't tell you. . . . Did I tell you what she said the last time I. . . ."

Rudolf is always very courteous and grave with Miss Buffington, more than I'd have the patience to be. When I ask him about that, he says that in his hometown in the South there are lots of ladies who run on like that. He, evidently, knows dozens of great-aunts and cousins and the like, quite unlike my family, where everyone is in Europe.

"I wish I could tell her we're not married. . . . It bugs me."

"It doesn't really matter. . . . She enjoys thinking it."

At the lab the news of my impending childbirth has spread, probably not owing to gossip so much as just the sight of me in my ever-swelling state. The odd thing is that for some of the students I've become a kind of folk hero. After a seminar I give Tuesdays a girl named Lurleen Montofer came up to me. She's a peculiar girl, I think a Mennonite, who looks, though she's younger than I, like someone off a Grant Wood drawing, very severe face, hair coiled over her ears, long, dowdy skirts. Evidently she goes up to anyone in the lab who uses a "profanity" and begs him to refrain. Despite this, she's very bright and handed in one of the best papers in the class at mid-semester.

"Miss Van de Poel?"

"Yes?"

"I just wanted to say . . . I have so much admiration for you and . . . what you're doing. I think it's such a fine thing!" She has an ardent but slightly crazy way of talking, her lips barely open, as though she were giving away state secrets.

"Thank you, Lurleen."

"You're the best teacher I've had here and I just think this is the grandest thing I ever heard of. . . . I've written my mother and my uncle. . . . *They* say it is too."

"Really?" Lacking a context in which to place this information, I still find it surprising.

"If Mother comes up at Thanksgiving, she wants to meet you. I said to her, 'Mother, you *should* come up.' She's in this small town all year round, she needs to get away, you know, just needs a change of scene. . . . But Father just wouldn't budge, not an *inch.*"

"I hope she does come then."

"Me too! You know, Arthur and I are separated. . . . Did you hear? I guess you did. We're no longer together, I'm afraid."

"I had heard . . . I'm sorry." Her husband was another student, not quite so peculiar as she, but much less bright.

"Oh, no! Nothing to be sorry about!" She laughs peculiarly. "I'm *glad* myself."

"Are you? Well, that's good."

"It's so much easier alone," she says, "it really is. . . . You'll find that with the baby too, I'll bet."

What can she possibly know about babies? I can't think of anyone who would look less "right" with a baby in her arms. A pitchfork would be more like it. Still, you never can tell.

When she departs, I reflect, once again, on the irony of it all. There was a couple last week, two students that have been living together for ages, who also felt they had to say how much they "admire" what I was doing. I don't mind, exactly. Maybe in part I mind on the grounds that I'm a private person and now I feel that something quite personal about my life is public knowledge. Also, I'm not sure I want to be a folk hero. Better that, I guess, than lewd jokes and that kind of thing—though I'm sure that's going on among the older generation here, I just don't hear about it. I wish what I'm doing could be just an isolated act, of interest to no one, something quite routine.

Well, maybe for the generations that live after us, as they're always saying in Chekhov plays. Not now.

Rudolf is coming home at the end of the week. The day before he's due home we have a ferocious argument. I come to see him in the evening at the usual time. First, I go into his usual room and draw back in horror when I see a man stretched out, somehow gory—I look too quickly to see how, and I think, irrationally, it's Rudolf. It's as though I were coming to the hospital for the first time, not knowing how serious the accident was, and, in fact, it turns out to be as bad as I feared. I back away, my heart thumping, and go to the main desk, where they explain he's been transferred to another room. Why this should make me angry at Rudolf is anyone's guess. Partly I guess it revives that feeling of how scary it is to care enough about someone so that their well-being means something to you. I had had a flash of that when the hospital called, saying he'd been injured, but once it turned out it was just a compound fracture, that feeling receded.

Also, I had a most peculiar conversation with his sister, Ellen, last night. He asked me to call and tell her, now that any real fear for his life or something very serious is over. She was laconic, as always, but she kept implying that it had somehow been a suicide attempt, even though I'd told her the exact details of how it happened. Rudolf did say she had tried to kill herself several times, and maybe she likes to think of him as being just like her.

"I'm sure it wasn't that," I said. "He was just getting these bags out of the trunk and—"

"He's always been self-destructive," she said. "You just *look* at him and you know that."

Hell, I've looked at Rudolf plenty of times, and to me there's nothing "self-destructive" about his face. Sensitive, maybe, but that's not the same thing at all. "I feel quite certain it's an accident," I said firmly.

163

"Oh, it's the same thing with Daddy's mother. . . . Did you hear about that?"

"No, what?"

"Oh, it was crazy! Just plain crazy! Daddy's mother was in this car—he was with her, he was around five at the time—and she got stuck on a railroad track. The train smashed into them and she got killed instantly and he, Daddy, wasn't hurt at all. . . . How do you explain that?"

"Well, I don't know," I said. "Maybe the train somehow hit—"

"It's clear as beans to me that she got out and was hit right on. . . . They, none of them, will admit it, of course! Oh, no! . . . Rudolf's the same. Men *always* are. . . . They never admit anything."

"I just . . . really and truly think it was an accident," I repeated, sounding rather lame.

"Okay. . . ." She suddenly became silent.

I felt hurt. I had liked Ellen, and it's not that I want to block out anything self-destructive in human nature. I'm not a cockeyed optimist or anything, but I just feel she's bringing her own thing to bear on this.

"How's your baby?" she said after a while.

"Not born yet."

"Oh. . . . Are you scared of dying?"

"Excuse me?"

"In childbirth. . . . God, I was always scared out of my wits at that. . . . I guess it was silly." She laughed in her odd, barking way.

"Well, I think the chances of that today would be rather rare," I said carefully.

"Oh, sure," she agreed. "I'd have been scared anyway, though."

On the way to see Rudolf the next day that whole conversation plays back in my mind. I really do think what I said was

GIVE ME ONE GOOD REASON

true, that it was an accident, that Ellen was just bringing her own thing to bear on it, but somehow it eats at me. I just don't want Rudolf to be another self-destructive talented person who makes suicide attempts he can't admit even to himself. That would be so sad and depressing. The idea of it really wouldn't have occurred to me about him if she hadn't said it—now it's lodged like a thorn in my leg.

Also, the thing of his being so content in the hospital bothers me in an odd way. Why should he be like me, desperate to get out and work, do something? Partly I admire the fact that he can just lie there, reading, drawing, listening to music on his transistor radio. In the abstract I think that's fine, but in reality it bothers me.

I sit there, looking at him from my chair in the corner. Maybe I'm a sadist. The sight of him in that hospital bed, wounded, injured, incites me. I can't bear him looking so defenseless, and that, in a crazy way, makes me want to attack him. Talk about kicking someone when they're down! "Stop drawing!" I say suddenly.

He looks up in surprise.

"No, I mean. . . . If I come here, you might as well talk to me!" I guess I feel that too. My life is ruled by these crazy hospital visiting hours. Of course, no one says I "have" to come, but I do.

He puts down his pad.

"Ellen thinks you tried to kill yourself." God, I had sworn, practically taken an oath in blood, that I would not mention that to him. So the first words off my lips—

Rudolf looks bewildered.

"In the accident. . . . She thinks it wasn't an accident. That's what she said anyway."

"Well, that's understandable, I guess," he says slowly, thoughtfully.

Just what I had thought, but now I say fiercely, "How?"

165

"Well, her own. . . . I mentioned her—"

"Yes?"

He's silent a minute. "I don't think she's correct. . . . But she is a very perceptive person, that's true." He is brooding, actually ready to consider what she said, and for that I feel ready to kill him.

"Rudolf, it was an accident! You *know* it was!"

"Yes, I know. . . . I'm not saying I agree with her. I'm saying I think she sometimes has certain insights that are worth considering."

"So you really are a self-destructive person?"

"No, not at bottom, I don't think." That same calm, unflappable quality which at times I admire now drives me up the wall.

"Then why *don't* you become an artist, for God's sake?" I say suddenly, violently. "If that's what you love, you should do it! If you're scared of blood and hate being a doctor, why *be* one? That makes no sense!"

"I don't hate being a doctor," he says.

"But you like painting more. You've said that!"

He's silent a long time. "Look, Gabby, you have to get something straight. . . . Maybe I haven't been clear enough about it. . . . Yes, I do love to paint. . . . But Ellen isn't right in saying it was only because my parents twisted my arm that I went into medicine. . . . For one thing, I'm not sure I really have the talent to make a go of painting."

"You'll never know unless you do it, though."

"But, also," he goes on, ignoring me, "it's—well, my father is a very, he's what you said of me in that letter, 'creative, sensitive, an escaper'—was that it?" He looks at me wryly. "It's true—of both of us. . . . But he deliberately struggled to prevent himself from escaping, to involve himself in something he thought was important, and I think that made a difference in his life."

I say nothing. He must have read the letter I wrote to

Matthew saying those things. Did I deliberately leave it around, hoping he would? I didn't really mean to belittle him, but now I see it was a kind of betrayal. I don't tell Rudolf about Matthew's bisexuality, yet I felt free to analyze his character in that offhand way. It is inexcusable.

"You don't want to escape," he said, "so maybe you can't understand that."

I consider this. Yes, it's true. I feel part of the here and now. . . . I've constructed my life around virtues like directness and strength of character, but I'm not altogether sure that wasn't deliberate, a deliberate desire to bury my daydreamer side the way some children who've been seriously ill at an early age become athletes in later life.

"I'm sorry about that letter," I say finally. It's the hardest thing in the world for me to apologize about anything.

"That's okay."

Sometimes I feel Rudolf understands me better than I'd like him to. Being misunderstood is annoying, but also protective. Maybe he senses Matthew is not really a threat by reading between the lines, as it were, even without knowing all the facts.

The next day I arrive at eleven in the morning to help him check out. They insist he sit in a wheelchair right up to the minute we get a cab. Then he's given his crutches by Miss Buffington and another nurse and hobbles after me to the cab.

In the cab he says, "So our 'marriage' is over."

I looked at him, puzzled, then realize he means our marriage in the eyes of Miss Buffington, whose parting words to us were, "Let me know as soon as it happens!"

"It was certainly a painless divorce . . . or annulment," I say.

"Moderately."

I'm not sure exactly what he means by that, and I don't exactly want to ask. At home I get him settled—the bed is freshly made—and head off for the lab.

When I come home that evening, Rudolf says, "You've had four phone calls . . . all from someone named Eve."

"Huh. . . . Four?"

"She left this number."

I look at it. It's odd Eve leaving a number at all since, of course, I have their number. I call the number he hands me, and it's answered by one of those weird answering services where the person's real voice says, "Hello. . . . This is Eve Van de Poel. I'm not in right now, but if you'll leave your name after you hear the beep, I'll call you back as soon as I get in." I don't wait for the "beep." Those machines scare me. I decide I'll just try her later.

"I called the clinic," Rudolf says at dinner. "They said to come anyway. . . . They can find something for me to do."

December 1 is in two weeks. "You'll fly?"

"I called American Airlines."

Our voices—to me anyway—are sounding very stiff and polite and not quite real. "I guess American is one of the safest," I say.

"That's what I heard."

We finally abandon the topic as essentially undiscussable, which it may just be.

At eleven I try Eve again, and she's in. "What's up?"

"I don't want to talk now. . . . Can I come by?"

"When?"

"Now? . . . I'm right around the corner from you. It'll only take a minute."

Actually, I feel a little tired, but I put my hand over the receiver and say to Rudolf, "It's my sister-in-law. . . . She's in the neighborhood and wants to come over. . . . Are you too tired? I can tell her some other night."

I almost wish he'd say yes, I am too tired, but he just says, "No, that's okay."

To Eve I say hastily, "It's okay, only . . . well, we won't be alone, Eve. . . . I have a—a friend is here."

"Oh." After a moment she says, "Who?"

"His name is Rudolf."

"Hmm. . . . Well, let's see. . . . Maybe I'll come anyway."

"It's fine by me."

In about seven minutes Eve comes sparkling into the room. She looks tired, but electric, keyed up. "Hi, Rudolf. . . . You *are* Rudolf, aren't you?"

"I am."

Eve sighs and sits down. "Give me some very strong coffee, my dear."

"What happened?"

"It's odd you didn't hear. . . . I was sure Boris would've called your parents."

"You left him?"

She nods. "Yes, last week. . . . I left Miranda, too. . . . It was really a *great* idea. . . . I should have done it years ago. . . . You know, actually, Boris is extremely happy and Miranda is extremely happy . . . and *I'm* extremely happy." She looks at Rudolf. "Were you ever married?"

He shakes his head.

"Uh, you innocents! . . . Why were you never married?" She gives him her imperious ice-blue stare.

Rudolf laughs. I think he's taken with her directness. "Should I have been?" he says.

"That type," she says. "Answering questions with questions, huh? No, you should not have been. . . . You two are probably the only wise, sane people in this whole crazy city."

"How great," I say dryly.

"Never married. . . . You're what, Gabby, thirty-three—"

"Two."

"And you"—she squints at Rudolf—"you're thirty-four."

169

"Correct."

"And you've never, either of you, even once had the insane urge to wreck your life by getting involved with someone else? You should both go on TV. I mean it. I wish there were more people like you who were presented as positive examples: this is the way we should live. . . . Because it is! This togetherness thing is insane, and every decade it keeps whipping back in some new form. . . . I want marriage buried, once and for all, in a big black casket."

"What happens with Miranda after school?" I say, bringing out cookies.

"Let me see. . . . It's really very simple. . . . She goes to a friend's house most days, and on two others, I think, Boris picks her up. . . . Isn't that typical of Gabby?" she says, looking at Rudolf. "She always wants to know the details, never the theory. . . . Maybe she's right. . . . It's the details that matter."

"If you're happy, however . . . that's the main thing," I say, somewhat lamely.

"I am!" She looks at both of us. Her face is flushed but almost radiant in a tired way. "I think I'm just someone who ought to live alone. And yet crazily enough I've spent the last ten years of my life since I was twenty, practically, just hopping from one man to another."

"And now you won't?" Rudolf says. He's looking at her critically, like a zookeeper inspecting some rare, beautiful tropical bird.

She shrugs. "I don't know. . . . It will be awful if I do. . . . I'll hate myself. . . . I really want, this time, to see if I can manage on my own. Slap my hands, Gabby, if I ever come to you saying I'm going to marry again. Drug me and put me in a sack and don't let me out till the impulse passes." She looks at Rudolf again. "The fantastic thing with Gabby," she says, "is she's never even *tempted* to get married. Why can't I be like that?"

'Well, you're simplifying a bit," I say, annoyed at her flirting

GIVE ME ONE GOOD REASON

with Rudolf and at her seeming praise, but underneath slight condescension.

"Oh, well, you mean that time you and Matthew almost did it?" she says. "I don't know. . . . I kind of knew you wouldn't. . . . I remember your mother kept saying how amazed she was, and I kept thinking somehow I'd always known you wouldn't."

I've never gone into that episode with Rudolf, and his face is getting that supercritical look I hate. I wish I could get Eve to shut up for one second.

"You think Miranda will be okay?" I say to veer back to that, which is, after all, more the topic at hand.

"She'll be marvelous." Again she addresses herself more to Rudolf than to me. "Look, here's this little girl who adores her father. I mean, you couldn't say love, it's adoration. . . . And has since birth. . . . Since before she came home from the hospital. . . . If he held her, she stopped crying, if he made a face at her, she grinned from ear to ear. It's clearly inborn. . . . And now she has him all to herself. . . . I'm just a visitor, a guest. . . . What could be more perfect, really?"

Rudolf says nothing.

"Rudolf, why are you giving me that stare?" Eve says. "Does he always look like that, Gabby? You have a very disapproving expression. You think I'm an evil lady for deserting my child, is that it?"

"No, how could I? I don't know the situation."

"Oh, he is disapproving probably," I say suddenly, almost to my own surprise.

"God, men always are, aren't they?" Eve says. "Isn't it incredible? Fathers all over the globe can leave seven starving babies with an alcoholic, crippled mother, but if a mother leaves, with the approval, signed in *blood*, of everyone concerned, it's a sin, it's evil."

Rudolf says, "I'm sorry if you're right. . . . I think that is

171

bad. . . . Maybe there's a strain of moralism in all of us which we can't eradicate even if we try."

"Try!" she says, spreading her hands wide.

"I will."

"Can you live?" I say. "I mean, financially. . . ."

"I'll swing it . . . maybe not easily, but, you know, I can get a regular job, not just do free lance. . . . It's an exciting challenge, as they say."

"You won't get alimony?"

"Oh, no! . . . No, that seems too ugly. . . . And Boris is barely managing himself."

We all sit looking, for our different reasons, exhausted by this confrontation. Finally I say, "Eve . . . I have to get up at seven tomorrow. . . . Otherwise—"

She leaps up. "Oh, sure! . . . No, I have to go too. . . . I'm glad to have met you, Rudolf. . . . I'm like this. . . . Take tremendously good care of Gabby, who is a nut but a very lovely person."

"Eve!"

She tugs on her coat and is gone. I sigh and collapse on the bed. I tell Rudolf how she was someone I knew from college. "She's so pretty, I hated her for years. . . ."

"How could you have known her from college? Isn't she older than you?"

"Older? No, God, she's . . . well, four, three years younger at least! How peculiar you should think that."

"I guess it was her expression. . . . She looks very tense, that line on her forehead."

In fact, Eve has worried aloud to me about that line, should she have it removed by plastic surgery etc. "I think that's just a physical thing, it's just there, it's not due to being tense especially."

"I like her," he says quickly. "Very much. . . . I just don't think she's especially attractive."

I shake my head. "Rudolf, you're weird. . . . Most men think she's gorgeous, but a bitch. . . . I don't know if she'd love you or hate you for saying you liked her very much but don't think she's pretty."

We get ready for bed. "What was that time you almost got married?" he says, turning off the light.

I'm in the bathroom brushing my teeth. I spit out into the sink. "Aha! I knew we'd get to that." I click off the bathroom light while noting that the influx of roaches seems to be increasing at something beyond its normal rate. "No, I didn't do it in the end. . . . Couldn't go through with it."

"Do you regret that?"

"Not a bit."

"She said vehemently."

I climb into bed. "She said honestly. . . . Do you wish I'd *had* regrets?"

"You seem to make these decisions so firmly . . . not to have any of the usual tangled feelings the rest of us do."

"Who's 'the rest of us'? The rest of the human race, you mean?"

"Okay, that sounded too pontifical."

I curl up. Being pregnant does, in an odd way, make me feel self-sufficient and confident. I don't feel as shaken by this conversation as I might otherwise. "Of course I have tangled feelings," I say finally. "Of course I have regrets. . . . But on the whole for me it was the best."

"I guess I wasn't aware you had even. . . . Well, you always refer to Matthew as this somewhat distant . . . so the fact that you even came that close. . . ."

"Umm. . . . Okay, I did. . . . I came that close. . . . Did you ever come close with Barbara or whatever her name was?"

"Emily."

"Right, her."

Suddenly the topic wears both of us out. "Let's sleep."

Our lovemaking in the weeks Rudolf is home is strange. I'm so huge now that it's my eighth month that we would no doubt have to resort to strange positions anyway. But the added complication is that his legs are still not healed, and apart from endless types of mutual masturbation at which we become reasonably adept, the only thing that works is if I lie on top of him and we join together and move with incredible slowness, like something underwater, to a quiet, almost excruciating climax. The freakishness of it is part of the general peculiarity of those last few weeks before he leaves with all the unspoken tensions. There's the oddness of his being at home all day, somewhat like in the hospital, just reading, drawing, sitting in the park. When I come home in the evening, sometimes he's prepared a delicious meal, some kind of curry with rice, which we gobble up. We drink lots of wine at dinner. I can see that for him dinner is somehow the center of a rather aimless day, though he's still not discontent as I might be in such a situation.

"Maybe I'll buy a house out there," he says one evening. "I'm getting sick of apartments."

"Good idea."

I guess if we could find a way of discovering the real issue we could discuss it. If, for instance, I was against the "institution" of marriage and Rudolf was for it, we could have a great heated discussion about that. But I'm not. I don't think it's an ideal institution, but neither is democracy or any of the other institutions in which my life is enmeshed. So for me it's not a didactic problem. Nor is Rudolf especially "for" marriage in principle. . . . The trouble is, I can't say either that the issue is—should I try and rearrange my life around his, look for a job in California, say, somehow manage to make our being together a center of my life? Put that way it would seem to have women's lib overtones—*e.g.*, I am willing to rearrange my life, he's not willing to. But that's not the point either. I'm sure if I wanted, some accommodation could be worked out. It's not a matter of jobs or where to live or any of those rather solvable things. . . . I suppose it's the fact, which is even more true now that I'm pregnant, that I want to do it myself. I just don't feel willing, right now, and maybe ever, to include someone else in my life. And I know I will miss Rudolf tremendously, a fact I can't quite acknowledge aloud, even to him. So like our lovemaking there's a certain pain in our relationship now, a certain wariness, like two people stuck in an elevator both afraid it may break down or they may die of suffocation but neither willing to admit this central fear. We can't go forward, we can't go backward, nor can we remain in the same place, which seems to make things tricky.

Elizabeth and Timmy are coming this weekend. I go to pick them up with Rudolf, who is still on crutches. Bringing Rudolf to Calla and Julian's isn't hard. For this moment their flat, unassertive blandness is pleasant after Eve with her theatrics. Calla is feeling indulgent toward me because of my pregnant state. I find it a little much, but not so very awful.

"No showers this time," I say, winking at her.

She smiles. "Oh . . . well, I'm sorry I made such a fuss about that."

Rudolf and I take the children to the park to fly some kites that I bought last week. They're odd kites, big puffy plastic ones that sail magnificently even though the wind isn't too strong. It's chilly out and overcast, and we soon repair back home for an early dinner.

Elizabeth keeps looking resentfully at Rudolf. I think she doesn't like sharing me with anyone, whereas to Timmy it's a lark to have another man along.

"Why do you have those *things?*" she says, pointing to his crutches.

We are sitting on the floor with our hot chocolate in mugs near us. Rudolf has put his crutches beside him. "I was hit by a car," he says, "and I need them to walk."

175

She inspects them. "Will you need them forever?"

"No, I don't think so."

She stands up, feeling them. Maybe this weekend wasn't a good idea. I feel his energy since the accident is more limited, and he tries not to admit that.

In the evening Elizabeth showers by herself, using my shower cap. She dances out afterward, wrapped in a big green towel. "You know something," she says. "Lucille is bald as a billiard ball."

"She's supposed to be," I say, amused.

"I should get her a wig."

"It would be hard to keep on, I should think."

"I wish she was all furry like Gwendolen."

That's odd. I recall thinking pubic hair was ugly as a girl and hoping I'd never get it.

"Who are Gwendolen and Lucille?" says Rudolf, finally rising to the bait.

Elizabeth smiles slyly, enjoying our secret. "Should I tell him?" she asks.

"Sure."

She goes over and in a loud stage whisper says to Rudolf, "They're our vaginas."

Rudolf turns red. "Those are good names," he says with a slight effort.

Elizabeth has her steady gaze fixed on him. "Does your penis have a name?" she says.

He shakes his head.

"It should. . . . Why don't you give it a name?"

"Okay. . . . What should it be?"

Again a short pause. "I think I'd have to see it first . . . to tell what its personality was."

I give a hoot. "Nuh-nuh-nuh. . . . Your mother would have a cow."

She looks aggrieved. "You can't just give it *any* name," she

176

says. But despite this, after a few moments of intense thought, she says, "How about Sylvester?"

"Sylvester?" I look at poor Rudolf to see how he is bearing up under this inquisition.

"Okay, Sylvester is good," Rudolf says.

"Sylvester, Lucille says hello to you," Elizabeth says.

"As long as all she does is say hello," I mutter. "Okay, folks, how about one more round of bingo and then bed?"

Elizabeth is a bad sport. She hates losing with a passion, but I somehow cannot bear the idea of deliberately letting her win, love her though I do. Besides Timmy, Rudolf and myself, her Barbie dolls, Malibu Ken and Malibu Barbie, are playing.

I make Barbie talk in a high squeaky voice. "Oh, boy, I never do well at this game, I don't know what's wrong with me."

"Now, Barbie, be a good sport," Elizabeth says. "You can't always win."

"I want to, I want to always win," I make Barbie leap up and down, yelling.

"Barbie, you can't play if you're bad," Rudolf says. "Pipe down. . . . I'm going to spin. . . . Okay . . . the big number is—G nine."

"We had that already," Timmy says.

"Okay, let's give it another try. . . . What will it be? The wheel goes round and round and lands on . . . B six."

Timmy lets out a shout. "Hey! I got bingo."

Elizabeth glares at him.

"Barbie's got B six too," I say, filling in her card.

"Well, I don't," says Elizabeth. "I just have B seven, and it's been sitting there empty for a hundred hours."

We play until everyone's card is filled. Then there are "prizes" for everyone, which Timmy takes to bed with him. They are sound asleep in about two seconds.

We have coffee in the kitchen, talking softly. "Is this wearing you out?" I say.

"No," he says slowly, but he does look tired, run-down. After a moment he says, "She seems very fond of you, Elizabeth."

"I'm very fond of her. . . . I don't know why. I just love her. . . . I mean, I don't really love Timmy, though he's a very sweet kid."

"Well, love is a peculiar thing," he says.

Silence.

We carefully retreat from that topic. I pick up Malibu Barbie and walk her slowly down the table. "Did you ever think how odd it is that dolls don't have genitals?" I say. "It's especially odd with these Barbies that are so deliberately sexy and busty . . . but nothing between their legs."

Rudolf smiles. "I could imagine a great movie," he says. "Two children asleep and on the floor Malibu Ken or GI Joe or whatever. He wakes up, comes to life and spies Barbie, gets all excited, rips off her clothes and then suddenly realizes there's nothing he can do about it. . . . So he starts searching in his knapsack. . . . Surely it must be there, somewhere. He takes out his canteen, his flashlight, you see him tossing one thing after another out of the knapsack until he discovers it's empty. . . . Then he bursts into tears."

I let out a hoot of laughter, then subside. "That's great. . . . But, you know, that's a rather masculine fantasy, if you'll pardon the expression. . . . I mean, even if he had a penis, it woudn't do him much good because she doesn't have a vagina."

"True, true."

We get into bed and lie quietly side by side. Rudolf begins stroking my breasts. After a second I whisper, "We better not . . . do anything."

"Oh, sure. . . ." But he keeps stroking, which for some reason I find almost painful. I guess I really don't like being turned on unless there's something I can do about it. I suppose we could, if we were terribly quiet and stealthy, attempt something, but given Calla's prohibition on showers, I feel this would be the last straw. And trust Elizabeth to wake up at the least convenient moment.

"I'm sorry," I murmur.

"Don't be silly. . . . It's perfectly all right."

The next day, Sunday, is sunny, but cold. We have breakfast on the floor. Elizabeth is "conversing" with Rudolf, evidently trying her damnedest to make a friend of him as long as he has to be around.

"You know something really silly," she says.

"No, tell me something really silly," Rudolf says.

"I used to think my Daddy had three penises."

He stares at her.

"You know," she says, as though explaining something to a very dumb child, "there are those things hanging in back, and I thought *those* were penises too."

We get past that one, bundle up warmly and go to the playground. In this very familylike setting (there are many couples with children out, despite the cold) I feel the sense I did in the hospital of our being a pretend family. Only this time the pretense is even greater since we now have two children and Rudolf has the same reddish coloring Timmy does, while I look quite remarkably like Elizabeth. We look more like the real parents than Calla and Julian. Plus being pregnant. We remind me mentally of a poster in the bus about planned parenthood which shows a couple first alone, then with one child, then two, then three. I even see a woman staring at me as I watch Elizabeth swinging. Elizabeth won't let me push her, unlike Timmy, who is hooting with glee as Rudolf pushes him very high up. The woman next to me says, "We thought of a third, but I don't think I would. . . . The population thing is just too important."

I'm tempted to say, "Bug off, lady," since I hate stranger's intimacies, but I just mutter, "Umm," and try to focus on Elizabeth.

"Anyway, you have one of each," she persists, "a girl for you and a boy for your husband."

"These are not my children," I say finally, in a detached, cold voice.

"Oh, are they adopted?"

"No, they're my sister's children. . . . I'm not married, and that is not my husband."

There's a long silence. "Oh," the lady says. She looks very embarrassed, and I feel a little guilty. Well, that'll give her something to mull over for the rest of the day. I, however, still feel bugged.

We "return" the children at around five. Calla asks us in for coffee. She's been very friendly since hearing of my pregnancy, a kind of sisterly bond which I wish I could accept at face value. Lots of questions about my doctor, the hospital, whether I'm going to nurse or not. Over coffee she suddenly says, "God, did I tell you about Ginnie Adolf?"

Ginnie Adolf was in my class at high school but went to the same college as Calla. I scarcely remember her. "What about her?"

"It's awful, she has cancer, and they have to remove her breasts! Isn't that ghastly?"

"Yes, it's. . . . Still, I think the survival rate is fairly good on those operations."

"But imagine having no breasts!"

I don't know if Calla does things like this just to annoy me or what. "I can imagine that a lot more easily than having no life!"

"It's the same thing."

"Calla! Come on! You'd just as soon *die* as have no breasts?"

"Well, not die maybe, but I think it would be the most terrible thing."

"Why?"

"Why? To have no breasts! How could you—you'd feel so unfeminine?"

"I would *not.*"

"Well, *I* would."

"Simply because you had no breasts, your whole sense of being a woman would vanish?" I say, furious, despite myself. "That, if true, is utterly incredible."

"You mean, you could just have yours cut off and wouldn't care at all?"

"Of course I'd care. . . . But it wouldn't destroy my life or my sense of myself as a woman."

"That's typical of you." She glares at me, then stares meaningfully at my figure.

Okay, so I'm not big-busted. Do I get put in jail? I like my breasts, I'm very fond of them, but Calla's attitude offends and horrifies me, and I can't but feel that it's connected to the whole thing of my not nursing. It's as though to say: You don't even *deserve* breasts, you're not even going to use them.

Meanwhile, whatever discussion had been going on between Rudolf and Julian has ceased. We all sit in an uneasy silence. I guess what I feel at bottom is I wish Calla and I could have rapport on something other than this level of motherhood, nursing, breasts. I have the feeling that deep down there are other things she cares about, but that she's roped them all off, at least as far as I'm concerned.

"Did you like her?" I ask Rudolf after we leave. It's freezing by now and we decide to go to an Italian restaurant nearby and have wine and spaghetti.

"I didn't get that much of an impression. . . . She seems slightly ill at ease with men."

"Did she remind you of your girlfriend Emily?"

"Your sister? . . . Oh, no, well, Emily was very . . . she had a very good figure, she was very feminine in a certain way."

"And Calla didn't seem so?"

"Not to me."

A week later there is a very typical-of-my-parents Thanksgiving dinner, which Rudolf attends. Before Calla and Boris were married to their respective spouses, my parents never had relatives for Thanksgiving dinner. Of course, most of the relatives are in Europe, but even the few that aren't were never invited. It was always a strange conglomeration of friends, other European couples, single men who worshiped my mother. There was never a turkey, always goose. Goose is fantastic, especially as my mother cooks it, all crisp and brown with wonderful apple stuffing. It's a huge rich meal, but this year there just doesn't seem much room in my stomach. I only pick at everything, which for me is atypical.

Boris has come with Miranda, but not with Eve. Miranda sits right next to him in a burgundy velvet dress, her black hair fastened with a gold barrette, like a Spanish princess with her upright posture. Boris cuts the goose for her, very carefully, into small pieces. No one mentions Eve at all; she's become a ghost.

"What kind of abortion clinic is this, that you'll be working in?" I hear my father ask Rudolf. I'm reclining on the couch, slightly knocked out. I should, perhaps, be napping in the afternoon, but that's just impossible at the lab. Even if I closed the door, Lobochowski would no doubt pop in on some irrelevancy just as I was dozing off. Now I start dozing almost involuntarily, hearing the conversation at a great remove.

". . . months after she is. . . . That sounds very. . . ." That's Calla. Is she about to sail into Rudolf on grounds of aborting women too late in their pregnancy? Why is everyone in our family so argumentative?

Rudolf is explaining, justifying, holding forth. The room is very warm, and I feel I'm drifting into no-man's-land, catching up on all the sleep I've missed in the past two months.

182

"I heard you saw Eve," Boris says, coming to sit next to me.

My eyes fly open. "Huh? . . . Oh, right. . . . She visited us the other night. . . . Do you, are you in touch?"

He shrugs.

"But it's working okay, your having Miranda by yourself—"

"It's working. . . . It's not ideal, but neither was the other."

We don't discuss his "business" because I don't want to hear about that right now. But Boris keeps looking at me critically. "Your face looks the same," he says finally, which clearly wasn't what was on his mind.

"Well, why not?"

"Some pregnant women get a kind of funny look—"

"Which means they're going to have a girl," I finish up for him.

"I wasn't going to say that."

Elizabeth races over and flings herself on top of me. "Roo, take it easy, okay? . . . I don't want to go into labor right now."

"Why? Then you could have it right here and I could watch."

"Would you like to watch?"

"Yes!" She snuggles up to me, putting a pillow on top of my belly and resting her head on that. "I wish children could watch," she says.

"When you have your own baby, you can watch. . . . They set up mirrors, and you can see it coming out."

That idea fascinates her. In the background I can hear Calla talking to Rudolf about natural childbirth. I feel as if I'm in some movie where a drowning man hallucinates about everyone he's ever known. If Matthew were to suddenly appear in the armchair opposite, talking about Baudelaire to Mother, it wouldn't surprise me one bit.

Calla usually describes her natural childbirth experiences the way some Hemingway-type men describe their biggest catch. Blow by blow, every breath and pain and moment of exhilaration. I'm torn between loving Rudolf for listening so intently and respectfully and wishing he'd put her down in some way.

"You're not nursing, I guess?" Boris says.

"No, why?"

"I didn't think you would. . . . Eve didn't either."

I suppose Boris gets some satisfaction out of lumping Eve and me together, the two "career" women, the two castrators. I feel sensitive to his taunts, as always, but reluctant to get into defending myself.

I am delighted when my father, passing by, says, "This whole nursing thing is nonsense. . . . I mean, if a woman wants to do it . . . okay. But it couldn't matter less as far as the baby is concerned."

"How do *you* know?" Boris says coldly.

"I'm stating an opinion, of course. . . . But I've known many doctors who've said—"

Boris gets a contemptuous expression as though to say, "We know those doctors!"

Meanwhile, Calla, who has tuned in, blurts out, "How can you *say* that, Daddy? Every doctor I've ever met says there's no other way a baby can get that sense of warmth and well-being."

"Not so," Daddy says in his bluntly genial way, pouring some cognac.

There is a dismayed silence.

"With bottles the father can join in," I say, much to my own distaste. I hate the way almost any topic becomes a family-hitting-one-another-over-the-head thing.

"So how does that apply to you?" Boris says coolly.

"I didn't know we were discussing me," I say.

"We're not!" Calla blurts out. "You're not the only person that's ever been pregnant, you know!"

"Aren't I? I thought I was."

Suddenly Julian says in his soft tentative voice, "Calla loved nursing."

"No, I don't say no one should do it," I say. "Let those who want to do whatever they like."

"Everything is the same to you," says Calla.

"Huh?"

"I mean, you never think anything's better than anything else," she runs on incoherently. "It's all the same. Do this, do that."

God, I feel weary, slightly drunk and overcome by an immense desire to be an only child.

Rudolf gets up and sits next to me, putting his arm around my shoulder. His physical presence is immensely reassuring, also the fact that he's a stranger in this family circle and has no ax to grind.

"The thing is," Calla says after a few moments of dead silence. "I just think aborting five-month-old fetuses is terrible."

How did we get to that? I wonder.

"Rudolf, would you like some cognac?" says Daddy, as though we were having a perfectly civilized conversation about nothing at all.

"I think I—"

"Did I tell you I'd seen Eve's jewelry at Bonwit's?" Mother says, coming in from the kitchen. "I love those new silver things she's doing."

Boris just looks at her.

"Have you seen them?" Mother runs on. "They're really something new, something—"

"I like Eve's jewelry," I say. I sink against Rudolf. I want to disappear into him, I want him to be pregnant with me, I don't want, for this moment, to have a physical identity at all.

I am disgusted by my family.

"They're all individuals, that's all," Rudolf says when it's all over and we're downstairs, resting.

"That's no excuse!"

"Your being pregnant sets them all off."

"Why should it? What's it to them if I'm pregnant or if I nurse or if I have natural childbirth or anything? It's none of their goddamn business!"

He is fixing coffee and says over his shoulder, "What's odd to me is that for someone who puts such an emphasis on being independent, you care so much about what they say . . . or think."

I've been over that in my own mind enough times, but I still have no really good answer.

"You should leave New York and really be independent instead of just talking about it all the time."

From Rudolf that's unusually strong. I look up in surprise. "Yes, Doctor. . . . Only who says just moving geographically makes one independent?"

"It makes a difference."

"Wouldn't it be stronger in a way to feel free without moving?"

"It's not possible."

"It must be for some people."

"I never met any."

I ponder this. "So maybe I want to be the exception."

"Do you really think you can be?"

I shrug my shoulders. "It is odd, though, that I care about Calla and Boris."

"Not that you care. . . . But their motives, toward you, are so transparent."

"Are they?" It's funny how one never really gives other people credit for powers of observation. So I'm surprised that Rudolf has taken all this in during one Thanksgiving dinner.

"They both are dying for you to fall flat on your face."

"Well, I won't."

"Of course you won't. . . . But why plan your whole life

around proving that to them? I should think better if you had the courage to fall on your face for a change."

"I can't." Somehow that reply pops out of somewhere deep inside me, as though he were about to push me off a cliff and I were, at the last moment, holding back.

"Just let go," he says after a second.

"Rudolf, stop that."

"What?"

"Just let go! . . . *You* try letting go, if you want! I have my life and I know it has these faults, but don't tell me how to run it."

"I'm not. . . . I'm saying just one thing. . . . You say you want to be free, then you go tie yourself in knots. . . . That doesn't make sense."

"Well, maybe those particular knots are ones I think I can handle. . . . No, not handle, but I'm used to them, I know them." I feel our whole conversation has a curiously Henry James-like indirectness. Why aren't we talking head on about this instead of circling it so circuitously? I know why *I'm* not—I don't have the courage. As for Rudolf, at times I feel he's like a careful hunter, knowing me well enough to know I'll bolt, emotionally anyway, if it becomes too direct.

The last few weeks pass by rather quickly, the weeks before Rudolf is to leave. They aren't pleasant, but they pass, and in an odd way I've begun looking forward to his leaving. Just as one might feel about some dreaded operation, to get it over with. The way I used to think about tests at school—tomorrow at this time it will be over.

I feel having the baby's coming so close is good because it means there's one big thing that won't be over after he leaves. I can begin to focus on that with all my energies. Not that I don't have enough to focus on at work, as well, but that's all much more handleable.

I've begun the natural childbirth classes. It's just women, but still I feel a slight resistance to the idea of meeting in a group like that. The teacher, a rather blunt but not so genial nurse, encourages everyone to pour forth their personal feelings about being pregnant, their fears, their worries about how their life will change. I guess in some ways I feel about being pregnant the way Matthew feels about being homosexual—I don't want to merge my identity in a larger group. I don't want to feel aha when someone "confesses" her doubts that her child will be born normal. It's this human, all too human thing, and maybe I feel I'll have more problems than these girls, being unmarried, and their problems seem rather trivial, I can't get involved. No, your child will not be born with six toes, I want to say, and if it does, it won't matter. To me they're like a bunch of girls before a dance—will anyone dance with me?—and in a snobbish way I want to say, either they will and your worries will be over or they won't and you'll accommodate to that. I guess such an attitude covers a lot of ground and obviously to these particular girls it does matter. . . . Maybe it's their being in their early twenties, on the whole, which makes their problems seem trivial to me. They seem so young—in a sweet way, but also somehow untouched. . . . There are one or two who seem to have professions and have raised questions about how they will deal with this after the baby's birth. The teacher seems almost disapproving of the idea of a mother continuing to work after she has a child. Here she's obviously unmarried and rather masculine in manner. Well, maybe that's an explanation rather than something too surprising in view of her attitude.

I've never mentioned I'm not married. I don't have any desire at all to get into that. Once Rudolf picked me up, and some of them saw him, so I assume they assume he's my husband. That's okay.

I certainly don't think I'd prefer a class specifically for unwed mothers. That would drive me even more up the wall, feeling part of some special weird little group. Here the only saving grace is that I can feel apart from these girls. If I had to identify with them, I'd go off the deep end.

However, just from the point of gathering information, the class is useful. Sometimes it seems too basic biology—*e.g.*, diagrams of the human body, parts pointed to with a long stick, this is the uterus, it is used for etc. But there are some details I hadn't known which are interesting.

The night before Rudolf is to leave is Saturday night. December 1 is a Sunday, and he's leaving at eleven in the morning. So I'm driving him to the airport at nine thirty. I'm no longer "allowed" to have intercourse, so we perform our "last rites" in one of our peculiar ways, developed over the weeks since Rudolf came home from the hospital. I put cold cream between my breasts, and he moves his penis back and forth between them until he reaches a climax and ejaculates. It sounds kind of awful, but is really rather nice. I like squeezing my breasts up so they seem large and moundlike. Then he caresses me, and we lie side by side.

"It's lucky you're leaving just when I'm out of commission anyway," I say.

Those words sound not quite right. He doesn't reply. Talking is getting progressively harder, and finally we turn over and go to sleep.

In the middle of the night I wake up. I'm having contractions. My stomach tightens into a hard ball, then relaxes again. No! I won't allow it. I won't allow myself to be in labor, I just won't, and that's that.

"Once the process of labor is set in motion, nothing can stop it." Quote unquote. . . . I don't care, I won't let it happen. I'll stop it by sheer force of will. I lie on my back, grim. I haven't even gone through more than one or two natural childbirth classes. We haven't even gone into the breathing, the exercises, I'm not prepared. . . . But the main thing is I don't, don't want Rudolf to be here when I give birth. There was a time when I was glad he was a doctor, thinking that if the baby did happen to come very quickly, he'd know what to do, he has delivered babies after all. . . . Whereas I'm not sure I'd have the presence of mind to do it all myself, cutting the cord and all that. I know that's not likely, having a first baby come so fast, but I used to be glad he was there just in case.

But now that he's about to leave I've gotten used to that. This whole pseudomarriage thing would be even worse if he were to accompany me to the hospital. I decide that even if I keep having the contractions, I'll try not to mention them. I've heard they can go on for hours. So I might even be able to drive him to the airport and back and not give birth for another day.

I get out of bed and go to the bathroom. I click on the light, and dozens of roaches scurry off in all directions. I don't have the aversion for roaches shared by most city dwellers. In fact, I rather respect them. They're one of the oldest forms of animal life, after all, almost like tiny dinosaurs, and they really do no harm. I think people's aversion to them is more esthetic than because they could carry diseases, which they don't. . . . Sitting on the toilet, I watch the last few straggle off to their subterranean chambers.

Am I in labor? That's the other thing. I just don't know. I guess with a second child—not that I'm exactly planning for that at the moment—you know just exactly what "the real thing" is like. But if you haven't been through it before, it's hard to say. I gather there are false contractions, false labors, every variation.

"Gabby."

"Umm." I push the door open a crack. Rudolf is propped up in bed, squinting at me.

"What are you doing?"

"Going to the bathroom."

"You've been in there a hell of a long time."

"I didn't know you were up."

"I woke up when you got out of bed."

"Oh." Another contraction comes, and I must grimace inadvertently because Rudolf says, "What's wrong?" and gets out of bed.

"Oh, it's. . . . I don't know, I. . . . Well, I feel these slight contractions. . . . I don't think it's the real thing, though, I just—"

"Are they coming regularly?"

"I don't think so. . . . It's hard to tell."

I go back to bed and lie down. "Look, I doubt it could be. . . . I'm not due for a month."

"Premature babies aren't that uncommon."

"I just have a hunch this isn't it."

Much good my "hunches" have been in the past.

We lie there, he holding my hand.

"It would be awful to be in labor now," I say.

"Why?"

"I have to drive you to the airport."

"Darling!"

"Well, I do."

"I'm not leaving if you're right in the middle of labor."

"You are so!"

"I certainly am not."

"Rudolf, you have to leave. . . . I mean it. . . . I won't let you stay."

"Damn you!"

"Why? Now look, you just have to understand my point of view."

"I understand that you're the most incredibly pigheaded, selfish human being I've ever met in my life."

"Look, you said you'd leave on December first and it is December first."

"So what?" He's still looking furious.

Oh, fuck it all! Do I have to go into labor in the midst of a raging argument? I want a nice, relaxed, simple labor. "You

191

know what I'm like. . . . How can you act surprised now? . . . It doesn't make sense."

"Maybe because I don't see how you can one moment be warm and responding and lovely and the next minute like this . . . an automaton."

"I'm not."

"What?"

"Either of those . . . warm or an automaton."

"Yes, you are."

"Look, I'm probably not even *in* labor. . . . Why are we having such a stupid argument?"

"Because you are a—"

"I'm an eight months' pregnant lady. . . . You're supposed to treat me with care, right?"

"Bull."

"I'm not in labor!" I shout.

He looks at me a minute. "Are you telling the truth?"

I stop a minute to see if I am. "Well, they seem to be dying away."

Neither of us speaks. I sigh. "All that for nothing."

"Not for nothing."

I can't say to him, "It's not your baby," because I know that's not the issue. I lean against him. "I'm sorry, really. . . . I wish I wasn't this way."

"Then don't be! Stop saying it and do something about it!"

"It's not so easy."

"It's not impossible."

We both try and get back to sleep. I take a Miltown, which helps a little. The contractions really are subsiding.

When we wake up to the alarm in the morning, it's pitch black out, like the middle of the night. Partly winter, partly an overcast day. But by ten it's beginning to clear and is even sunny, so sunny I have to wear sunglasses driving to the airport.

For some reason I think how, the day Kennedy was assassinated, I was in Boston visiting Boris and Eve, who were just married. It was gray too that day, and I recall Eve saying as we stepped out of the car, "That's a pathetic fallacy . . . it being a gloomy day," and Boris saying, "Eve, for Christ sake!" and my thinking Boris must be the right person for Eve because he was the only one who could talk to her in that tone of voice.

"What are you thinking?" Rudolf says.

"About Kennedy being assassinated."

At the airport there's some time before his plane leaves, so we have breakfast, which we didn't think we'd have time for. My toast comes burned, and Rudolf says I should send it back.

"No, I don't want to. . . . Really, it doesn't matter. I like burned toast."

He shakes his head. "You are incredible."

We have said all there is to say about writing etc., though he does add, just as we are walking to the gateway, "Call me from the hospital . . . when it really does happen."

Usually I would balk at that and say why from the hospital, I can write when I get home, but I have enough sense or maybe I'm just too exhausted to say that now.

At the gateway we have a long kiss, and I'm beyond caring as I usually might if people are watching or what they'll think. My arms hurt where he's held me as he walks away. I stay there just a moment, watching him walk toward the plane. Then, just as he's about to climb up the steps, he turns to look at me. Luckily, my eyesight is getting worse, but the expression on his face, anguished, caught that way for one second before he turns around again makes me feel as if someone, out of the blue, had come up to me and socked me in the stomach. It's like the end of one of those French movies where they catch the hero in a still frame, his face while running.

The four hundred blows. I feel as if I'd had more than four hundred. I drive back and, upon getting home, fall into a dead sleep.

When I wake up, it's four thirty in the afternoon, and outside my window it is black and very cold-looking. I get up and make myself some coffee. Usually I like this time of year, late fall and winter, when daylight savings is over and the evenings begin early, around four. It always seems cozy to be indoors when it's so bleak and cold-looking out. But now it seems too cold, too black, as though the room I were sitting in were a space capsule flying to the moon. There's hardly a soul on the streets. I don't feel lonely, it's more an acute feeling of being alone, as though I were the last person left on earth.

The dogs are stirring, and since they haven't been out since I left for the airport, I leash them up and take them down.

I want to get my research in a certain shape before the baby comes. It's never as complete as one would like, but I'd like to have enough done so that if I do end up staying at home more the first few weeks, I can work on a paper I've had in mind for a long time. If I mention casually about this to anyone, some laugh and say something to the effect of, "You'll never have time to work once the baby's born," and others say, "Of course you'll have lots of time, especially if it's a good baby."

Ye gods, a "good" baby. I wonder what that means, what a "bad" baby is. If people use those terms, they always add hastily that, of course, no baby is "bad," only, perhaps, colicky, fussy, a screamer.

I try asking Dr. Hattie about this now that I'm seeing her once a week. "Oh, it'll work out, whatever," she says.

I guess after one has five kids, those differences tend to blend together. For now that the event is so close, I have odd moments of utter terror, of wondering how on earth I decided to do a thing like this, given my personality, my way of life, my job. It's not at all as though I didn't hack through all those things before, but it's like saying you're aware you will die someday and then having, at times, that more acute definite awareness: one day I will no longer be alive.

Comparing childbirth to death! Help, am I that bad? It's not like Ellen's fear of dying in childbirth, I have no fears along that score, just a genuine curiosity. It's only the fact of it that strikes me like death, an irreversible change in one's life, nothing you can do about it.

Then, on other days, I feel a tremendous, almost insane excitement that this thing is going to happen to me, that that's allowed, that at least I live in an age where, despite not being married, I can do this, I'm "allowed" to.

I miss Rudolf very much. Gwendolen, for her part, is, for the moment, inconsolable; she's gone into mourning. I do wake up from erotic dreams, my hand between my legs. All this despite the fact that, even if he were here, we couldn't do much. But I miss the whole physical closeness, sleeping in the same bed, all the peculiar variations on lovemaking we concocted. . . . He writes, but not the way Matthew does, more little poetic notes, descriptions of things that have happened during the day, sketches of things.

After he left, I discovered in a drawer, left behind either on purpose or by chance, a series of drawings he did of me in the nude. Actually, my face is blurry, just quickly sketched. They're more sketches of pregnant women, and I like them. It strikes me I've rarely seen paintings of pregnant women, photos occasionally. But seen this way, I can appreciate the beauty of a pregnant woman's body, the usual curves exaggerated, but almost more interesting for that reason. I guess even though I'm pregnant now, pregnant enough so that men even offer me seats occasionally on the bus, I'm not aware of how I look to an outsider, I'm only aware of my own feelings about being pregnant. But while at the lab, say, I can forget about it altogether, just concentrate on my work, and be surprised when my belly bumps into a table which I was thinking of as being farther away. . . . Then I wonder—will Rudolf recall this moment in his life as, oh, that was the time I slept with a pregnant lady biochemist? Will it be filed away under that odd heading, an interesting memory, unique certainly, but . . . ?

Christmas is almost here, and I do a day of hectic shopping, buying everything that one day. For Elizabeth I hesitate long and hard over an immense rack of Barbie dolls which I find in a doll store. I can't believe the range, the number of types, the extent of the costumes. It goes on and on, row after row, and I spend nearly an hour, staring at them with a kind of horrified fascination before picking one she had mentioned coveting. Live Action P.J. They all look alike, except for hair. It must be peculiar seeing them put together on the assembly line, long plastic bodies screwed into place, wigs clamped down, talking mechanisms inserted. Calla may be mad at my picking such an ugly present, but I've always hated the idea of parents forcing attractive unwanted toys on children.

The week of December 10 we draw lots for being Santa. Lobochowski has all our names in a hat and also the name "Santa." Whoever draws the "Santa" name has to dress up in a genuine Santa costume on the day of the big lab party and read aloud the poems composed by everyone. We each, also by drawing lots, get the name of someone else in the lab—this includes everyone, technicians, glassware washers etc.—and for that person we must buy a small present and compose a poem. Some of these "poems" are quite amazing; reading them aloud is a real test of strength since you can't laugh, no matter how insane the grammar or the substance of the text. Not that I should talk. I can barely put four lines of poetry together myself.

Guess what? I draw the "Santa." I look at Lobochowski—he couldn't have planned this, but finding out, he gets a sly little smile on his face.

"You won't need any padding," he says with a wink.

"No, it's awfully convenient, isn't it?"

God, this thing is insane. But there's one nice part of it which I remember from earlier years. "Santa" goes in to get dressed and is supposed to consume a bottle of champagne along with the "Santa's Helper," supposedly to get into the properly festive mood. I do like champagne a lot, even if this is American champagne. That part should be nice. I pick Frances to be my "Helper," and she, naturally, gets a big boot out of its being me.

The day arrives, a Friday, as it always is by time-honored custom. We have a regular working day, but at four o'clock Frances and I disappear into the ladies' room to get into our costumes. Hers is like an elf, bright red with a peaked hat, which suits her small, perky face.

We go over the poems together. I get the biggest kick out of one someone has done for Lobochowski:

> It is good to speak or write about a joyfull man.
> Who put his self out to do the best he can.
> One thing about him he never
> try to make an early start
> but he always turn out
> very smart.
> To look at him at work, one would take him for a joke
> But to me I know he can do
> some very smart work.
> I think of this dear one
> What can you call him but very good.
> But for sure you can call him
> Dr. Leonid Lobochowski.

Frances has to pound me on the back, I start laughing so hard.

"What in heck did they mean by he never tries to make an early start? He's usually here at eight in the morning."

"Maybe it's to rhyme with smart." Frances is busy rouging her cheeks and drawing her eyebrows in black and surprised-looking.

197

"But why one would take him for a joke? Poor Leonid."

She glances at me. "Well, one would, wouldn't one?"

I'm sitting on a closed toilet, drinking champagne out of a paper cup.

"Get cracking, Gabby. . . . We start soon."

"This champagne is so good."

"I don't like champagne."

"You don't? How can you not like champagne?"

"It makes me want to sneeze."

"Jesus! I'll have to finish the whole bottle myself." I pour another cup.

"You'll pass out, you idiot."

"Nooo, don't be silly. I never do. . . . I hold my liquor very well." I'm feeling, already, marvelously drunk. I have a theory that you never get unpleasantly drunk from champagne, just very giddy and foolish and maybe, at the end, sad. But never headachy and rotten-feeling or raucous and boorish.

"Have I told you my theory about how you never can get really drunk from champagne?" I say, glancing through the other poems.

"You have. . . . Gabby, listen, do you want me to dress you? I can help you with your beard and makeup."

"Thanks, kid." I sit patiently as Frances attaches my white cotton beard with some rub-in glue. It feels ticklish and funny. She gives me big, heavy grayish eyebrows with some drimark pens she has in her bag.

"Hey, you're good at this," I say, watching my face change in the mirror. "How did you get so good?"

"I used to do stage makeup at college. . . . I love it." She shadows my cheeks so they look puffy and sagging, then gives me big gleaming pink circles. "Try a ho-ho-ho."

"Ho ho ho. . . . Did I tell you, Frances, that Lobochowski proposed to me?"

"Proposed *what?*"

"Marriage!"

"Oh, come on. . . . You're drunk."

"I know I'm drunk, but it's true. He did. I swear it. He offered to give me his family name."

At that point Leonid pokes his head in the door. "Almost ready, girls?"

"In a minute," I croak out.

"Hey, you look darling," Frances says, standing back to admire her handiwork. "You make a perfect Santa."

She's right. I'm adorable. My belly sticks out just enough, and my hair in front has been powdered a nice grayish white. A kind of androgynous Santa. I have vague fantasies of a children's play. Santa is really a lady, a secret that's been well kept all these years. She's always pregnant, that's why her belly is so big. And all the elves are her children. . . . Who's the father then? One of the reindeer?

I stagger out. I still haven't finished the champagne, but I'm afraid Frances is right—I may get too drunk to read the poems.

Outside, in the library, everyone is dancing. Leonid waltzes a few of the women around in a stiff old-fashioned step. Some of the younger staff are doing wilder, freer dances. It all, as they say, passes in a whirl. I'm warm in my costume, sweating but actually feeling quite jolly.

I get out the big sack and begin reading the poems, then handing each person his gift. I guess everyone knows who I am, but I feel quite different, not myself at all. I've hardly ever acted, but I suddenly see what it's all about. How delightful, how very nice it is to become someone else. I have visions of snow, my ancestral home.

When I'm done, Lobochowski kisses me gingerly on the cheek. "Thank you, dear Mrs. Santa," he says.

"Ms., please!" I croak, but he doesn't catch on.

"And now let us all partake of the delicious refreshments!"

Everyone flocks over to the big table on which cookies, cakes, canapés, have been laid. I snatch up a bunch of cookies and pour myself a little more champagne.

"You can change," Lobochowski says softly in my ear.

"What?"

"Out of your costume. . . . You look warm."

I touch my forehead. It's streaming with sweat. "Oh, well, I feel good, but maybe. . . ."

I go into the ladies' room, and Lobochowski's two technicians are there, Karin and Ulrika, one tall, blond, stately, the other rather squat with a faint genuine mustache on her upper lip.

"You were darling, Santa!" Karin says, giggling.

"Thanks." I go into one of the booths to make a pee. Suddenly, as I'm reaching to pull down my pants, there's a sound like a loud pop, and I double over in pain, as though someone had punched me unexpectedly in the stomach.

I'm in labor. There's no doubt this time. Now I know that the difference between that earlier time, with Rudolf about to leave, and this is all the difference in the world. The pains are much more severe, so strong that while one is passing I just sit back and close my eyes, feeling I'm being pressed down by some giant, relentless steamroller.

I feel frightened. Why did I get so drunk? I'm not sure it matters really, but why? I wanted to be calm, cool, alert. Did getting drunk cause this, or did it just happen? I'm ten days from my due date, but. . . .

"Gabby?"

"Frances?"

"What are you doing in there?"

I wait for the particular pain to pass, then open the door. "Listen, this is crazy . . . but I'm in labor. . . . Could you get me a cab?"

"Your baby?" She looks frightened, too. We've never really talked about it in detail, and even though the evidence is there for all to see, maybe it didn't seem real until this moment.

"Sure, but, gee, what. . . . Should I call your doctor?"

"Why don't we get to the hospital first?" I say breathlessly. I don't seem to *have* much breath. "You don't have to come, if you—"

"Don't be silly." She steers me out and somehow blessedly past the party. I see a few people glance at us, but I think they assume I'm just in a bad way from too much champagne. Just as the elevator is about to come, Lobochowski, of all ill luck, dashes out into the hall. "Where are you two going? The party's just begun!"

I open my mouth to speak, but a contraction comes along and sweeps away all my consciousness but it. I hear Frances saying, "She's having her baby."

My eyes flicker open to see Lobochowski looking terrified, even more so than when I first told him I was pregnant. "Gabrielle . . . I didn't know it was so. . . . Will you be all right? Can I—"

Somehow we are in the elevator and Lobochowski is no longer there. I love you, Frances, I will love you, forever, for this. That thought, then pain, alternating all the way to the hospital.

At the entering desk, they stare at us as though we were pulling some gag. "This is Dr. Gabrielle Van de Poel," Frances says in her crisp voice. "She is in labor and wishes you to contact her doctor at once."

The nurse behind the desk stares at me. I'm sweating like mad from the heavy costume, from the champagne.

"She was at a Christmas party," Frances says, staring her down.

Still the nurse says nothing. Is she trying to decide if it's some kind of practical joke? In a detached way I don't blame her, but I also feel immensely relieved when Frances, raising her voice, says, "Are you just going to just sit there on your ass or get us a wheelchair?"

Suddenly the nurse comes to life like a wind-up doll and rushes stiffly off.

I'm alternating between taking everything in, the hospital corridor, certain people passing by, the elevator opening and closing, and taking nothing in.

The nurse comes back with a wheelchair. My body is streaming with sweat. I try to yank off the Santa jacket, and it gets stuck. "You can do that later," the nurse says, coldly.

Frustrated, ashamed, I rip off the beard. It's like a huge Band-Aid being ripped off, but at least my face feels better.

Everyone we pass or meet stares at me either with amusement or disapproval. When Dr. Hattie finally appears, some time later, I begin to cry loud, mawkish crocodile tears.

"Well, my dear, you picked a fine moment, didn't you?" she says.

"Oh, Dr. Hattie, I'm so sorry, I'd never have gotten drunk if I'd known. . . . Will it hurt the baby? Will it be bad?"

Now that I think of it, maybe a baby would be better off being drunk while being born. Like taking a few drinks on an airplane because one is afraid of flying. Surely being born is as nerve-racking as flying. I imagine the baby floating, inebriated in its liquid sack, grinning, somersaulting. Then, as she comes out, the nurse checking her over and saying sternly, "Why . . . this baby is drunk! Take her away and sober her up! It'll set a bad example for the other babies." And my baby being wheeled off, finally being placed next to all the other sober, neat babies, lying there, grinning happily in a champagne daze.

"You'll be fine. . . . Let's just get you fixed up. . . . Out of this—outfit."

"Where is my friend, Frances?" I ask, trying to sit up.

Dr. Hattie and another nurse struggle to get me out of the Santa suit. The zipper sticks in back and they finally have to yank it off.

"What friend?" Dr. Hattie says.

"Did she leave then?" I try and remember when exactly I last saw Frances, but all I can remember is that at one point she was here and now she's not.

The Santa hat is bobby-pinned into my hair, and they begin yanking out bobby pins to get it loose. Another nurse appears and begins shaving my pubic hair. Oh, dear, I feel as if I'm in the Army getting an unwanted crew cut. Poor Gwendolen. What an indignity. Also, I have a horrible fear they will hurt Gwendolen, injure her in some way, and I stiffen involuntarily. It must be like some weird fear of castration since they're just shaving the outside, but I still feel relieved when it's over. Then an enema.

I sit, still drunk, on the toilet thinking how sad to precede a glorious event, childbirth, with things like shavings and enemas.

"How's it going?" Dr. Hattie says when I'm lying down again. "Is it hurting?"

"Oh . . . it's okay," I say finally. It is hurting, but until it becomes downright unbearable, I think I'll try and stick with it.

One second later, or is it hours later—wait, it must be a long time because I've been lying in the room, sometimes almost asleep, then awake again—I'm wheeled onto a bed and then wheeled down a hall. Then another hall, then another. Where are they taking me? It's all very Kafka-like. I'm wheeled through about a hundred corridors, bumping along, onto elevators, off again, by someone whose face I can't even see. I have some fantasy that it's all a mixup, like that scene in *The Lady Vanishes* where they bandage up the old lady to take her off and do a ghastly experiment on her. Some unknown person for some unknown reason has bought my body for experimental purposes. Only no one will know until it's too late.

"Where am I going?" I say to the faceless person behind me.

"You have to be X-rayed," says the voice.

A likely story!

Still, a short time later I find myself in an X-ray room, where they prop me up, X-ray me and plunk me back on the table with wheels again. By now the contractions are worse, and the pain of being shifted around like some great carcass of meat is painful, as well as humiliating. Back we go, down more corridors. Lord knows where I'll end up. It seems to take hours.

Then I'm back in the room, and for some amount of time it's very quiet and peaceful as though they'd decided to push me out to sea on a raft one quiet sunny day.

Then, without warning, I'm on that table with wheels again and again corridors, no face behind me.

"Where the hell are we going?" I yell.

"The X ray didn't come out. . . . It has to be done again."

I don't believe it. I hear someone—it's got to be me, not the faceless voice—screaming at the top of her lungs, "I will not have another X ray taken! Get me off this goddamn table! Get me my doctor!" I'm yelling obscenities so loudly that I hardly notice that they have, in fact, stopped wheeling me.

Dr. Hattie's round, beaming face hovers into view. "We won't bother with the X ray," she says to whoever. To me, "I'm sorry, Gabrielle. . . . The baby's position seems to have shifted. We may have to have a breech, in which case there'll have to be anesthetic. . . . And I was a little worried because if you've been drinking, there's a chance you may vomit during labor. . . . But I don't think it's likely."

I'm so ashamed! It's like being drunk on your wedding. Here is a day I've been planning for for months, and how did it happen that on this one day I'm wheeled in drunk? For all anyone here knows, I'm drunk constantly, this is just my normal state. In fact, they probably think so. . . . She couldn't even stop drinking long enough to stay sober for the childbirth. . . . Or if they know I'm unmarried, they'll think I was drinking because of that. "Unwed mother has breech birth while under the influence of alcohol. This is most irregular," hospital authorities are quoted as saying.

204

I'm glad I screamed. I'm not usually a screamer, but I'm glad I did it. I couldn't have faced another X ray.

Dr. Hattie is bending over, pressing my stomach, which hurts like hell. "You're almost there," she says.

Almost! I feel as if I've spent the better part of my life in this place. My body must be black and blue from all that tumbling from one bed to another.

"You'll be unconscious just for a short time," she says.

When I was seven, I had my tonsils out. I had spent years of getting colds, and this was to be the cure. What I remember was lying in a small room, and suddenly a man rushed in with a mask, threw it over my face, and I lost consciousness. The suddenness of it was what scared me, and even now, twenty-five years later, I have some of that kind of fear as they wheel me into the delivery room.

I have the impression someone is throwing cold water in my face; then I pass out completely.

When I come to, I'm in a room by myself again. I *think* I'm by myself. At least it's quiet. It's all over. It must be. But why is no one here?

A nurse strolls by and I say, "Umm . . . I, did I . . . what did I have?"

"Oh, a lovely little boy. . . . They showed him to you, but I guess you don't remember."

I don't. I don't at all. I raise myself up to stare at her. A what, did she say? A little what?

"Boy, did you say?" I repeat, but she's gone.

After some time she reappears and wheels me down another corridor. I somehow can't get myself to ask again what I had. Instead I say, "Will I see the baby again now?"

"Oh, soon enough, I expect. . . . I think they bring them in at noon."

"What time is it now?"

"Ten thirty."

A day and a half have passed since the Christmas party, since Frances and Santa and champagne. It seems years ago, centuries ago. I'm in a bright, sunny room looking out on the park. "I imagine you'll want to wash up," the nurse says, leaving me.

I get out of bed, very carefully, and stumble over to the washbasin. At first I almost keel over when I look in the mirror. Has my hair gone white from this experience? Then I remember Frances powdering it for the party. I look incredible. I can't believe it. Huge gray eyebrows up to my ears, smeared insane pink cheeks, the whole makeup blotched together, half wiped off, half still on. God, how terrible. I wash my face six times with hot water and soap, try to rub some of the gray out of my hair and finally collapse back into bed. I don't want the baby to die of shock when it first sees me.

At one, after I've gobbled up a huge lunch, they wheel in a small basket. "Here he is!" the nurse says cheerfully, handing something to me.

He! It really is a he! I sit there dumbfounded, looking down at the wool-wrapped creature in my arms. It can't be! I was going to have a girl. It was all planned. It can't be a boy, it just can't. I can't even move, I feel so distressed, as though they had handed me a two-headed child. How can it be a boy? Explain that to me, please. Okay, I'll explain it. There are two sexes. When a woman becomes pregnant, she has, roughly, a fifty-fifty chance to bear a child of either sex. I had a fifty-fifty chance to have a boy all *along*. Why am I so shocked, so horrified? Where is all this much vaunted common sense that I always attribute to myself?

No one would believe this, but I have never once, in all these nine months, seriously considered for even one *minute* that I would not have a girl. Not once. How is that possible? I'm not that kind of a person. I'm never taken by surprise, I always foresee all possibilities.

But I wanted a girl! I don't want a boy. Oh, no! A boy! How

can this have happened? The whole point of this was to have a girl, a little girl like Elizabeth, not someone to raise grossly in my own image, but that was there, sure it was, someone who would be like me, whom I could joke with, have fun with.

A boy? What will I do with a *boy?* Boys like baseball cards and motorcycles and. . . . Jesus, where do I get these stereotypes? Usually I fight them tooth and nail, but deep down I do believe boys, little boys anyway, can't be as much fun as girls. They mature slower, they have more emotional problems, they aren't as verbal. . . . It's true! It's all true! I can cite thousands of examples.

Anyway, that's not the point, I *wanted* a girl. Most people if you ask them what do you want say, "Oh anything . . . as long as it's healthy." I *never* said that. Are there any witnesses? I never said it, not *once.* I always said I want a girl. Wasn't anyone listening? It was already a boy, right when I was saying that, it was growing a tiny penis, it was all over right then, only I didn't know.

There ought to be a way to set this right. There must be dozens of women right here, right in this hospital who wanted boys and got girls, whose husbands wanted boys. Maybe a little switch? No one will know. Why not? We won't tell anyone. The nurses won't notice if the armbands are switched.

So why didn't I adopt a child? Wouldn't that have been easier? Then I could have specified the sex. No, I wanted my own. I really did. I wanted the experience of childbirth, and I wanted my own child. I knew my peculiarities. I knew I might not be the mother type, and I felt if it were my own child, that would make a difference. I still feel that. I don't really want to trade him.

I just feel overwhelmed. I won't be a good mother for a boy, I'll be awful, I'll be a *disaster.* Here is this child barely eight hours old, and he's already doomed. I would have been such a good mother for a girl! I know it, I thought about it in detail . . .

but a boy? How can a woman want a boy child? It's a fact a certain number of women actually would prefer a boy. How can that be? I can see, easily, a man wanting a son. It makes sense that someone would want a child of his own sex. But one of the opposite sex? Daddy always said he wanted girls more than boys. There are those exceptions, but. . . .

Maybe he'll be atypical. Don't let him be a kicker, a biter, a screamer, don't let him be "masculine" in any of those ways. Please. Can he be quiet and gentle and shy and like books and hate baseball? Could you do that much? Even let him be homosexual, only not one of those wild, brutish, mean little boys I see in the playground when I take Elizabeth and Timmy, the kind that ram their motorcycles into other people and that kind of thing.

Girls do those things, too. Yes, I know, only in a girl I wouldn't find it so hard to take. In a girl I'd find a way to accept it. That's a curious point. You'd really rather have a boy who was homosexual than a regular, normal, red-blooded American boy? Look, no one will know but you. I would, I really would. Oh, dear, maybe they should take this baby away from me, for its own good.

I peer down at him. He knows nothing. Nothing of me, nothing of life, nothing of anything. The terrifying aspect of being that innocent suddenly overwhelms me.

Maybe Calla will prove right. Maybe he'll be a "blank slate" on which anything can be written. Maybe he can still, despite being a boy, be witty and odd and nice. Is that possible? Let it be possible.

After an hour they take him away, and I fall into a long, deep sleep. When I wake up, late in the afternoon, I feel wonderfully well rested, not hung over at all. See, everyone, I was right about champagne. You can't get drunk from champagne!

Dr. Hattie comes in. "So, you did well, Gabrielle."

"Did I? Did I not throw up?"

"Not a bit of it. . . . You were fine. . . . And he's right as a trivet, a great little fellow."

"Is he?" I feel weakened, lapping up all this praise so eagerly.

"Didn't you notice? Not a blemish on him. That only happens in breech births. Otherwise, he might have marks from the forceps and so on."

"Oh, well, I didn't. . . . I've never seen that many babies."

"Have three more!"

I smile, helpless with pleasure. "I'll think about it."

"Okay, Mrs. Santa, I'll see you tomorrow morning. . . . Your 'outfit' is in that locker over there. . . . I'd get some regular clothes sent in by your mom or something, for going home and so on."

The nurse wheels in supper.

"Eat hearty, my dear. . . . See you in the morning!"

They bring the baby in again right after dinner, but he hardly stirs. Too worn out. Too hung over, more likely. . . . Poor old fellow, what a way to be born. I'm sorry. I didn't mean it. Never again.

I don't get to feed him for another twelve hours, the nurse says. Okay.

It's over. It happened. It really did happen. Alone in the room, after he's wheeled out, I suddenly feel a small rush of insane happiness.

I think I'll call him Bruno.

PART THREE

G OD is a lady and a scholar. No doubt about it. Otherwise, I'd be hard put to explain my baby, my Bruno. He's a wonder. No, this is not just the usual maternal crap. You'll have to take my word for it, you'll have to believe me. This is no ordinary baby. I'm not saying he'll grow up to be a genius or especially handsome or charming, but he is not just your everyday garden-variety baby. No, sir.

He's three months old now, and I want you to know that he never once, not once, has let out a cry. You've seen those screaming, insanely angry babies, red in the face, twisting, turning. This baby never cries. Even before he gave up his middle-of-the-night feeding, when he was about six weeks old, even then I had to put his crib right near the door so I'd hear him when he woke up. He'd just make these soft, mewing sounds, just to let me know he was there and hungry and wanting to be fed, no screaming, not a bit of it.

On Sundays I can sleep till eleven if I want. When I wake up and go in to him, there he is, lying on his back, smiling at the mobile over his crib, cooing to himself, "commenting" on things. And when he sees me, there's this big grin as though to say, "Gee, nice of you, Mom, to look in on me like this." Not, "Where the hell have you been, a fine mother *you* are, sleeping till eleven."

I don't know I really believe in him. I often feel he must be a figment of my imagination. He's like a baby from a mail-order catalogue. I think, though I must have forgotten it, I just wrote in to some Giant Heavenly Sears, Roebuck, "One insecure, uncertain thirty-two-year-old unwed mother desires quiet, charming, genial baby, bright, lively, with no major complaints about life." We go everywhere together, I just put him in this canvas baby holder that I have, and we walk the dogs, go bicycle riding, have picnics. I don't even boast about him that much, partly because I've always hated that kind of thing in other people, partly because I don't think anyone will believe me if I do tell them.

He drinks his premade bottles, guzzles them down and then sleeps. That's all there is to it, though now he's beginning to be up more. He's as fat as can be, has four chins and looks like James Cagney. There's not a hair on his head.

When I glance up at him, say, some Sunday morning when I'm in Matthew's robe, leafing through the Sunday paper and Bruno is in a clean stretch suit, sitting in his infant seat, waving his hands around as though he's conducting a symphony, I wonder: does he know something I don't know? He seems so wise, so contemplative, like a small Buddha. He looks at me and gives that smile which always seems to me to say, "Cool it, Mom! Isn't this easy? There's nothing to it." I wonder where he gets his calm. Is it something babies are born with and then lose? I've rarely met an adult like this, which seems sad. Will he, too, at some point lose it, a kind of downward path to wisdom?

The odd part is that his "wisdom" doesn't seem naïve. I really feel he seems to know more about life than I do. He has a certain flexibility which I've never had but have always admired. If it's creamed spinach today, okay. But if it's yukky gray mushed-up baby-food veal, that's okay, too. I don't think it's sheer dumb-ness or just an autistic kind of who cares what it is. It seems as though he really can somehow see the virtues of different things.

I always feel I'm so hung up on how things should be, so rigid. If my plans go awry, it's so hard for me not to be very angry. I wish I could learn from him. Maybe in time I will. I hope that's possible, rather than that he'll become affected by my drive and nervous tension.

It also puzzles me that a "person" who doesn't speak can seem so aware of things. I suppose I put too much stock on mental things, on talking and intellectual subjects, and yet his life seems as full as mine, as interesting, more so, if anything, even though he can't be thinking anything very complex.

I've changed, too. I feel reluctant to admit it, but I always said I wanted a baby just to see what it really was like in a way I'd never know just hearing about it from someone else. I think one thing that always used to puzzle me was the way my father would say when I was little that of course any parent would give his life for his child. I just couldn't imagine how I could ever feel that. I always knew my own life would mean more than anyone else's. And now, without any great mental leap or tortuous inner process, I understand what my father meant. I would give my life for Bruno. I don't know if I approve of that, but it's so clearly true I have to accept it. And if it's true of me, with all my hangups about wanting to hang onto my own identity, it cer-tainly must be true of many other people, even those who would die rather than admit it.

Bruno makes me feel that way partly because of his babyhood in general and partly because of his particular personality. That is, he has that helplessness which awakens the desire to protect him, and I find I feel that just as much even if he's a boy. He's no less helpless owing to his sex, which may be just as well in establishing that basic, primeval bond before one has a chance to think about it or argue about it. Also, because he seems so undemanding and yet has made my life so much simpler than it might have been, I feel a kind of gratitude. Because I see now, as I didn't before, that this is a complicated thing, trickier in many ways than I really was able to imagine.

The day care center, for instance, where I leave him every Monday through Friday from the time I get to work to when I go home, isn't all I would like. I wanted that particular center for practical reasons. It's near the institute. I can dash off and pick him up at lunch, and we can have lunch together in a small quiet park nearby. I feed him and then lay him on his blanket and then have a sandwich myself. In the early months when it was chilly, we sometimes ate inside, but now that it's March and warming up, it's nice to get some fresh air. After I eat, I wheel him around in a carriage till it's time to go back to work.

But the day care center is not so great. I was writing Rudolf about it a few weeks ago, and somehow putting down my dissatisfactions on paper made them seem more real than they had until then. I guess before that I kept trying to rationalize them away. Actually, for babies they are not bad, and it's true that when I go to pick Bruno up, he's always sitting cooing by himself; he doesn't seem to suffer. I just feel sorry for the older kids, the ones of three or four who are plunked in front of the TV, sucking their thumbs. Many of them come from broken homes, so maybe the shock of suddenly having the parents break up accounts for their looks of anxiety. Rudolf claims that out where he is the centers are better. Maybe. I guess up till now I'd always thought of day care centers as a vague political issue. Now I can see there is vast room for improvement, even with a relatively good one like this.

But I don't think I'll change right now. As I've said, Bruno seems okay, and I would hate to leave him all the way at home, where I couldn't even peek in at him. This way I find I have many pockets of time where I can just whip over where before

I might have gone to the library and read some tedious articles. He seems to take my sudden appearances and disappearances in his stride, the way he takes everything else. I guess that's what's meant by being sheltered, the feeling that everything is going to be okay. It almost makes me nervous, how certain he seems of that. Is it an intellectual idea that comes later—there is danger, deceit, cruelty—or are some people, babies, just born with some gene for security which it would take a lot to shake?

I suppose most basically I feel I know or am learning things about the development of life, of what it means to be human, that I'd otherwise never have known. Since Calla and Boris are relatively close to me in age and since my work doesn't bring me in contact with babies or children, I'd probably never have known even as much as I know now except this way. And now that seems so strange, that one could go through life without this most basic knowledge. I guess I feel somehow sorry for Matthew, as though his hating babies has deprived him of this, without his knowing it. He "knows" so much about such abstruse, intricate subjects and nothing at all about something so much more important and fascinating in the general scheme of things.

On Sundays my parents take him. I arrive at one, just before he has his nap, with a bag of supplies, and there they are, waiting right at the door, like anxious party givers who are afraid their guests won't come. Mother grabs him at once and rushes off, as though afraid I'll change my mind and take him back. It's a little obscene, their eagerness. I love him, but clearly to grandparents babies are something too important even to talk about. Maybe especially with parents like mine who won't admit openly to any of the usual desires for offspring to live after them and that kind of thing.

"I'll see you at five then?" I say.

"Oh, anytime," Daddy says expansively. They keep urging me to take a weekend trip, though, in fact, there's no place I want to go, so they can have a whole weekend to drool over him.

"If the nipple seems clogged, pick it out with a toothpick," I say.

"We know all that," Daddy says. "What do you take us for?"

I used to feel this day might be too rich for Bruno, like suddenly being fed plum pudding after having only crusts and water, but he seems to love it. When I come to pick him up, often Daddy is lying flat on his back on his bed and Bruno is lying beside him, staring, as though Daddy were a huge sea turtle that he'd come upon on the beach. Bruno pokes tentative fingers at Daddy's ears, eyes, exploring, cooing to himself while my mother sits in her rocker, doing needlework and sipping sherry.

I'm very proud of myself. I'm sorry, I can't help it. I feel I've done a great, a really magnificent thing. People who see him and make no comment or just seem to have that so-here's-another-baby-so-what? expression, which I recognize so well from having felt the same myself before this—such people I hate at once and have no forbearance for.

One odd thing. I meet people from the institute while wheeling him, and they'll say to me, "I didn't know you were pregnant." Even people who saw me every day in the halls while I was huge.

I take a special pride in the fact that my work is going so well now. Not only did I manage to do that paper on my past work and have it accepted, but since then so many things have dropped into place. I feel I think more clearly, as though a lot of deadwood or anxieties which must have been hindering me without my knowing it have been cleared away. While I'm working, I feel much calmer, as though I had some special, almost psychic touch. I know that's nonsense, but feeling it seems to help. I think I may have enough for another paper by the spring.

I even, crazy as it seems, toy with the idea of having another child. I love Bruno, but I'd still love a girl, in another way. But if I had another boy, I'd be prepared for that and wouldn't mind. I wouldn't be as naïve as I was this time. When I say "toy," I really mean just that. I don't think of it as something I'll definitely do, but as something I may do if I feel like it. I guess I expected having the baby would be a case of pride going before a fall. Instead, it's been in some ways the opposite. I have an insane, undoubtedly illusory feeling that there's nothing I can't do.

I seem to be heading for a fatuous middle age. Well, why not?

Monday at work I get a call from Calla. That's unusual; she rarely calls me at work, as part of what I feel is her desire not to acknowledge my work.

"Would you, um, like to have lunch?" she says, sounding tentative. She must be calling from a subway station—there's a lot of roaring in the background.

"When?"

"Well, like, today?"

I glance at the clock. It's nearly twelve. "What time?"

"I happen to be very nearby," she says. "I could come anytime."

"Let's say twelve then." I tell her the name of the day care center, and we agree to meet there.

It's in an apartment building—they use two rooms toward the back since there's also a play area outside for the older children. Calla goes with me as I collect Bruno, who looks sleepy.

We wheel him over to Second, where we pick up some sandwiches at a delicatessen, then back to York and the park I go to.

"You don't mind eating out?"

"Uh-uh."

Bruno has a jar of apricots and a jar of ham. He eats like a ravenous bird, opening his mouth every second and bolting the whole thing down. It takes about three minutes.

"Lord, does he look like a Van de Poel!" says Calla. "Look at those chins."

"I know, isn't it obscene?"

"Remember those pictures of us Mother had framed—the three little pig ones?"

"I always thought Boris looked like a balloon, the way the photographer took him kind of looking up at him, his head looked so tiny."

"I'm so relieved Elizabeth isn't huge. . . . I thought she would be as a baby, but she's lost it."

After this burst of chatter there's a silence as we unwrap our sandwiches and eat them. Calla takes something out of her pocket. "Read this!" she says.

I glance at it. It's a letter from the School of General Studies at Columbia stating that one Camilla Nicole Unterman is accepted as a matriculating student for the year of 1973–74. "Terrific," I say, handing it back to her. "I didn't know you were, you never mentioned wanting to go back to school."

"Yes, I've wanted to for a long time," she says quietly, not looking at me, "ever since the abortion, actually."

The who? Which one? Can I ask that or would it be rude?

She looks at me finally, though it clearly costs her an effort. "You know, I had an abortion in January," she says, "right around when you had Bruno."

I feel utterly taken back. "How come? You used to say you wanted lots of kids."

"I used to say a lot of things. . . . No, I know two is enough for me, but still it took some thinking about to go through with it, especially since . . . well, Julian felt I should have the baby."

It's utterly unlike Calla to say anything about Julian which implies any disagreement or rift. I feel touched at that and say hesitantly, "Did he . . . in the end go along with your decision?"

She bites her lip. "I don't know. . . . Yes, yes, I think so. . . . He said yes, it was fine. He saw my point. . . . But, you know, it's just different if you've never had a baby. You can't quite see it the same way."

I nod, aware that three months ago I would have taken such a remark as a putdown: *I* know, *you* don't.

"Did anyone else know except Julian?" I say, thinking of that awful Thanksgiving dinner and wondering if Calla's mood then was due to worrying about this.

"No, I didn't want to tell anyone. . . . I don't want them to know. Don't tell Mother and Daddy!" she adds with sudden vehemence. "Promise!"

It's funny that now, married with two kids, with abortion legalized, Calla should have such qualms about telling them when before, unmarried, childless, with the whole mechanisms of abortion so tricky as they were in the sixties, she always seemed so blasé, wanting to affront them almost. "Do you really think they'd mind so much?" I say after a moment. "I won't tell them, I promise. . . . I just—"

"Of course they'd mind!" she says, flaring up.

"Why? They're fairly liberal. . . . I mean, about Bruno they've never—"

"Oh, with you it's different," she says cryptically, looking away.

"In what sense?"

"Anything *you* do is okay."

"It is?" I look at her. "Come on, Calla. . . . You were always Daddy's favorite, don't be silly. . . . I used to hate you for it."

Calla stares at me. "His favorite! How can you say that?"

This is really odd. Being the children of the same parents is a bit like having been in the same squadron during the same war with someone but having different memories about how certain battles were actually fought. I can remember clear as day my feelings all during that era when I was ten, eleven, twelve and

221

Calla was five, six, seven, how Daddy always said she reminded him of Mother, the way she ate with her hands, her dreamy sensuality, love of food, the way she didn't do well at school and had to be transferred to a special arty kind of school where you could take weaving for credit, all the "shows" she put on at home with her dancing like a small plump Egyptian princess, draped in Mother's old sari, and me galumphing around in some idiotic horse costume. True, now, it may have shifted somewhat, but I remember feeling what an oddball I was, not the "boy" of the family but somehow endowed with all the "boy" traits, being good at chess, science, being well organized. "I always thought they regarded me as a freak," I say now bluntly, stuffing the paper from the sandwich in my bag.

"You? They adored you! Christ, anything you ever did was this great production. . . . Anything *I* ever did was this great disgrace. . . . I know they hated my marrying so young and marrying Julian, I *know* it. . . . Mother's said as much to my face practically a million times."

It's true that Mother disapproved of Calla's marriage, but I always thought that was because she married so young herself and regretted it. And, true too, Julian wasn't—which may be why Calla chose him, in part—the type who would flirt with Mother and win her over. He always seemed a little scared of her, and she could never forgive him that. "Well, Mother's funny," I say, musing. "You remind her of herself."

"Only I'm not beautiful," Calla says doggedly, "and I'm not 'artistic' . . . so where's the big resemblance?"

"Still, it's a more general thing."

"What I'd like to do," she says, "is go into city planning."

I consider this. "You'll be good, too, I bet."

Calla, with me, always has a slight chip on her shoulder, as though she expects me to be critical. Maybe when we were younger, I did lord it over her. Anyway, when I say anything approving, as now, even if it's said casually, off the top of my head, she looks so pleased I feel ashamed. I hope Calla will be a good city planner.

"Mother is so . . ." she begins. "Did I tell you how we went shopping the other day with the kids? . . . There she is, taking charge of everything, and there I am, trailing behind, like the *au pair* girl or something. . . . I swear everyone thought she was the mother. . . . And talking to everyone in her la-de-da voice. . . . One saleslady asked us, 'Where do you come from?' and she said, 'Why don't you try and guess?' "

I laugh. I can imagine the scene perfectly. Mother does have this great accent, half English, half Russian, a wonderful, subtle blending of a million nationalities which no one can recognize. "Do you wish you were like that?" I say.

"Are you kidding?" Calla makes a face. "Julian would go into shock if I ever pulled one of her bits."

"Only you wouldn't have married Julian if you were her."

"True. . . . No, I give her credit. . . . She is charming. . . . Only it's too much of a life-style. . . . Maybe she should have kept up with her painting."

"I think so," I say before I have a chance to think. Then I realize I needn't feel bad since Calla is at least contemplating doing something with her life. I wonder if her decision had anything to do with my having Bruno. As though, now that I've acknowledged I need something in my life other than my work, she can acknowledge she needs something in her life other than her kids. I'm no longer Superscholar, she's no longer Earth Mother.

Calla is looking at Bruno, who is gradually getting sleepy. His big dark eyes are drooping shut. "He seems a good baby."

"He is . . . just lovely. I don't know why."

"You probably know how to handle him better, being older. . . . God, I was so young with Elizabeth. . . . I was scared of everything. I didn't know which end was up."

"It certainly turned out well," I say.

"I've no idea why."

"Maybe one never does."

I am glad of the sisterly rapport that exists now with us, though I doubt it will ever be without certain tensions. "How's Rudolf?" Calla asks.

I grimace. "He's well, fine, healthy. . . . We write."

"And?"

"And? . . . And, I don't know."

"Maybe you're just too old and set in your ways," Calla says, eyeing me. "I thought he was perfect for you, if anyone is."

"Thanks."

"Do you think you are?"

"Are what? Am what?"

"Too set in your ways?"

"To make room in my life for Rudolf, you mean?"

"Umm."

"I haven't decided yet."

She looks at me, eyes twinkling.

Luckily, by a glance at my watch I ascertain it's time for me to get back to the lab. I wheel Bruno over to the center, and Calla walks me to the lab.

"Elizabeth and Timmy would love to visit you here again," she says. "They liked the white rabbits."

"Okay, anytime. . . . Thanks for coming down, Calla. . . . That's great about G.S."

It would, in a sense, be a supreme irony if Calla turned out to be an eminently successful city planner with her own office and staff.

Back at the lab, I realize I won't be done by dinner. I call Jessie, and she says she'll pick up Bruno, bring him home and baby-sit till I come. She's been great about this, though I'd never have expected it.

When I get home, she's there with her "boyfriend," Ivan

Liss. Ivan's parents are old friends of my parents, and Jessie has been friends with him in a purely platonic way for years. I think it's still largely platonic on his side—he's a year older than she, fifteen—but she's confessed she wishes he would regard her as girlfriend. They make a great couple. They're both small, Jessie with her boyish, shaggy blond hair and Ivan with his shoulder-length dark hair, like some unisex brother and sister.

"Was Bruno okay?" I ask.

"Oh, fine. . . . We gave him that leftover stuff in the refrigerator. . . . Is that okay?"

"Sure, as long as he ate it."

"He seemed starving," says Ivan.

"He always does," I say.

"He's certainly fat," he says, frowning. "Should he be so fat?"

"Oh, it doesn't matter. . . . Thanks kids."

Jessie says, "We started to watch this murder mystery"—she always brings her own portable TV—"but we got scared so we turned it off."

I pay her and they leave. She's getting adolescent, her skin is breaking out. I think Jessie will make it through adolescence more easily than Calla and I did; I hope so.

Almost every week Mother appears at my door with new outfits for Bruno, elaborate sailor suits with gold buttons, corduroy jackets, denim workman's overalls. They're all charming, usually much too expensive and sometimes just too much for my taste. I accept as many as I can, but this Saturday I realize that I'm never going to put them on Bruno, and I might as well return them. She looks hurt but gives me her Bloomingdale's credit card so I can credit them to her account.

I'm not a big shopper, and Bloomingdale's on a Saturday is my idea of a special kind of very fashionable hell. It's almost grotesque the number of extravagantly elegant people there are in New York whom normally I would never see, couples, single ladies, women with dogs, with carriages.

In the baby department I fling my things down on the counter and wait for my existence to be acknowledged. While waiting, I notice someone staring at me, a girl off to my left who is clutching a snowsuit.

Finally she comes over and says, "You were in that natural childbirth class at Mount Sinai, weren't you?"

I nod. I think I recognize her. Somehow everyone in that class became a blur to me. Maybe I was so eager not to be recognized, that I blended them all into one faceless pregnant lady with interchangeable hair color, hangups etc.

"What did you have?" she asks eagerly.

"A boy."

"So did I!" She seems taken by this coincidence. She sits on a stool near me. "It's ridiculous to come here Saturday," she says, "it's such a madhouse, but I have to, I work."

"What do you do?" I'm not sure I really want to know, but I feel trapped until someone removes these things of my mother's.

"I'm a librarian at the Brooklyn Museum."

"Oh."

"You know, I'm not even married," she says suddenly. "I don't have a husband, so I have to support my baby myself."

I do a double take. That's almost too odd to believe. Wouldn't it be a gas if all the girls in that class had been unmarried but all afraid to admit it and assuming everyone else was married? I mind a little her stating she has to work just because she isn't married, but decide to let that pass. "I'm not married, either," I say.

"Really?"

"Really."

"How weird! . . . You *never* were?"

"Never."

"You mean you. . . . Isn't that strange? I just assumed you were. . . . You had a kind of married look."

"Me?"

"Yes. . . . I just thought. . . . And that guy who always used to pick you up."

"Rudolf."

"Is he the father, are you living together, is he giving you child support?"

I lean back from this barrage of questions. "No, he's not the father and we're not living together and he's not giving child support."

"Oh, just a friend, huh?"

"In a sense." The truth is, as usual, slightly too complicated for me to want to go into now with this girl.

"Are you getting child support from *anyone?*" she persists.

I shake my head.

"Isn't it awful? God, I couldn't believe it—there's just plain nothing you can do to get those bastards to give a cent. . . . It's amazing. I mean, you'd think there'd be some law!"

"Isn't there?"

"So there's a law! Big deal! Look, I chased this guy from here to Kalamazoo and back and what good did it do me? My lawyer says there's nothing you can do."

"If you'd known that, would you have had the baby?"

She looks puzzled.

"I mean, do you regret . . . the whole thing?" I say. "The baby and so on?"

"No! No, I do not. . . . Why, do *you?*"

"No. . . . Only I never counted on child support."

"Well, you're smart, let me tell you that. Never count on *anything* from those bastards. . . . If you do, you ought to have your head examined."

I feel more than a little uncomfortable with this girl and

utterly trapped, as though we were stuck in an elevator and might never get out. She lets out a sigh and flings her snowsuit on the counter. "One thing I can tell you, I'm never getting married. . . . Ever!"

"You don't think if, say, you met someone. . . ."

"I wouldn't marry the King of Saudi Arabia," she says. "I don't care *who* he is! . . . Look, there's a guy who wants to marry me now, right this minute. . . . I could go out and get married this afternoon if I felt like it."

"Only he's not. . . ."

"It's not *him!* . . . I don't trust those guys! They give you shit one way or another, no matter what they say. . . . This guy, he's divorced, he's really sweet, we go bowling together, you know, I like him, he's a really nice, nice guy. . . . So what! They're all nice guys in the beginning."

Suddenly I get up. "You know, I wonder if I'm waiting at the right counter," I say. "I really came to return something."

"Oh, no, the return stuff is over there," she says. "Listen, nice talking to you. . . . What was your name?"

"Gabby."

"Good luck with your baby."

"Same to you."

I manage to stagger over to the return counter and after about an hour stagger out of Bloomingdale's. If Mother gets more stuff, I'll keep it, the heck with it.

Why did that girl bug me so much? Is it seeing an alter ego, a mirror image, but distorted in some unpleasant way? In a sense we're "in the same boat," but how I hate the idea that I might in any way seem like that girl, that belligerent down-on-men thing, the suspiciousness, the anger. I'm sure it's all justified, she's no doubt been "ill used" in all the classic senses, but how sad, and I want no part of it. Even she couldn't see me as anything except a version of herself. "Are you getting child support?" In an odd way, wanting to like me, to sympathize

with me, she still seemed immersed in stereotypes, "those bastards." . . . I'm not such a trusting soul myself. It's just that
seeing mistrust carried to that extreme makes me uneasy.

I don't know the answer.

It's getting to be spring again. One whole year ago Bruno
already existed, one whole year ago I had just found out I was
pregnant. Before that, the era of before I'd even thought of
having him seems too far away, another life. But I can
remember very well last spring, Matthew's leaving, the whole
who shall I tell, when shall I tell thing.

There seems something fitting about having a winter baby.
It's like hibernation. Now, as it gets warm, he's big enough to
take almost anywhere.

I said I'd take Elizabeth and Timmy to the zoo one Sunday. I
don't think Elizabeth has quite forgiven me for not having a girl.
She was very sulky for a long time as though it had somehow
been my fault. I tried to tell her I had wanted a girl very much
too, but I could see she didn't quite believe that if I'd wanted one
enough, I wouldn't have had one.

Watching me diaper Bruno, she says, "Boy, you know what
he did before?"

"What?"

"He peed right in my eye almost!"

"Well, that happens, Roo. . . . You have to kind of hold his
penis down like this or else learn to duck at the right moment."

She looks disgruntled. "He should go on a diet. I never saw
anyone so fat, it's disgusting!"

"Babies are often fat, Roo. . . . They're just like that."

"With a hundred chins?" She looks scornful.

"I was a fat baby."

"You were?" She stares at me.

"Sure. . . . I'll show you my baby pictures one day."

"I bet you weren't *that* fat. . . . You couldn't have been."

Maybe it's plain old garden-variety jealousy, which she was too young to feel in as developed a form with Timmy, being barely two when he was born. Anyway, I forgive her, as I always forgive Elizabeth everything.

We go to the merry-go-round in Central Park. It's a lovely day, unusually warm for April, so warm we hardly even need sweaters. Timmy and Elizabeth hop ahead while I walk with Bruno in his backpack, sleeping.

"You come on, too!" Elizabeth insists, so I do. I sit on a large red horse with a beautiful big purple eye and we whirl around and around. The only thing that bothers me is the music, which is horrendously loud. After one ride, I get off and sit on the grass nearby, while Elizabeth and Timmy go around and around. Suddenly I spy another familiar face—Eve. She's sitting sidesaddle on a reindeer, dressed in some strange but charming outfit, shocking pink blouse with a big black egg in the middle of it, an egg cracked and ready to break which is done in alarmingly realistic detail.

"There's Aunt Eve!" Timmy shrieks, spotting her, too.

"Hey, Auntie Eve!" I yell. "Yoo-hoo!"

"Hi!" Eve says breezily, but then she vanishes as the merry-go-round keeps going.

When it stops finally, she jumps off and comes over to me.

"I didn't know you were a merry-go-round fancier," I say.

"I'm not. . . . It's Ian. . . . His boys love it."

"Ian?"

She waves a casual hand at the merry-go-round. "He's over there—only they're going around again. . . . I'll introduce you later."

Elizabeth and Timmy want to go around again too, so I sit beside Eve and watch all of them. Ian, from the glimpse I get of him, is a tall hulk of a man, yeomanlike with a wild mass of red brown curls and a grin that literally goes from ear to ear.

230

"We're not getting married!" Eve says suddenly. "I won't let myself. This time I've learned."

"I didn't know you were even divorced yet."

"Well, just about . . . to all intents and purposes, as they say."

"Who's Ian?"

"He's a Scotsman. . . . Isn't he gorgeous? He's a painter, and he's had two wives who both killed themselves."

"Great, great. . . . Where do you find these creatures?"

"I don't have to even look. . . . I seem to attract them like a magnet. . . . If you can tell me why, please do!"

"He looks fantastically sexy."

"Doesn't he? . . . It's all an utter hoax, however. . . . He's lousy in bed."

I feel a pang of pity for poor Ian, whirling past us with his wild grin. "What a waste."

"It's an *awful* waste, let me tell you. . . . Everyone thinks he's such a hunk and he is . . . but he more talks a good show. Look, I don't care. I'm hooked, I adore him. . . . It's just one of those usual ironies in the life of Eve Hammerling."

"How'd you meet him?"

"Stop asking me that. I don't meet people. . . . I'm not like you. Suddenly it happens, and that's all."

"Does he earn a living of any kind?"

"Of some kind. . . . Over in England he's well known. . . . Oh, he's a mess, Gabby, he drinks, he's lazy. . . . I don't blame his ex-wives one bit."

"He didn't drive them to suicide, did he?"

"He might have in his own insane genial way."

"But you really 'adore' him?"

She looks at me. Jesus, she is a pretty girl—pink cheeks, big eyes. She ought, by rights, to have everything, if the American myth is true. "I do. . . . I'm a nut, did I ever say different?"

"*Why* do you?"

She makes a face. "Because he has a great antic grin. . . . I love it. . . . When he smiles, I forget the whole other mess."

I stare at her, puzzled. How strange. I guess it's like my mother, in a different way, this thing of "adoring" one man after another, whether in marriage or not. . . . And all for an antic grin. Someday in a later reincarnation I want to be the sort of person who can feel things that way, who throws everything to the wind so easily, I want to know what it's like, not to have "common sense," if one can even call it that, stitched into one's skin like a scarlet letter. Abstinence, not passion; withdrawal, not abandon.

Ian and his two boys get off the merry-go-round and join us.

"Hi, love!" he calls to Eve, squeezing her. "Who's this charming girl?"

"My sister-in-law," Eve says, "and she hates madmen, so don't go through your usual bit."

He shakes his head. "Isn't she a prize! What a tongue! I thought American girls were so docile, I've had a terrible education with this creature, she's a spitfire."

I smile. They seem very fond of each other, hugging all over the place, that fine careless rapture. And he is gorgeous. Despite all Eve has said, I can see leaping into bed with him, whether he's impotent or not.

"She's been telling you my life story, I can tell by your face," he says to me. "Well, it's all true. . . . I'm worse than that! Much worse!"

"Oh, well. . . ." I feel embarrassed.

"I'm a killer," he says. "I am. . . . Women should stay away from me, I told her that."

Eve makes a face at him. "Don't pose."

We're passing the Central Park lake, and suddenly Ian snatches Eve up and runs with her to the edge of the lake. "I'm going to toss you in right this minute," he yells gleefully. "Shouldn't I? Isn't that what she deserves?"

232

Elizabeth, Timmy and the two other children rush along, excited.

"Look, Gabby, he's going to throw her in!"

"It's just a game," I say calmly. Bruno is stirring, and I take him out of the backpack.

"Ian, you bastard, will you cut it out?" Eve is shrieking, flailing her arms.

"Look at Aunt Eve. She'll get all wet."

He really does throw her in. There's a big splash, and there's Eve, sputtering and gasping and wet to the bone. Lucky it's a warm day. She climbs out with a menacing expression while Ian is roaring with laughter. "*You* are a swine," she says. "Go away, never come back."

"You didn't think I'd do it."

"I did. . . . Now leave, I mean it!"

But, of course, soon he's cuddling her and joshing her and Eve is drying in the sun and we all have ice-cream cones. The kids think it's the greatest show they've seen. I can tell they'll be talking about it for years.

"Gabby's an unwed mother," Eve says, wrapped in Ian's jacket, looking as tiny girls always do in men's clothes, ultrafeminine and adorable.

"Ah, a little bastard, eh?" Ian says, but tenderly. You can tell he loves babies by the way he handles Bruno and plays with him. Eve watches him suspiciously. "He's a charmer," he says to me. "You should have another."

"I may." I forgive him all his eccentricities for being so admiring of Bruno.

At home, after having delivered Elizabeth and Timmy to their parents, I feel terribly horny. I guess just seeing Eve and Ian together, whatever she says about the reality of their sex life, that thing was there, that magical sense of two people hugging and kissing and squeezing and I want some! It's spring and I haven't been laid in four months and I want some. Damn, the

233

eternal problem. I try to conjure up the ghost of Rudolf, but that only makes things worse, much worse. Oh, Lord.

Poor Gwendolen, what can I tell you? I know your life is sad. From rags to riches to rags again. That's just how it goes. I know you don't care how many papers I write, what's that to you? And I recall Calla once saying how much more sexy she felt since she's had children, a certain sense of being in bloom, of getting it all together physically. Yes, ah, yes.

On May 1 I get a letter from Matthew. Here is how it goes:

April 19, 1973

GABBY, DEAREST,

I have the feeling the letter I'm about to write is one you may have contemplated writing me at some point during this long year. So maybe I deceive myself in thinking that for that reason you'll find what I have to say neither all that surprising now, nor, and this I hope most of all, that hurtful.

I'm living with someone. At least I will be by the fall. His name is Roger Voight. He's just your age, actually, which struck me as an odd coincidence, and, odder still, I suppose, he's a scientist also, but he's in the history of science, he doesn't do research. I've often thought of how the two of you would get along, though that may seem a strange thing to think about. Like you, he can be very headstrong, and for that reason you might clash. He has your dogmatic streak and very vehement opinions on all sorts of things I couldn't care less about. . . . But, as with you, I think I enjoy being with someone who cares that much.

I've never done this sort of thing before, and I really have no strong convictions one way or the other about its chances for being something lasting, even in the short range. What makes me hopeful is that I don't think I have insane desires anymore, I don't want everything. He has his own life, and if we can, apart from our lives, find something together, that's fine. That's enough. But even such hedged arrangements are tricky, as you know. What can I say except that for now I feel hopeful? There are no happy endings, anyway.

I am going to stay another year at least, maybe longer. My letters this year must have been oddly schizophrenic, hating the place at times, then loving it, going overboard in various directions. I don't know I've completely resolved all that. The English are different, and that will always bother me slightly. But my work has been going well. I hate to even get into that for fear of putting a hex on it. So let me just say I think it's possible, just possible I really will get the Baudelaire into some kind of shape. That's what I hope, that's why I'm going to stay, to make sure I don't break the spell or whatever has made it possible.

Roger knows about you, of course. He could hardly help it since I carry those photos of Bruno everywhere and show them to everyone like a doting daddy. I have to admit, now, that though I knew you always wanted a daughter, I can't help feeling a special pride it was a boy. I'm sorry, darling, don't hate me.

To me he looks like my father, though I know you say you think he looks like yours. Maybe it's a touch of both of them. In any case, he has that calm, patriarchal, wise expression which seems so extraordinary in a child. It's clear, as of course we knew, that our genes make a splendid combination. I feel we owe it to the world to have several more, don't you think?

I hope sometime, in the next year, you'll find time to bring him over. I'd hate to think of never laying eyes on him at all till he's twenty. That seems too remote, even for me. See if you can swing it.

I must say you seem to be managing marvelously, not that that's unexpected. I wish you'd get someone to take a picture of you with Bruno. It's always him alone, as though he had no mother!

Tell me really what you feel about all of this. I'd like to think we could still write and be close and that this doesn't signal an end, just something which, as I feel, we both probably had to come to terms with somehow, being apart so long. I hope you have a "Roger" too.

Be well, darling,
MATTHEW

*   *   *

Hmm. I read the letter quickly, then slowly, then tuck it in my pocket and take the dogs for a long walk to think it over. Is it unexpected? Now that it's happened I'd say no, not entirely. . . . I do feel jealous. It's funny. I feel that for Matthew it is an excellent thing, that if I had only his welfare at heart, this may well in the long run be a better solution than me and him. He never seemed to be able to swing such a thing before, with another man, and if I were his true well-wisher, I would hope he can do it now. I guess in my own possessive way I wanted him to lead a celibate life for as long as he was away, which doesn't, I realize, make much sense, considering my own activities.

I dreamily envision going over there, a scene with Roger, whom I see, for some reason, as a starkly handsome, self-righteous person who would scowl at Bruno and be disgusted if he spat up and Matthew looking on, flustered, alarmed, wanting us to like each other. It would, as I see it, be an utter disaster. No, better just keep on writing and sending photos.

I recall how I used to say I didn't want to convert Matthew, how I prided myself in thinking that. I wanted him "to find happiness on his own terms." I still, deep down, think I feel that, but I wonder if that's something for which I should credit myself or the opposite. I just feel maybe there was, is, too much forbearance between Matthew and me, too much excusing of each other's failings. We didn't, don't, demand enough. It's all too civilized and too "understanding." I feel we should both have someone who would call us to account, who would force us to a more committed no-holds-barred relationship.

Well, easy to say. We both resisted that very much, that's why we never had it. Maybe Matthew will get it with Roger. If he does, more power to him.

But, as with Eve and Ian, I once again have this sense of the animals entering the ark and the water is rising and I don't want to be left behind. I don't mean marriage, just some kind of pairing, some bond. For Eve that's easy. She doesn't even really think twice about committing herself, even to someone riddled with faults, and I admire that. I want to go over Niagara in a barrel, but I won't unless someone pushes me.

It must have been hard for Matthew, too. I wonder how much he resisted it and fought against it. Not because it would seem too unconventional, but for all the reasons I would, because it's easier, for people like us, to be alone, not to have to make compromises of any kind. Good for you, Roger, I'm glad you broke through. I still hate you, but that's my privilege.

Did I ever mention Rudolf to Matthew? I guess I did without really spelling out just what our relationship was. And now I wonder how I could quite say what our relationship is.

Good question.

Mother and Daddy are giving a birthday party for Miranda, who'll be five on June 15. They don't really know her as well as they know Elizabeth and Timmy. Neither do I. Partly it's that Eve and Boris always kept more to themselves, perhaps owing to their marriage and not feeling as at ease in family groups. Also, it's Miranda's personality, somehow more inward and sullen.

To me, even seeing her on this presumably exciting day for a child, a birthday, she still has that quality. She's much happier-seeming since Eve left, but there's still that black, brooding quality, that feeling of some inner wound that will never be healed that you sense in her big, dark, solemn eyes.

She's dressed very formally, in a dark dress with a big lace collar, white tights, patent-leather shoes. Mother takes her aside and fixes her hair, fastening it with a barrette on top of her head. To me she says, "You can always tell when there's not a mother by the way their hair looks. . . . Though why men can't learn to fix hair is beyond me."

"I guess they could if they wanted," I say.

The house has been all fixed up, a large donkey for pin-the-tail attached in the front hall. Miranda comes to the door as each guest arrives and carefully takes each present, which she deposits in a big pile. There's none of that frantic eagerness which you usually sense with children at parties—what will I get, will it be what I wanted?

After the cake and ice cream she sits down on the rug, and the others, seven boys and girls, sit around her and watch her open her presents. They seem much more excited than she does, letting out whoops of excitement as each gift is unfurled. "Hey, can I play with that? Can I, Miranda? Please?"

Mother is in the back, gathering up wrapping paper, which she loves to save in her pack rat fashion. Miranda, upon opening each gift, says a quiet "Thank you" to the person who gave it. It would be impossible to tell which gift she likes, if any. The children, seeming affected by this, become a little more silent than children usually are on such occasions.

Finally all the presents are open, or almost all. Suddenly Boris comes rushing in with a giant red rocking horse, covered with sequins. It's hardly a toy, but it's lovely, really a magnificent thing. For the first time Miranda's face opens a little. "That's lovely, Daddy." She just touches it delicately, doesn't try to ride it or sit on it.

"Where did you get it?" I ask Boris. "It's gorgeous."

"Oh, a store downtown I found. . . . It's Eastern, Arabian, I think."

The party begins to break up. I go down to check on Bruno, who is being baby-sat for by Jessie. Then I come up again, carrying him in my arms.

"I want to go for a walk," Miranda suddenly announces. All the children are gone. Mother is bustling with papers and clearing the ice-cream dishes. It's three thirty.

"Why don't we all go?" I suggest. "Bruno needs some air too."

Miranda comes to look at Bruno. "Why did you name him that?" she says. "It sounds like a bear."

"I like bears," I say.

She seems to accept that.

Daddy and Mother stay behind, and I go to the park with Boris and Miranda. I push Bruno in his carriage since he's wide awake and enjoys looking around at passersby.

"So, do you like the new job?" I say. Boris is now working for the city government, helping to get black businessmen set up in their own companies. Since he has business contacts from his years on Wall Street, it's not quite as though he were starting afresh.

"I do." He's silent a moment. "It's chaotic, and there's too much work, but I like it." He walks beside me, hands clasped behind his back. Tall, heavyset, dark, he looks, with his small eyes and ears, like a whale, I've sometimes thought. His face can look menacing, but that's deceptive. I think Boris, for all his sarcasm with women, is really rather unaggressive. I can see how he would be no match for Eve. As he walks with Miranda by his side, they look like a very old-fashioned nineteenth-century papa and daughter, both curiously formal and silent, absorbed in their own worlds. She walks next to him, holding herself with excellent posture, looking at passersby but with that same detached, intent look. One could never tell what she's thinking.

"You seem to be managing well," he says finally, as though with an effort.

"You mean with Bruno?"

"Yes. . . . I never thought you would."

"Thanks."

"Well, you're hardly the type . . . wouldn't you agree?"

"To be a mother?"

"Umm."

"It depends on how you look at it. . . . I think I'm 'the type' as much as a lot of other people." I'm trying not to sound defensive, although with Boris that's not easy.

"Anyway, you seem to like it, that's what I meant. . . . That's good."

I nod, willing to settle it at that.

We walk down to the pond at Seventy-second where people are already sailing boats.

"Do you . . . see any girls?" I say after we pass some girl who smiles at Boris as though she knows him.

"Oh, sure. . . . All disasters of various kinds. I guess I shouldn't."

"Shouldn't what?"

"Even see them. . . . Some of them, they're so young, it isn't fair. If you sleep with them once, they get so excited, it's . . . better not to do anything, probably."

"For the moment. . . . I wouldn't think permanently that would be the answer."

"Who knows?"

It's curious that in some way Eve seems to have bounced back from their marriage so much more easily, whereas with Boris, maybe because he's so superficially undemonstrative, one senses it will take years longer.

He buys Miranda a balloon shaped like a cat with a little bell on one end. She carries it in one hand, but suddenly, inadvertently lets it go. It instantly is carried by the wind and sails up, up in the air to catch in a tree. Miranda lets out a wail and begins to sob, heartbroken. I look at her, amazed. That phlegmatic, silent child so upset over a lost balloon. Instantly Boris is at her side, squatting next to her.

"Darling, I'll get you another," he murmurs. "Don't cry, please."

"I want *that* one," she sobs. "That was mine. . . . That's the one I want."

"I know, sweetheart, but I can't get it. . . . See, look how high up it is. . . . It's too high for Daddy to get. . . . Let me get you another."

"No, no, that one, that one!" She is sobbing, sobbing as though her heart were actually broken. The expression on Boris' face as he tries to comfort her, the tenderness, the grief, the helplessness, is too much; I have to look away.

I can't quite believe it. Boris, who's always so inward and caustic with women, so defensive, suddenly spilling it all out, as though where that came from there was much much more, more than one could possibly imagine. I reflect again how peculiarly, how unexpectedly parenthood affects people, how utterly unpredictable it is.

He holds her, just holds her for a long time and finally she grows silent and the tears disappear.

But she won't accept another balloon.

It's odd at the lab. On the one hand, I feel that there's been less reaction to my unwed motherhood than I might have expected. Perhaps some goes on behind my back, but I think on this subject I'm sensitive enough, maybe hypersensitive, to sense what people's real reactions are, and I'd say on the whole they just accept it. But what bothers me is the feeling that no matter what opinion they have, I'm somehow typecast in everyone's eyes as the Woman who . . . the Scientist who. . . . Maybe that will fade in time, but it bothers me, I hate being identified according to this one fact of one life which ought to be my own business and no one else's. It's not that I didn't think of this before, but sensing it now makes me more uneasy than I would have expected.

Lobochowski, for instance, with whom I used to have merely strained, superficially cordial relations, now feels he must from time to time take me aside and ask me meaningfully how things are going, how I'm managing. It's all quite touching, and maybe if I were a different person, I'd just say, okay, he's being sweet,

GIVE ME ONE GOOD REASON

he's in his own queer way concerned for my welfare. But I
don't feel that way. I resent it acutely.

The other day when I was showing pictures of Bruno to
Frances, Lobochowski passed by and insisted on looking at
them too. After looking, he said, "You're so lucky, Gabby! You
must have been born under a lucky star."

"How so?"

"You know, I have four sisters and none of them have
sons. . . . Xenia has two daughters, Patricia has one, Zina has
three, and Stefania has none so far. . . . They've all been to
doctors, they go through special rites, and they simply cannot
have a son. . . . They would give anything. I tell you, Xenia
would give her right leg, I tell you this seriously, she would, for
a boy."

"That's a pity."

"She would give anything! And here you, on the first shot!
It's remarkable."

"You know, I wanted a daughter," I say, but that washes over
his head.

"He's such a fine-looking boy. . . . Will he be a biochemist
someday? What do you think?"

"I really don't think that far ahead, Leonid. . . . I hope he'll be
whatever he wants."

"He'll follow in his mother's footsteps, I'm sure he will!"
He's so beaming and pleased with the idea, with himself, that it's
all I can do to restrain myself from socking him. What the hell
business is it of his if my son is a ballet dancer? What business is
it of his that I even have a son!

I wonder if I should look for a new job. I've been saying that
for years and each time I figure what the heck, things aren't so
bad here, I have relative freedom to do what I want, a good
salary, the institute has money, one doesn't have to go through
all the business of getting grants, which is so time-consuming.

Elsewhere I feel I'd have more administrative work, which would be a pain. Still. . . .

In the early summer there's a tumor virus meeting at Cold Spring Harbor. I decide to go and give the paper on the work I'm just completing. Also, in the back of my mind is the idea that I can keep my eye out for job offers if any should come my way.

It's beautiful summer weather and a relief to be out of New York. I haven't left the city since last July, when Rudolf and I went camping. Jessie comes with me to look after Bruno since her school is out and her camp hasn't begun yet. There's a whole klatch of mothers and babies who gather on the beach, sunning themselves and swimming. The mothers all look tan and healthy, the husbands all pale and flabby.

In the afternoon, which is free, I go out in a Sailfish with an Israeli scientist named Pinhas Zuckerman and another woman scientist named Molly Jackson. I know Molly slightly since we got our doctorates at Columbia together, though she was older than I. She's married and has no children, a thin, repressed-seeming girl with not too much of a sense of humor.

Zuckerman is large and booming, gray-haired, probably in his sixties or late fifties. He's onto his third marriage, so he tells us with a lovely girl, a former student who is back at Stanford, where he works.

"How can you stand to live in New York?" he asks me. "It's such a dreadful place. I lived there twenty years, and I can't tell you how glad I am to leave! I feel twenty years younger."

"Do you like the setup where you are?" I ask cautiously. The wind is strong, and we're zipping along at a fairly fast clip.

"I love it! I can do whatever I like. I'm my own master. . . . There's hardly any teaching. It couldn't be better."

Of course, Zuckerman is the type who waxes enthusiastic about things in general. I don't know that I trust his judgments completely. "You should come and see us," he says.

"Lobochowski is crazy. . . . How can you work with him?"

I laugh. Most scientists hedge more when discussing Lobochowski. "Why do you think he's crazy?" I say, smiling.

"Are you kidding? Look, my dear, you're too young for all this, but I had a student who worked with Lobochowski when he was at Einstein and this man almost had a nervous breakdown. I tell you, this was not a neurotic man, this was a very healthy, excellent . . . well, you must know. Don't tell me you don't know."

"California must be so strange," Molly says suddenly, quietly.

"Why? Why strange? After New York nothing is strange. . . . No, the point is, you have fresh air, you can swim, you can ski, you can have a real life. . . . Don't tell me about New York. I know, I lived there from the age of forty when I came over from Israel to the age of fifty-five. . . . I know! I know all about it!"

He has a broad, beefy face, handsome in a rugged, crude kind of way. As I recall, he used to drink a lot, so people said, and he has that reddish complexion of a former drinker.

That night, after the meetings, when some of us are having a drink in a local bar, he again says to me, "At least come out and see it. . . . What can you lose?"

I look at him. What I gain or lose is nothing to you, I think. "I'll think about it," I say.

I wonder, privately, what he'd be like to work for. He's certainly not an innocuous person, and though I'd insist on having my own lab and being independent, I wonder what it would be like to have Zuckerman in constant residence. It might be a refreshing change, it might be a disaster.

Lobochowski, for his part, thinks Zuckerman is crazy. I refer just casually to the paper Zuckerman gave at the meetings, after I return, and Lobochowski says dismissively, "He's a buffoon."

"You don't think. . . . I thought his point about—"

"Gabrielle, I would not go near a man like that. . . . His work is completely off beam."

It's really impossible to weed out how much personal animosity is involved in the low opinion each of them has of the other. In the scientific community at large, I'd say Zuckerman probably has a better standing than Lobochowski, partly because, though he has, it's true, been wrong on some fairly important things, he's also been right, more willing to take chances than Lobochowski, and I admire that.

Maybe I'll go to California. I want to see Rudolf again. It's foolish to deny that plays part in my decision. I want him to see Bruno. He was there throughout so much of my pregnancy that he's somehow, willy-nilly, connected to it. Oh, hell, I just want to see him. No need to find excuses.

I'm not afraid of airplanes. I don't know why. Everyone I know is, but for my own part I feel much more uneasy in a car. Maybe it's the feeling that death, if it came, would be instantaneous. Whatever it is, I get a kind of high when, as now, we rise slowly into the air.

I've taken Zuckerman up on his offer. It's vacation time, anyway, and this way I can see his lab and have another few weeks to play around with as I wish. The dogs I left with Calla and Julian. I felt as though our usual position were reversed, my leaving my pseudochildren with them instead of their leaving Elizabeth and Timmy with me. Though I must admit that love the dogs though I still do, since Bruno's birth my feeling for them isn't quite as intense as it used to be. I hate like hell to admit that. I used to fight tooth and nail the idea that the dogs were child substitutes, but now I wonder if there wasn't something in that. I recall those afternoons when I lay with Sasha in my arms, smelling her doggy smell with rapture, and I realize those days are gone. I'll always love dogs and animals in general, but there's a subtle difference somehow.

Bruno is watching the movie for which I have not bought earphones, a Technicolor Western. He seems to find it fascinating and gurgles, "comments," smiles at all the inappropriate moments.

I feel mild regret at not having taken Elizabeth with me. She begged and pleaded, wanted me to take her to Disneyland etc. I guess it's partly that if I'd taken her, I'd have had to take Timmy, too, and it would have been a little too much to handle.

Palo Alto is lovely. The air does seem mysteriously cleaner and fresher, but more than that, Zuckerman has a very nice setup for his work. It isn't a huge lab. On the whole he probably has less expensive equipment than Lobochowski, but most of our equipment just sits there anyway as part of Lobochowski's "empire," hardly serving any function.

"Your last paper was extremely interesting," Zuckerman says over lunch. "But what you're doing has nothing to do with Leonid's work or D'Angelo's. . . . How is that?"

How indeed? The fact is, Lobochowski and Paul D'Angelo have been doing work for years which has only the most peripheral relationship to cancer research, only they've never been called down for it. And it does bug me. I feel they are unfairly wasting the institute's money. "I haven't minded working on my own," I say cautiously since I don't entirely feel like airing dirty linen in public.

"But who do you have to talk to there?" Zuckerman persists. "Stenard? Mendolson?"

Okay, he's right. But I just say, "There are things there I'm not that happy about. . . . I wouldn't be here now otherwise."

"Okay. . . . Fair enough." He evidently senses my not wanting to make any instant commitment.

Despite this, the way he describes what it would be like if I came here is more than slightly tempting. I'd have several rooms to myself and a post doc. We could try to lure some other people out here to collaborate with. "How about Chorberg?" he says. "I know he doesn't like Einstein."

"You think he'd consider coming?"

"It couldn't hurt to try. . . . Yes, I think he would."

After we've talked about it some more, we stop. It's six o'clock. We drive back to his house for dinner.

Gloria, his third wife, must be younger than I am by a couple of years at least. She's a quiet, soft-spoken girl with blond, straight hair and granny glasses, a very good figure, dressed simply in blue jeans, a shirt, sandals. But what I like is that, despite the age difference between them, which must be close to thirty years, it doesn't seem the classic "Me big daddy, you little worshiper at my feet" type relationship that one might expect. She's quiet but very sharp, and there's a kind of bantering but affectionate rapport between them which is very nice.

"Has he been offering you the moon?" she says as I take Bruno into their bedroom to change him and settle him in for the night.

"Sort of."

"No, he'll do it, if he says it," she says. "He's crazy, but he tells the truth." She peers at Bruno. "How old is he?"

"Six months."

"Gosh, how do you manage with him and working and so on?"

"As best I can." I arrange the pillows around the bed so he won't fall. "Will you have children?" I ask.

She shakes her head. "No, well. . . . You know, Pinny has a son from his first marriage and another from his second. . . . I don't think he'd feel like starting all over again. . . . And to tell the truth, I don't especially want children. I never did."

"I think lots of people feel that way," I say. "They're just afraid to admit it."

"Do you think so?" She looks pleased. "I feel guilty admitting

247

it. I guess I feel I ought to say it's a great gap in my life, but it isn't. . . . Our life here is very good, we don't feel we need anything more . . . for now."

Zuckerman is in the kitchen making giant drinks. "I don't drink anymore," he says. "You know, I did. . . . Did you know that? I was almost an alcoholic at one time, but I've completely changed."

"How did you manage it?" I say, taking a few sips. "It's very good, whatever it is."

"I just. . . . My life changed and I stopped."

"I didn't make him," Gloria says.

"No, she said, 'Do what you like, I'm not going to convert you.'. . . How do you like that?"

"Would you have liked it if she'd tried to convert you?" I say.

"I'd have killed her!" he roars with laughter.

"Bull," she says, poking him.

"You know, this girl has no respect for her elders," he says, grinning. "It's the most terrible thing."

"Very touching," Gloria says. "Now clear out of the kitchen."

I sit in their living room, which is beautifully furnished, very simple and open with only a few pieces of modern furniture, and Zuckerman chats on about the lab, life here, politics. My mind is wandering, but pleasantly so. I enjoy being with them and don't feel embarrassed when, after dinner, sitting in a deep chair, I actually fall sound asleep.

I stay another day, meeting the various other members of the department. Then I plan to go to San Francisco. Before leaving I call Rudolf. I call him at work since it's three in the afternoon.

"Gabby? . . . Where are you?"

"I'm at Stanford. . . . I'm out here for a job interview."

"Why didn't you write me you were coming?"

"I wanted to surprise you."

248

"Well, when are you coming?"

"Give me directions. . . . I have a car."

An hour later I'm driving up to Rudolf's house, a large, rambling structure with green shutters. He ambles out, still on crutches. He is in a denim shirt and jeans, and his eyes are still beautiful. We have a long kiss, managed as well as it can be with Bruno in his pack on my back and Rudolf on crutches. But it's a good kiss anyway.

"It's taking longer to heal than they expected," he says of his leg. "There's no pain, though."

"How do you like having a house? Isn't it odd, being alone in such a huge thing?"

"No, I like it. . . . I tried an apartment, but it was so cramped."

"What do you do with all those rooms?"

"Nothing much. . . . I use one to paint in. . . . It's nice not to have to clean everything up when you stop the way I used to."

Bruno has dinner with us in the kitchen. He smiles and accepts a chunk of fresh bread from Rudolf. "Why is he so friendly?"

"Don't know. . . . He's promiscuous. He loves strangers."

Rudolf eyes him. "Does he look like you? It's hard to tell."

"No, like himself, I think. . . . Not like anyone."

After dinner I feel a fantastic headache coming on. It's been lurking there in the back of my head all day, and suddenly it hits me, as though a refrigerator had fallen plunk on my head.

"Could I lie down a little?" I say, reluctant to admit how lousy I feel.

"Sure, go inside. . . . What should I do with Bruno?"

"You couldn't . . . do you think you might give him one of those bottles in my bag. You just unscrew the top and put one of those nipples on."

"Does he get the whole thing?"

"If he wants it."

Inside I lie on Rudolf's bed in the dark and feel as if I am dying. A migraine headache to end all migraine headaches.

Rudolf, carrying Bruno, looks in on me. "What's wrong? Are you okay?"

"I hate happy endings!" I yell suddenly.

He's walking back to the living room. "Who says we'd be happy? . . . Oh, Jesus!"

"What?"

"He threw up on me!"

"You should wear a raincoat when you feed him," I murmur, faintly.

"Well, it's too late now."

"Can you handle it? Just change him or whatever and put him in that car bed." I turn over on my stomach and hang over the edge of the bed. Will it be better if I throw up? Rudolf is bustling around in the next room. I hear his footsteps, very loud through the pain in my head. "Rudolf, I love you," I mutter so low he can't possibly hear.

A few moments later he appears at the door. "Did you say something, Gabby?"

I raise my head. "I said . . . do you have any aspirin?"

He looks at me suspiciously. "They're in the top bureau drawer."

But somehow I cannot manage the trip from the bed to the bureau, which looks about a thousand miles away.

After what seems a long time Rudolf comes in. He lies down next to me and puts his arms around me. "So, shall we get married?"

I still freeze a little at the sound of that word. "Not yet. . . . I just can't. I'm not ready."

"Will you ever be?"

"Maybe not. . . . Is that okay?"

"Sure." I can imagine, rather than see his smile in the dark-

250

ness. "I got you all the way across the country. That's a start, anyway."

I follow the pain down a long winding road which finally, imperceptibly leads to sleep. In the middle of the night I wake up. Rudolf is sleeping, one arm thrown out to the side. I tiptoe into the living room. Bruno is asleep, in his car bed, smelling faintly of sour milk. The house is quiet; my headache is gone.